# Zainab

By Mohammed Hussein Haikal

Translated by

John Mohammed Grinsted

DARF PUBLISHERS
LONDON

This edition first published in UK 2016

By DARF PUBLISHERS LTD
277 West End Lane
London
NW6 1QS
United Kingdom

Copyright © Darf Publishers 2016

First published in 1989

Translated by John Mohammed Grinsted

Cover design by Luke Pajak

www.darfpublishers.co.uk

ISBN-13: 978-1-85077-290-3
eISBN-13: 978-1-85077-292-7

Printed and bound in Great Britain by Clays Ltd, St Ives plc

# Translator's Introduction

"Zainab" was written in the year 1910–11 while the author, Mohammed Hussein Haikal, was studying law in Paris. Published in 1913 by Al-Jarida, an Egyptian newspaper, it was the first authentic Arabic novel to appear in Egypt. Because the new genre was itself a 'revolutionary' concept in some circles, and perhaps also for the criticisms levelled at some of the traditions and institutions of Egyptian life, the work first appeared without being ascribed to the author. Haikal chose instead to use the title 'Misri Fallah', meaning 'a village Egyptian', by which he was able to conceal his identity, while at the same time expressing his sympathy with the village people of his country.

Apart from the historical significance, Haikal's book is also a highly creative achievement in its own right. The portrayal of Egyptian rural life and customs is both realistic and perceptive, set against the perennial backdrop of the Egyptian countryside. The often beautiful descriptions of nature help the narrative to flow at a natural pace and give the reader the feeling that he or she is actually experiencing some of the day to day events with which the story is inextricably interwoven. The result is an appealing story which can only rouse one's sympathy for the 'heroine' of the book, Zainab. In fact, it is a poignant attack on the tradition of arranged marriage, which still exists in Egypt today.

In translating this work I have found it necessary to make a few omissions and some revision in order to assist the flow of the English text. Otherwise it is faithful to the original and I would like to thank Dr. Mohammed Enani, Professor of English literature at Cairo University, for checking and commenting on the draft of my translation.

My appreciation also goes to Ahmed Haikal, for his encouragement and cooperation in the publication in English of the first truly Arabic novel. I hope that it will be as enjoyable and rewarding an experience for the reader as it has been for the translator.

*John Mohammed Grinsted*

# PART ONE

*The farmlands spread out before his eyes, covered with green clover and the new shoots of cereal crops, tender but full of life so that when the wind passed over they bowed before it as one body.*

# Chapter One

It was the time when the world comes back to life; when the total silence which reigns over the peasant villages during the night is broken by the call of the muezzin and the crow of the cockerel. Animals were awakening from their rest and as the darkness stole away, morning appeared from behind the veil of night. In that hour Zainab was stretched out on her bed and in the still air she could just hear the sighing of somebody else getting up. On either side her brother and sister were still asleep and Zainab snuggled between them, glancing round with sleepy eyes. The morning breeze did not draw her from her place, instead she leaned on the pillow, trying without success to see into the courtyard. Turning her head towards the closed door, there was no sound to be heard apart from the muezzins calling to one another across the village.

For a few moments she remained motionless then she stretched her arms and sighed, letting herself fall back into the dreams which the breeze revived until she heard her mother returning from her first journey to the canal. Zainab shook her sister to wake her up but the young one was in a deep slumber and paid no heed, merely turning over as though annoyed with whoever was disturbing her. Finally Zainab's mother called:

'Zainab . . .!'

'. . . Yes.'

That was her only word in reply.

After waking her sister she turned to rouse her brother and gazed towards the East where the horizon was rosy and the sun appeared blood red as the sky took off its cloak of night. Zainab got dressed and lit a fire, placing a small loaf of bread for each of them on the grill, not forgetting her parents.

Presently her father returned from the mosque, having read

3

the invocation and prayed el-fajr.* No sooner had he crossed the threshold than he called 'Mohammed!' to see that he was up and ready for the day ahead.

The family gathered round the basket and they each ate a loaf with a pinch of salt before the father left for work with his son. Zainab and her sister stayed behind, waiting for Ibrahim who would accompany them to Sayyid Mahmoud's lands in order to weed the cotton fields. They were hoping today to clear the land to the west of the canal or, as the chief clerk had said: 'From Section 20 to Section 14 . . . by Tomorrow!'

When Ibrahim approached with a group of their fellow workers they went to meet them and exchanged the customary greetings. They made their way down the alley to the village path and out along the country road, arriving at Section 20 just as the morning train was passing. With no hesitation they took their places in the line, in the same positions they had occupied the day before. Finding that Saada was absent from the row beside her, Khadrah turned to Zainab on her right to enquire but she simply shrugged her shoulders.

The sun rose above the trees when they had cleared two lines and its rays immersed the young cotton bushes that received more care from the proprietor and the farmers than their children, even at this early stage of growth. Moving on to the third row, which lay beyond a drainage ditch, Ibrahim made a point of telling them that this patch had more weeds and therefore required special attention. He warned them that he would be supervising meticulously and that anybody not doing the job properly would be in trouble.

In the afternoon the clerk came to record their names and tying up his donkey, he made for the centre of the field to see the workers for himself. Some wanted to ask for money but he glowered at them and remained indifferent until he had finished his business. Then he informed them that there would be no pay until market day.

On the eve of the market the clerk was in his office with

* The dawn prayer.

a twelve year old boy to help him in his work. In front of them the accounts were spread out on a white wooden desk illuminated by an old lamp, its dim light further hindered by layers of dust on the glass. Next to it stood an inkwell and a copper pen holder and on the far side a small bottle, half filled with ink. A group of workers surrounded the desk, the waterer holding their workslips in his hand, while some tried to ask the number of days they had worked. At the window a number of younger workers, boys and girls, began to mutter between their teeth, showing their dissatisfaction with the clerk who was making them wait for their pay. But after keeping them waiting for another hour, he announced that he would pay them in the market the following day.

Now their anger spilled over and from different corners voices were raised in protest:

'And what about those who aren't going to the market?'

This and similar expressions were voiced in vain until some were so annoyed that they resolved to go to the proprietor to submit their complaint. But at that moment one of the proprietor's relatives, who was much loved by the workers, chanced to pass by. This encouraged them and the bolder ones surrounded him to explain their problem whereupon he assuaged their fears with pleasing words which did not, however, benefit them at all.

Eventually most of them left, content that they would receive their pay the following day, although some went back to see how much was due to them. Khalil Abu Jabr had worked six days which meant eighteen piastres while Atiya Abu Faraj, who had been sick for much of the week, would only receive six piastres—and he had a wife and young daughter to support as well as a frail mother who had no other sons but him left to care for her. In spite of the ragged manner in which he and his family dressed, there was nothing he could do to improve their situation as long as the wages remained so low. But he praised God in any case, especially for not allowing his buffalo to die as had befallen Mabruk Abu Saeed, a neighbour of his, leaving him in narrow straits for some considerable time.

In the morning many of the workers returned, only to be regarded disdainfully by Sheikh Ali saying that he did not have any 'small change'. With the insistence of some and the declarations of others they were still pestering him when the proprietor himself arrived. As the clerk was still refusing to listen, some went to air their grievances to Sayyid Mahmoud even though they knew that he usually turned a deaf ear to their complaints. However, on this occasion he called his clerk and took over the task of paying them himself. This brought smiles to their faces and having received their pay they glanced back at Sheikh Ali, winking to one another. But he had forgotten all about them, upset now over a mistake his master had found in the accounts for which he had been rebuked.

At last the workers were free to leave, most in excellent spirits, especially after seeing the clerk humiliated in front of them. The majority headed for the marketplace where Zainab's father was waiting to collect his children's wages. Sheikh Ali was not long in coming; having received his master's orders he went to pay the others their due—after getting some 'small change' of course.

*  *  *

The days passed by and Zainab continued to clear the cotton fields under Ibrahim's supervision until it was time to harvest the wheat. Then she worked with her sister at night in the charge of Hussein Abu Saeed. Sleeping in the fields with the other workers they would get up at midnight and head for the huge field of wheat, holding their sickles in their hands. At this hour the stems were soft with dew so that they would not snap at the touch of a hand. It was one of those wonderful sleepless nights when the moist summer breezes blow and shining stars glitter in the sky. The farm labourers compensated for their inability to travel like the rich by going instead to the most beautiful plots of land where they would substitute their blankets for the protection of the sleepless moon. In the silent darkness of the night they gave voice to their hopes and the scented air would carry their songs on its wing, filling the spaces between the heavens and earth with music.

On nights like this the daughters of the fallaheen* found an arena for their aspirations and the stronger ones would forge ahead, forcing the others to hurry along behind. Even among this poor group, who needed cooperation more than anybody, competition drove them to work more earnestly. But nature's wish is that we should serve her, to advance the progress of the world, and she draws man away from himself in order to exploit him for her own ends. Whatever a person may endeavour to accomplish and however much society tries to make him an individual he remains subservient, driven to serve the group in spite of himself. Whatever man's selfish intentions the natural drive is to work for the good of all. Would it not be better then, to exchange those intentions?

Nature excelled itself in Zainab, crowning her in a way which set her apart from her companions. If fortune favoured, you might step out into a moonless night on a summer's eve with the stars shining overhead, lightening the darkness though unable to dispel it. Or if you were luckier still the moon would accompany you as you set out across those open spaces. Soon you would find yourself following a path without knowing why, attracted by a force which you could not resist, your feet following your impulse. Such an attraction and the beautiful night air would soften your mood, making you hum between your teeth, cry out in delight or call to the night to be answered by its echo. Moving on in pursuit of your heart's desire, you would reach a spot where your feet refuse to take you further. Craning your neck to see, the wind playing on your heart, you would be overwhelmed by the beauty of the world. Then the voice which drew you unknowingly to this place would rise again and you would strain your ears in rapt attention—to hear the voice of Zainab singing encouragement and her workmates answering her in their turn. On these magnificent nights, their songs of love revive the sleeping world and comfort the hearts of the sleepless workers. Echoing in the darkness, their voices stir the soul with a beauty to relieve all burdens.

* Country folk of Egypt.

Continuing your journey and following the sound of the voice until you are close to it, you would see the young girls and boys silhouetted against the moonlit sky. Bending over, they grasp with their left hands the stalks of wheat that lean against one another as though intoxicated by those qualities of the night which bring relief to the oppressed. In their right hands they hold their sickles—those semicircles of iron which have been in use from the time of the Pharoahs up to the present day.

And there you would see Zainab, at the head of the group, the others spread out in two wings behind. Singing while they work, the air carries their music in all directions, proclaiming their message in the silence of the night. The moon meanwhile, as though too in some drunken daze, descends in the sky, casting down a pallid light to embrace the green cotton bushes, still in the prime of life.

Zainab was at an age when nature smiled on her like a lover and she would lower her gaze accordingly, out of deference, raising her eyelids cautiously to see to what extent she could flirt with this mysterious love. Then she would lower them again, her heart filled with happiness by everything she saw. Her beauty mingled with the beauty around her so that existence itself seemed to admire her and she in turn became ever more enamoured with her love for the world. At moments like this the beauty of nature touched the depths of Zainab's soul and the image remained imprinted on her heart. In this way they complemented one another; only the nature of their contentment was different.

The contentment of the world is born of years of experience and an acceptance of reality acquired through the ages. To delimit the boundaries of life with threads of the imagination leads to confusion in the face of infinity. The most profitable attitude is to live for the present and to let the future follow. As for Zainab, she was helpless and bewildered in her happiness but at the same time she rejoiced in her situation. She knew that she wanted to claim for herself, from the great unbounded world, one human spirit that would mingle with her own, a soul to flow alongside hers. Then the world could pursue its course while their new found love increased their mutual happiness. That was the sum of her dreams and hopes and if time was in no great hurry to realise them, it never once occurred to her that it was in the power of events to prevent the fulfilment of her desires.

When morning came, the rising sun cast its light over the world and the dew shimmered beneath its rays. Then, as though filled with pride and dissatisfied with its lowly position, it soared up in the sky leaving the stalks of wheat below to revert to their former brittleness. The workers packed the harvested crop into sacks and some waited for the camels which would carry the grain to the barns while others made their way to their houses. They would pass the day with little rest, tending the beasts in the pastures for the days of ploughing which lay ahead. Only by the banks of a stream or canal might they spend a few hours asleep beneath the trees as some recompense for the labours of the night.

When the days of harvesting were over they moved to new work, exchanging the dreams and hopes of that moonlit place for the heat of the day beneath a burning sun. However much they suffered they had become accustomed, like their fathers before them, to this environment and heritage which was their lot. They were used to that state of eternal bondage in which they lived their lives and submitted to it without complaint or misgiving. Toiling endlessly, they would regard the results of their work with shining eyes while the proprietor alone gathered the fruits of their labour. His only concern was to sell the cotton at the highest price and rent out his land for the best return while at the same time exploiting the farm workers in accordance with their lowly status. The thought never occurred to him to raise them from the miserable conditions in which they lived as though he did not realise that his workers might be more efficient if their standard of living was improved or if they had an incentive to work in order to live at a more humane level.

The proprietor did not trouble himself with such matters. He was also accustomed to accepting things as they were and never considered for a moment to exchange the customs of his forefathers. When he spoke about the past it was with an air of respect and reverence, regretting that the cost of labour had increased by one piastre during the winter and longing for the return of the time when everything had been simple and cheap. Not that he complained about the burden of duties upon himself—from this point of view he much preferred the present—but he wished that wages would fall to their previous level, so that he might derive even more profit from the workers while they remained in their servile position.

# Chapter Two

Sayyid Mahmoud, the owner of these lands, came from a large extended family, his deceased father having left behind four wives when he died apart from two others who had passed away during his lifetime. In spite of the large number of offspring that had died before the age of six—twenty-five as far as Sayyid Mahmoud could remember—there remained twelve children, of both sexes, on the day of his death. Such circumstances meant that the children differed greatly in age, from the eldest who was fifty to the youngest, a child aged three and still at its mother's breast. They had all inherited a portion of the estate but in view of Sayyid Mahmoud's position as the eldest male he had acquired by his own efforts, and with the help of his father, considerable wealth and was now head of the family and legal guardian to his younger relations. He was a kind-hearted man with a clear conscience, loving towards his brothers and affectionate with the children. In spite of the mistrust which existed among those born of different wives and the dissent that was sown between them by their respective mothers, Sayyid Mahmoud treated all his brothers as his sons. Besides his own good nature, this attitude may have had something to do with the instructions his father had given him from his deathbed. Unable to hold back the tears which fell from the corners of his eyes as he took a last look at the world he was leaving, he had said in a trembling voice:

'I have entrusted your brothers to your care Mahmoud, now treat them as your sons.'

As for Sayyid Mahmoud's own children they were eight in number, all from one wife, consisting of four boys and four girls. He took a keen interest in their welfare and sent all his sons to school as soon as they were old enough but as to exercising any control himself he was more inclined to leave them to themselves, an attitude which cannot be attributed to one clear cause. He was a respectable man and it would have been quite reasonable for him to keep his children under strict supervision, as was the custom, or at least make them examples of obedience and good behaviour when they were in his presence in accordance with the requirements of Egyptian politesse. Certainly he appeared very stern when they came to him but he lacked that aspect of fearsomeness that his contemporaries possessed in front of their children. For this reason, and also because he belonged to the wealthy class of Egyptian notables, it is difficult to say whether his liberal attitudes were the result of a particular theory of education. Maybe he held Spencer's* view that children must be their own teachers as far as possible and that one should not object to anything they do unless there is some grave danger to themselves.

Accordingly his sons passed the days of their summer holiday in the fields and often spent the nights there too during the harvest, enjoying the air and the songs of the working girls or sitting beside the perpetually humming water wheels. Only Hamid, the eldest of them, differed in this respect, being more inclined to stay in the village and spend his time with the people in the guesthouse. The reason for this lay in his early upbringing when his father had devoted himself to him entirely, making sport in which he revelled without restraint. In moments of joy, he gave his heart to this child whom he loved more than anything and felt to be a part of himself, caressing him contentedly. In moments of anger, when he might have beaten him, the child's grandmother intervened and prevented any discipline of this kind. As a result, when Hamid was only five years old he was very spoilt, often crying and always the centre of attention. Despite his age he was often to be seen carried on the shoulders of the men and womenfolk. His favourite times were the hours he spent playing with Aziza, his cousin, when she came to the village with her mother.

* English philosopher (d.1903) who upheld the doctrine of social laissez faire.

Although he was two years older, his fondness for her was evident and it was not long before the women of the house had decided that one day they would be bride and groom.

Hamid's father sent him first to Koran school, then primary school. The years passed and he remained the focus of affection among his family who were proud of the merit he achieved in his studies. Bur his habit of staying within the walls of the village persisted at a time when his brothers and uncles were out in the fields. On the few occasions he accompanied his father, he neither knew his whereabouts nor the extent of the lands which belonged to them.

In the forenoon of one burning hot day when Zainab was working with her companions weeding the cotton bushes, Hamid did venture out with his younger brothers whose youthfulness made them zealous and fired them with a keenness to exert authority. They would only participate in the work for a short time however, before retiring, their brows covered in sweat, to shelter beneath the trees or rest their backs against the tree trunks. No sooner had the sweat dried on their foreheads than one of them would be on his way back, shouting to the workers as he approached that they were and not working hard enough. But on reaching them, something prevented him from working himself, as though he feared that he might become tired and thereby undermine his authority to order the others.

Hamid made his way over to the workers, scrutinising their faces and putting the occasional question to Ibrahim, the foreman, about the progress of the work. But after an hour he could not bear tire heat of the sun and retreated to the shade of the trees where he sat talking with one of his brothers. When his brother left, Hamid sat by himself, observing the boys and girls sweating in the heat as they toiled over their work. If they so much as raised their heads, Ibrahim or one of the 'gentlemen', as Hamid's brothers and uncles were known, would call out. Then they all slipped from his mind and he was alone in his own world, remembering the day Aziza had departed not long before, having spent a few days in the village. He had often sat with her in the company of his aunt and Aziza's brother and their conversation was always pleasant and merry. Recalling that day it seemed that the talk of the women who had made a 'couple' of them in their childhood still echoed in his mind, and the feeling grew inside him that one day he would possess this girl and have her to love.

In this Egyptian environment and with an upbringing such as Hamid's, it is not uncommon for young men to grow up with a false view of life. They often live in a land of fancy, creating their own happiness and suffering while painting the present and future with their own desires. Relying on such imaginings to get them through their work, many boys colour the outside world in a contradictory manner. Although their senses may belie their imaginings, the power of their fantasies is strong enough to overcome them, making them disbelieve what they see or distorting their judgement and estimation of what stands before them. So if Aziza was very thin it was because of the daintiness of her stature and however lacking in beauty she may really have been, to Hamid she was as beautiful as a flower. If she was somewhat empty-headed then that was due to the very purity of her love. In this way they roam behind their dreams, believing that their future wellbeing will accord with the world they imagine, filled with joys and delights. A world in which one can sit with one's partner, loving her lawfully while gazing at the stars or listening quietly to the voices of the night. When reality brings them back to earth or work forces them down from their splendid illusions, despair enters their souls and takes the place of those far-reaching hopes.

Aziza had been taught reading and writing by her father until the age of ten then she was sent to a sewing and embroidery teacher with whom she stayed for another two years. Her education ended when she started to wear the veil and this also prevented her from further meetings with many of her acquaintances. At the age of fourteen she began to read various books which fell into her hands and whatever difficulties she may have experienced in reading them, tales of romance are always appealing and enjoyed by every girl and boy. Would

that she had read something better though, than these romantic
love stories but regretfully there was nothing else available.
Moreover, only the private and intimate conversations of the
lovers attracted her attention while she ignored the plainer
parts which bored her or occasionally made her feel downright
annoyed! Since childhood she had always been physically weak
and as the inactive life she led did nothing to improve her
strength, she remained so. When she was no longer allowed
to go out by herself, her colour paled and her body grew even
thinner so that after a year had passed she was in great need
of a change of air. She also fell victim to the dampness of the
large house in which she lived and this affected her most
adversely, especially in winter. Consequently her health never
improved.

Unbiased nature knew that this was not her fault just as it
is not the fault of girls in similar situations and upon becoming
secluded at home something awakened in the soul of one of
her relatives, who had always been kind to her as a child.

Stirred by his dreams, Hamid imagined Aziza to be everything he wanted. He remained under the tree until the sun
reached its zenith, signalling the time for the midday break,
and the workers had only to finish the row they were on
before taking to the shade with their meagre lunches. At the
same time Hamid and his brothers' dinner arrived, brought
by their servant and they sat down to eat it without delay.

When the rest period was over, the boys and girls returned
to work followed by Hamid's brothers while Hamid stayed
behind and stretching out in the shade of the trees, he fell
asleep. An hour later the afternoon train passed by, waking
him from his slumber, and he got up to see what was happening
in the fields. Because he sometimes liaised with Ibrahim in
the office there was a degree of familiarity between them,
rather than the indifference that existed between himself and
the majority of workers from the village. For this reason
Ibrahim answered Hamid's questions plainly, with a permanent
smile on his face. When some of the boys saw that Hamid
did not appear too proud to be approached, they thought
they might score over their companions if they tried to speak

to him. But Hamid sent one of them back to work without listening to a word and shouted angrily at another, who believed himself worthy of his attention but whose hopes were dashed by this rebuke from one of the 'gentlemen'.

Examining the faces of the nearby workers, Zainab's beauty caught Hamid's eye and he wondered who she was and whether she usually came to the fields. Back among his family however, such thoughts were soon forgotten.

As the days passed by and the work continued, the fallaheen never complained about the heat of the sun when it burned down upon them during the day. They remained constant, living a life of patience and enduring what their forefathers had endured before them. Their steadfastness, with its roots in history—passed on from generation to generation from the time of the Pharoahs through the rule of Ismael* to the present day—grants to this unfortunate group some degree of happiness in their lives so that even in the face of eternal poverty, they bear their burdens with smiles of contentment upon their weathered faces.

The farmlands appealed to Hamid when he saw how beautiful they were: the plants, trees and streams, the fresh air—and the sturdy working girls. He began to go there every day before sunset and gradually forgot about Aziza. His particular happiness lay in returning from the fields with the workers, enjoying the sensation of freedom he experienced then and release from the cold and heavy chains of custom. At the same time he was less inclined towards girls of his own social group because of the veil which makes boys of his age, in the prime of life, turn elsewhere for natural affection. In reality, his attraction for the working girls was far more healthy than the pursuits of those who jeopardise their feelings and wealth in order to satisfy their carnal desires. And just as we cannot condemn those young men for what they do, it being more the fault of Egyptian society and its adherence to the veil, neither can we begrudge Hamid whose inclinations were only nominally harmful.

* Ismael Pasha, viceroy of Egypt 1863-1879.

After some days the workers were accustomed to Hamid's presence and he would return from the fields by the side of Ibrahim or Zainab, conversing freely with them. Zainab's simple nature revealed a spiritual beauty no less appealing than her physical charms so that whenever he looked at her wide eyes, protected by her pretty eyelashes, he felt as though he were gazing into another world, full of love and desire. As she strode along with firm footsteps, her dress seemed to indicate the luxuriousness of her body and this fancy was strengthened by the softness he noticed in her hands, even though she worked with them.

Hamid soon got used to frequenting the fields, in fact he was so attracted to Zainab that he hardly let a day go by without going where he knew he would find her. And as though Zainab too, enjoyed his presence she never missed a day in the fields, preferring this to the building work available in the village which most of the country girls preferred. The truth was that he was very gentle with her, as any young man would be with a girl he finds agreeable. In spite of her humble status her beauty spoke out on her behalf and Hamid's kindness and affection, something Zainab had never experienced before, drew her out of herself and captivated her. But although he was the only person who spoke to her in a way that expressed a measure of love, Zainab regarded him like any working girl regards her master, with an air of submission expressing both fear and caution.

One evening as the workers were returning from a distant field, Zainab was walking beside Hamid, conversing with him in her customary manner while he listened with pleasure to everything she said. And in that hour after sunset when all things appear as hardly discernible shapes, he put his arm round her waist and drew her towards him. Letting go of herself for a moment, their lips touched and she experienced all the warmth that there is in a kiss. Then pulling away, she said:

'My sister will see us and tell my parents.'

Hamid felt a tremor run through his body. Aroused at first by desire, his mood changed abruptly to one of pride and arrogance as though all the traditions and customs of the past had been heaped together and thrown down upon his head. His face reddened in embarrassment as he backed away from Zainab, lost in strange thoughts and no longer aware whether she was speaking or not.

Leaving the workers at the entrance to the village, Hamid went straight to the guesthouse to drink coffee and quickly dismissed what had taken place. As for Zainab the kiss filled her with happiness, bringing her many pleasant dreams that kept her from talking to Hamid along the way. However much the peasant mind may tremble at the mention of the word honour, the natural instinct of the human heart to love is a compulsion much stronger than social convention, as long as the deed remains out of sight, safe from the judgement of men. When we examine the human condition with all its hopes and desires, we find that it demands what nature drives it to; food when hungry, water when thirsty and so on, so that even if a person achieves their heart's desire, it is often due to forces beyond their control. At the same time man can only attain what his social position allows him to. Thus to a greater or lesser extent, he lives in a permanent state of conflict according to the amount of freedom his situation grants him in the way of achieving his aims and desires.

Hamid did not stop going to the fields, or returning by the side of Zainab, but he was more cautious in his conduct and less talkative. For her part she simply accepted his quietness as an expression of their closeness to one another. The natural pride which her beauty inspired restrained her from feigning conversation or stooping to the level so many girls would have stooped to if they had someone like Hamid to listen to them. As a result he found that he could kiss her from time to time without being shaken by shame, saying to himself: 'Isn't it natural for a boy to kiss a girl whose beauty pleases him?'

# Chapter Three

With the approach of autumn, the summer holidays came to an end. Hamid went away to school with his brothers and as the days passed by he settled down to his studies which began to occupy his mind. His memories of the village and the people in it faded except when he met travellers from his neighbourhood and was stirred to ask about events. Did Zainab still remember him or did she, like so many others, let the past lie fallow until the future dispersed it? Did she feel anything of the meaning of separation or did the present keep her from thinking about past times?

In fact they were both of a similar disposition. Oblivion spread its cloak as they both became preoccupied with the world around them. But when Hamid was alone and had the opportunity to reflect on the countryside and its beauty, the fields appeared before him as though he were present among them. He would picture the gentle streams traversing the open country, bordered by trees in their radiant attire and the water wheels turning here and there, emitting their sad and plaintive sounds. Sometimes he visualised the clear blue sky, split by the light of the brilliant sun. And when it set, stars twinkled in the heavens while the gentle breezes carried the happiest of dreams to the resting world. Sometimes too, he remembered Zainab and those whom he associated with her.

Zainab moved from one day to another in her usual manner, each much the same as the day before and as time flowed gently by, adding to the great age of the world, each brought with it the dreams she needed to resign herself to the next. Waiting patiently for her hopes to be realised she looked expectantly to the future but as it came it passed, adding another chapter to the history of time.

Autumn drew to a close and no crops remained safe in the fields of grass and clover stretching as far as the eye could see. Empty of people and workers the land was now a pasture for the animals that had laboured during the season—and how glad they were of the rest which nature granted them! They looked as if they were on holiday, raising their heads from time to time, bending the silent ear of nature with their noises. Then the birds of the air would answer; turtledoves and sand-grouse pouring forth their winter warblings, singing out in gentle melodies and filling the air with music to dispel all fear and return the world to a state of tranquillity.

In the corner of a field stood a shelter of dry straw, white now white after the wind and rain had washed it clean of dust and through the narrow opening which served as a door, black motionless shapes huddled within. A fire was alight in the hearth around which the fallaheen, their brown faces just visible beneath their cloaks, sat talking together, glad of the warmth of the shelter and the protection it offered against the strong winds which prevail at this time of year. Occasionally one of the younger ones would go out to see to the cattle grazing in the pastures and apart from the occasional passer-by, the roads were deserted.

Just before sunset on one of those December days when the cold chaps the face and teeth chatter, two boys were returning to the village discussing what they intended to do that evening:

'Let's go to the fakka* at Ammi Said's house,' said one. 'We can watch Mustafa and Ummu Saad's daughter dancing.'

'That reminds me,' replied the other. 'It must be nearly time for their wedding. The contract has been written for almost two years now, although no one seems to know when the wedding will take place.'

'I've heard it will be about two weeks after Eid,* which is in three days. So within twenty days they should be married!'

The gathering had become something of a regular event and when Hamid came to spend Eid with his family he heard about the music and dancing and wanted to witness it. He found a companion to accompany him and they set off

---

* Village gathering with music and dancing.
* The end of Ramadan, the month of fasting.

together, laughing in anticipation of what the evening might hold in store. Making their way through the alley-ways of the village they passed the mosque which stood as a silent and dignified reminder of death and the life to come. At times of prayer, voices resound in veneration and glorification as the devout remember what lies beyond this world in which men seek their pleasures and follow their reckless ways.

The two friends however, were unaffected, laughing in their youth without a thought for that fearsome day which lay waiting for them as it lies waiting for us all. Their only concern was to enter the hustle and bustle of Ammi Said's house where the shrill laughter of the village boys betrayed their empty-headedness and simplistic minds.

Crossing the threshold with his companion, Hamid saw before him a large gathering consisting almost entirely of boys. Those girls who were present kept to the edge of the ragged group, some of whom conversed eagerly while others sat quietly or nodded sleepily. The only sad aspect to the merry atmos-phere of this dancing-house, as day by day they anticipated the approaching festival, was the dismal lamp which cast a feeble glow over everything. The faces that appeared in the reddish light were rugged from the harshness of the sun and the cold of winter, but although devoid of softness they still retained their smiles. Drowning out the voices of those who were talking was the sound of a darrabuka,* drummed by experienced hands while the eyes of the attentive audience focused on the dancers in the middle of the ring.

When Hamid saw the workers he remembered the days of summer and on recognising a group of boys and girls whom he had known at that time he strolled across to ask how the work was going. They replied that things were no different from before and no sooner had he left them than they turned back to their friends and forgot all about Hamid and his questions. They wanted only to give themselves up to the pleasures of the moment—an opportunity not to be missed. There being no compensation for a lost hour of pleasure!

*A conical one-headed hand drum.

Scanning the faces, Hamid noticed Zainab's sister standing against the wall, in conversation with one of her neighbours. He went over to greet her and ask about her sister but she did not know if Zainab was up on the roof, where she usually sat every night, or whether she had gone home. In the hope of seeing her, Hamid made his way through the closely packed group, with hardly an inch of space between them, and climbing the stairs he found Zainab by the bannister, alone beneath the pitch-black cover of night. He stood beside her and with a gentle movement attracted her attention. Perturbed at the loneliness she had evidently brought on herself by leaving the noise and laughter of the house to sit alone at the mercy of this winter night, it was no surprise when she turned her head and he perceived her fixed eyes and obvious distraction. After a moment's silence he said:

'How are you, Zainab?'

But Zainab was too distanced from her surroundings to reply and shifting her gaze to him, she responded with an expression of such tenderness that Hamid was deeply touched. Were it not for the utter blackness of the night, near the end of the month, existence itself would have melted before such a look but the darkness could not share the sentiments that flooded Hamid's soul in front of that pained expression.

'How are you, Zainab?'

He repeated his question and feeling compassion he held her hands in his and gave her a brotherly kiss on the side of her forehead, aware that she was undergoing some kind of distress from which there was no one to console her. Her expression revealed that she accepted his sympathy with modesty and gratitude and when he saw her like that his feelings grew stronger. He drew her towards him and began to caress her whereupon she lost herself completely, unaware of the past or the present, and giving in to his gentle advances she allowed herself to lean against him. But no sooner did she remember that her heart was not her own to give than she began to tremble and her wide eyes clouded with tears which told of the sadness she was suffering and also the appreciation she felt for Hamid.

Time passes by while our hearts remain the property of some other force, its power so great that we may wish to devote our lives to it, but at the same time the knowledge that we cannot dispose of our hearts as we please saddens us. This spell on earth, with its happiness and suffering, joy and despair, is beyond our control. Our destinies lie in the hand of that other force and when we feel its presence we shudder, knowing that we are incapable of doing anything we want to do by ourselves.

The darkness shrouding the world was pierced only by the dim lamps which cast golden rays in narrow circles that looked like wounds in the body of the night or primitive weapons, unchanged through the centuries, to which the villagers turn whenever the sky forsakes them. The power of the night encompassed the whole of creation so that all creatures submitted to its authority and stood equal before it. That which was visible appeared obscure, edged with sorrow, and the two silent figures in the night were overcome with perplexity; one wanting to know what was troubling his companion and the other, the beautiful one, suffering an invisible torment which left her powerless and confused. In this situation Hamid eventually broke their long silence with a question about what had been happening during his absence and with a sigh of contentment at merely knowing there was someone in the world who cared for her, Zainab replied that she was happy and that nothing had changed. Then they reverted to their former quietude, turning their gaze in the direction of the dancers and merrymakers.

They sat together until the friend who had accompanied Hamid called up to him and bidding Zainab farewell he made his way down the staircase, his soul filled with peace. But in the midst of the noise of handclapping and the crazy merriment of the fakka, his heart shuddered as the sacred feeling that had filled his being while he sat with Zainab disappeared, shattered by the boisterous activity around him. Returning along the road, however, he soon began to laugh with his companion as they walked past the mosque which still stood in the darkness, warning of death and the life to come.

In the village, Aziza's brother had arrived on the last train to spend the days of Eid in the country and when Hamid learned of his presence he hastened to him and made his greetings. They stayed up for a long time talking or playing cards and backgammon before going outside to listen to some verses of the Qur'an recited elegantly by the faqih.* Then they returned to their homes to take an hour's rest before dawn.

Alone on his bed, Hamid reflected on what he had seen during the evening: the communal happiness in which the village boys revelled, the girls on the edge of the ring and Zainab, hardly speaking a word. Recalling his conversation with Aziza's brother, he also began to think about Aziza and in this way he imagined a confusion of many things, which mostly slipped from his mind as quickly as they came. However, the significance of such recollections is that important events take a more definite shape in the memory, overshadowing matters of no consequence so that while the images of the dancers and merrymakers only appeared briefly before passing into oblivion, the image of Zainab sitting silently by the bannister like a bronze statue, remained. Hamid had been moved by her sadness and wondered what could have happened to her but in the end he shrugged his shoulders, saying to himself: 'Well, what has it got to do with me?' As for Zainab, she was still thinking about Hamid's gentleness when the gathering came to an end and her sister called her to come down. But she trembled at her feelings for him—maybe there really is some divine element in the soul which perceives what the senses do not and that is what guides our hopes and affections, tracing out for us the path of our lives.

Although Hamid tried to forget, the image of Zainab looking to him for compassion filled him with sympathy and he wanted to know the reason behind her grief. He had always known her to be contented and happy so what could have happened, in front of all that boisterous merrymaking, to make her feel that she alone should bear the misery of the world? Maybe something had befallen her family which had

* Qur'an reciter.

saddened her, but what could possibly have befallen a family
who had always been poor and would always remain so?
Maybe someone had wronged her, causing her to be withdrawn
this evening, but then who?

Hamid remained with his thoughts until it was time for
sahur* which he ate downstairs before returning to his room
to continue his dreams. This time however, the images assailed
him so strongly that he could not face them and in dismay
he tried to retreat. Whenever he imagined himself with Aziza's
brother he felt so agitated that it was only sleep that finally
brought him rest from his anxiety.

Later in the morning, Hamid was still preoccupied and
decided to go to the fields in the hope of finding something
there to divert him. The farmlands spread out before his eyes,
covered with green clover and the new shoots of cereal crops,
tender but full of life so that when the wind passed over they
bowed before it as one body. The silky surface formed into
waves that rippled into the distance until becoming lost from
sight on the horizon. After walking a short distance he saw
smoke rising from the vicinity of one of the shelters and made
towards it, believing that a group of workers had lit a fire for
protection against the cold or to comfort themselves during
this, the last day of Ramadan.

Upon reaching them however, he found one of his uncles
looking on while the others roasted corncobs over the embers.
Hamid was shocked by what he saw but they were all laughing
merrily as they placed the cobs carefully and precisely on the
fire. Apparently they considered that this last day of Ramadan,
the feast of young people as it is called, was exempt from any
obligation to fast. As for Hamid's uncle, he took a fresh, ripe
cob of corn and offered it to him smiling. Hamid knew that
he should not just sit there and witness their arrogant behaviour but all he could do was look at them with contempt. If
only they had concealed their shameful conduct, but they
were doing it openly with no regard for anyone else's feelings
and even Hamid's own uncle dared to offer him a corncob

* Last meal before daybreak during the month of Ramadan.

when he knew that he was fasting. It was as though by his
action he wanted to show just how little he cared for the
obligation to which his family had been committed for so
many generations.

Hamid left them, making his way through the fields until
he arrived at the bank of a stream which was dry and empty,
waiting to be dredged. He stared for a while then looking up
he saw the clouds disperse, allowing the sun to cast its rays
upon the earth and transform the dull appearance of the
landscape. When it disappeared again, the world reverted to
that state of resigned sadness in which it had been since the
morning and as this scene repeated itself, Hamid was able to
find some diversion from his own concerns.

Retracing his steps to the house at the end of the day, some
of his relatives were playing backgammon with Aziza's brother
and he sat watching them until he became weary and went
to his room. On the way he passed his sister who stopped to
hand him some cards, which turned out to be greetings from
some of his friends. When he had read them he noticed that
she was looking very pleased with herself and as she was still
holding some cards he asked if she had received any greetings
herself. He knew how much she liked to correspond with him
when he was away, and with her friends when she found the
time to do so, and because she often shared her correspondence with her brother, Hamid sensed that she wanted to show
him what was in her hand. On opening the three cards which
she gave him to read, one was from Aziza, the others from
two of her school friends and as he held Aziza's card, looking
at the message she had written inside it he began to tremble,
which his sister might have noticed had she been more obser-
vant. It occurred to him to keep the card for himself but his
sister took it from him and held onto it tightly, determined
not to lose any one of her greeting cards so Hamid was obliged,
reluctantly, to let her keep it.

When he was alone in his room, Hamid's desire for Aziza
reawakened and he wished with all his heart that she had
come with her brother to spend the days of Eid in the village.
But she had not come, preferring instead to stay with her

family in the town even though she knew how strongly he felt for her! Such hopes and desires, which fill the heads of growing young men, occupied him for a long time until he passed into delightful dreams in which he imagined everything he wished for, planning a life of love with Aziza always by his side. He was only brought back to reality by a considerable commotion in the courtyard and looking towards the West, he saw the sun sinking to its rest as though it sympathised with the hungry world and wished to gladden it by bringing to a close this last hour of Ramadan. A moment later someone knocked on his door calling him to join them.

All his family were gathered together, one staring at the horizon in order to determine with his own eyes when the day had come to an end while another looked anxiously at his watch and a third stood with eyes closed, waiting for the last remaining minutes of the fast to pass. A fourth gazed at the rooftops as though there were something new there despite having seen them so many times while the younger ones could hardly keep their eyes off the table, laden as it was with plates of delicious food and sweetmeats which made their mouths water.

No sooner had Hamid taken his place among them than the voice of the muezzin rose above the silence of the village, proclaiming the return of freedom, and when they heard it they sighed in contentment and expressions of happiness appeared on their faces.

* * *

The following day was the Bayram, the end of Ramadan holiday, when people visit one another and exchange the traditional greetings, replacing the silent resignation of the world with activity and merriment. There were smiles on the lips of all the villagers as they passed to and fro along the roads, shaking hands with everyone they met, wishing each other a happy new year and good health and entering the houses of acquaintances and relatives to share with them the gaiety of the occasion. From time to time groups of girls and women emerged from the alley—ways bearing gifts of food on their heads. They wore their red

gallabiyas,* some with a black shawl round their shoulders and
as they walked peacefully one after another or side by side, they
talked together in tones which expressed their contentment.
On meeting friends they would stop to exchange greetings but
were too reserved to let the air ring out with their laughter on
that happy day lest it should be said of them that they were
wanton.

Hamid got up early and after praying the Eid prayer he
went to receive those who had come to greet him, some of
whom wished him a long life while the older ones laughed
and wished him a bride in his bosom by the next Bayram.
Then with a group of companions he joined the villagers in
their Eid celebrations, walking the streets from end to end,
stopping here and there to drink coffee before moving on and
whenever he saw a group of girls, Hamid did not neglect to
wish them a happy new year. Sometimes he called out to
those he knew by name but they would lower their eyes, and
covering their faces with their elegant headscarves, return his
greetings briefly before continuing on their way in an orderly
fashion. When Zainab passed by in one of these groups Hamid
looked at her but said nothing although her presence among
the other girls, who were all from the same family, attracted
his attention and that of some of his friends who called out:

'There'll be a husband for you this year, Zainab. Inshallah.*'

This did nothing to alter her earnest expression and she
walked on with her young companions, looking straight ahead,
her dark eyes shining beneath the arches of her eyebrows.
Hamid, who knew nothing of her situation and wanted to
find out asked one of his friends:

'Is Zainab to be married then?'

To which his companion replied:

'They say Ammi Khalil wants to engage her to his son
Hassan, and if you want my opinion I think she's very lucky.'

Their conversation was interrupted by another invitation
to drink coffee and they all sat together on a low stone bench

* Loose ankle-length garments.
* Customary Muslim expression meaning 'God willing'.

covered with a mat, while the sun's rays shone on their faces making them look even more radiant and joyful. The sunlight fell on the old white clothes of the fallaheen which they kept to wear on these special occasions and for a few hours they escaped the continuous hardship of their existence. Having enjoyed their company for a while Hamid and his friends got up to complete their tour in order to be home by noon so that they could rest a little before the afternoon prayer, after which the visits would begin again.

Hamid was happy on that festive day, glad to be free after the restrictions of the fast had been lifted and to return to his normal routine, sleeping at night and active by day. Happy also in believing that Zainab was soon to find a good match, something rare for girls of her station. As long as they did not wish for anything more than comparative comfort, what was in store for Zainab would be more than she could hope for. Hamid seemed to forget that as long as there are desires and longings in the human soul and that selfish emotion called love exists between men and women, it is not unlikely that we may find ourselves miserable, even in the lap of luxury.

# Chapter Four

Ibrahim was well respected by those who knew him. He was renowned for his diligence, and the good influence he exerted had endeared him to Sayyid Mahmoud and his sons and nephews so that they preferred him above the rest. Trusted by the proprietor, he was always placed in charge of work in the fields while at the same time left free to carry out the duties assigned to him and this trust made him all the more conscientious in his work. In spite of the pleasant manner in which he treated the boys and girls who worked under him, and the times he spent laughing and joking with them, he did not like to see time being wasted. He would urge them on, lending a hand if the situation required it and sharing in the work with them as an equal. Only when necessity demanded would he discipline them and then there appeared on his calm and gentle face the traces of a scowl which the workers never liked to see.

Zainab enjoyed listening to Hamid and conversing with him but she needed someone to whom she could give herself. Her aimless love needed somewhere to rest, in the heart of another to whom she could devote her life. In this respect Hamid was far from her thoughts. If she did think of him in her moments of longing she regarded him as just another stranger to her soul, hardly moved by him at all. As though the human heart, in its search for love, strives to find a partner of equal status so that the compatability between the two may assist their chances of happiness. Similarly, the longing inside us all for the spiritual partner that was separated from us on the day that Eve was created from the ribs of Adam gives us a special affinity with our own kind. A relationship exists between us and them which we do not experience with people from a different class; we belong to them as they belong to us and bonds of love and mutual affection draw our hearts together. For this reason we look for friends, lovers and marriage partners among our peers because more than any other group they represent the focus of our love and trust.

So it was from among the workers that Zainab would find the companion she wanted. Indeed, she had been feeling for some time that she had already discovered her partner in Ibrahim, whom she saw every day. Because she was the most beautiful, and the most skilful in her work, Ibrahim regarded her with a more kindly expression than he showed to the other working girls. When he said 'Good morning' with a smile on his lips, happiness filled her being and she would tremble from head to toe. Then she would go to the rows farthest away from him as though in the same moment that she wanted to fall into his arms she was cautious lest she should come under his sway.

With each day that passed Zainab felt more assured of her new found love. When she looked at Ibrahim, it was not in the way we usually look at something beautiful which pleases us, instead she lowered her eyes to visualise in the depths of her heart the image that she drew of him. In the end she became infatuated to the point where she would willingly have thrown herself into his arms were it not for the natural diffidence which stood in her way and deterred her from pursuing her goal.

Sometimes when sitting alone she would reflect on the happiness in her heart and ask herself: 'Is Ibrahim really the angel of bliss I imagine him to be, fluttering his wings over me? . . . If only he were!' As she became more enamoured she ceased to think about anyone else and hardly a moment went by in which her heart was not occupied by Ibrahim alone. His image would appear in front of her, gazing at her and smiling, his arms open ready to embrace her until the blood rose to her cheeks in embarrassment before such imaginings. Then she would shiver and her face flushed even redder as an overwhelming longing stirred within to go to him and hold him against her breast and possess him completely. Although she could think of nothing but Ibrahim, when she was under his supervision in the fields she worked calmly at first, anticipating the lunch break when she could sit with

him and the others beneath the shade of the trees. While the
workers chatted together she would raise her eyes towards him
then lower her gaze and return to her world of dreams.

A few days later, when her patience was running out and
she could scarcely keep herself to herself, she resolved to open
her heart to Ibrahim as soon as she could be alone with him.
She had to wait until midday for her opportunity, when the
workers had only to finish the row they were on before retiring
to the resting place for lunch. Hurrying earnestly she finished
her row before anyone else and hastened towards Ibrahim who
was standing a short distance away. But with every step she
took, a feeling of intense shame at what she was doing urged
her to withdraw until she no longer knew whether to carry
on or turn to some other place. Then her body began to shake
and no longer aware of what was in front of her, the air
appeared full of colours as the world spun before her eyes.
Stopping in her tracks she looked round to the right and left,
unable to see anything until she came to her senses and saw
Ibrahim making his way towards her, followed by her sister.
When Ibrahim saw that she was crying he took her by the
hand and led her towards the stream, signalling to her sister
to go back. He continued by her side in silence until they
reached the water's edge then he asked her what was wrong
and again the tears rolled down her cheeks. Indeed, if he had
not quickly thrust her hands into the water she would have
passed out there and then.

'If there's anything you want me to do,' offered Ibrahim.
'I'll do it for you, Zainab.'

The workers had no idea what was the matter and although
they obeyed Ibrahim's instruction to stay where they were,
they grew restless the longer they had to wait and when
Zainab's sister tried to get up she was only restrained from
doing so by the others. To pass the time they brought out
their lunch packs and putting them together, as was their
custom, they sat down to eat, practising amongst themselves
the true meaning of socialism.

Meanwhile Zainab had recovered a little but whenever she
looked at Ibrahim the trembling began again and she almost

fainted a second time. Holding her in his arms and resting
her head against his shoulder, Ibrahim sprinkled water from
the stream onto her face and gazed at her closed eyes.
Eventually she opened them as though coming out of a long
dream and saw the eyes of her companion looking at her, full
of love and tenderness. She could not restrain herself from
putting her arms round his neck but when he returned her
embrace she fainted completely. Ibrahim remained with her
until one of the workers, who had grown weary of waiting,
called out to him and rousing her as best he could, he led
her back to the others where she sat beneath a tree. The boys
all gathered round but time was short and the work could
not be delayed so when Ibrahim told them to return to their
lunch they did so, leaving Zainab's sister by her side.

Zainab rested while the others ate their food then she got
up quietly to have something to eat with her sister and when
they had eaten she returned to work, her mind still distracted
as she glanced from time to time at the green fields and carried
out her tasks in a mechanical fashion.

From that day Zainab emerged from her boundless imaginings
and her soul returned from its distant wanderings to see in
Ibrahim alone the beauty of the world and the fulfilment of
all her hopes. No longer did she look to the sun, the moon,
the planets or the fields for companionship because in all these
things she now saw the image of her beloved which remained
with her constantly. When she saw him in person her natural
modesty prevailed and she would lower her eyes, enjoying
within herself a pleasure similar to drunkenness which numbs
the senses. The kind of pleasure one gives oneself up to without
seeking to define it; the only desire being to remain in that
state for the rest of one's life.

As for Ibrahim, from the moment he led Zainab by the
hand to the stream and rested her head against his shoulder,
a tremor passed from the girl to himself. Seeing her distraught,
her beautiful face turned towards him, pale from her experience, he was barely able to restrain himself when she flung
her arms round his neck, something which gave him the

greatest pleasure he had ever known. Whenever he saw her afterwards he imagined the happiness that lay waiting by her side, but which would only be his if he could find a way to occupy that place.

It was about this time that Zainab first heard rumours about her proposed marriage to Hassan but she paid no heed to them. The joy she felt now left her no time for anything but Ibrahim. These were the happiest days of her life, when everything in the world gladdened her and thriving nature seemed to look upon her with a lover's gaze. The clear sky in which the stars of hope twinkled merrily, filled her dreams with gladness and in all things she discovered a beauty which enthralled her and which seemed to return her love. As day turned to night and night to day she found herself in a state of constant rapture either through seeing Ibrahim or in thinking about him, always looking forward to tomorrow when she would see him again and they would open their arms to each other, wanting to embrace. Each new day competed with its predecessor, pushing it into the past to take its place until it too elapsed and Zainab laughed at them all as they seemed to laugh with her. Nothing could detract from her complete joy and happiness.

When Zainab heard what was being said about her proposed marriage to Hassan autumn was giving way to winter. Nights were drawing in and the world appeared calm and resigned. The unremitting days of work were over, allowing the fallaheen a chance to rest and enjoy a period of relaxation during which it was not uncommon for them to nurture their limited hopes for the future. Children would think about new clothes and young men would contemplate possible brides while fathers enjoyed the sight of their families, gathered together again after the various activities of summer. Zainab did not concern herself with what she heard but gave herself up to the strong emotions which possessed her heart. Does love accept any encroachment on its territory or does it bring us so much happiness that we forget everything but the beloved?

The short winter days, folding and unfolding, soon began to claim back what they had lost to the night, unable to

tolerate such oppression any longer. This natural revolution
stirred those with a desire to live conscientiously, and activity
resumed in the fields as the farmers prepared for the new crop
of cotton, recalling their animals from the pastures to plough
the clover fields. The grass which survived faded quickly on
being exposed to the sun and as the life drained from it, it
blackened and died even before the second ploughing. A sorry
sight for the girls who sorted through it to take out the seeds,
leaving the best of it to be harvested or to be eaten by the
animals. The vast expanse of green which characterised the
countryside during winter was transformed into a desolate
landscape which seemed to glower in its nakedness as though
resentful of man's destruction of its beauty in pursuit of
financial gain. However, it was not long before the life-giving
water began to flow in the canals which spread across the land
and after a few days the shoots of the new crop appeared on
the surface of the earth. Owners and tenants rejoiced and the
world laughed with them—or at them. Such is the cycle that
recurs every year, since before we were born until long after
we have gone.

When the cotton shoots burst through, the faces of the
fallaheen shone with joy, knowing that this crop governed
their entire lives and offered the only solution to all their
problems. It provided their meagre incomes with which they
could look after themselves and their families. But how many
problems arose from day to day before the cotton crop was
ready to sell. How many young plants began their life and
grew bigger and stronger only to wither when they were about
to bear fruit. Rarely can anything be accomplished in isolation
from the power that rules the lives of the inhabitants of Egypt.

Again Zainab heard what was being said about her marriage
to Hassan, this time among her family and those close to her.
During the winter months, when the earth was devoid of new
growth, it seemed that the news had been suppressed but with
the approach of spring the subject was raised again and
rumours were diffused once more. However much she
pretended to forget about them when she was by herself,
preferring at all times to think only of Ibrahim, she could not

always escape them, not even in the strong emotions that flooded her soul. Sometimes they got the better of her, infusing their poison into her veins and putting her off her food, but she would soon return to a world of love in which she could dream to her heart's content. Then she would walk through the fields, filled with joy by the beauty around her, enchanted by the wonderful plants and the great trees in which birds make their nests. Perching peacefully among the leafy branches they pour down their songs of romance on everything below. At these times it seemed to Zainab that the world existed only that it might soar upon the wings of the angel of love, forgetting that over the centuries the hand of man has altered that which the Creator first brought into being. Nevertheless she lived with her dreams until the constant repetition of what was being said about her marriage finally distracted her. Then her feelings for Ibrahim only increased the pain of her anxiety and when grief began to take a hold, there was no refuge for her other than solitude. But loneliness only brings more suffering to those in distress and intensifies their misery.

Within a few days Zainab had become grief stricken almost to the point of despair and whenever she contemplated the misery that awaited her she bowed her head like one who has lost a well loved friend. Sometimes she became so weary of people; their conversation, their faces and everything about them that she longed to be alone, far from their evil ways and spiteful society. She would go to the fields in the afternoon and wander aimlessly, feeling that she no longer had a friend to turn to among the world of people.

When Zainab first started to go out alone, the cotton had grown a little but the shoots were still young and fragile. The spring sun lit up the clear blue sky above and the new leaves on the trees whispered in the afternoon breeze. In the midst of this scene ran a narrow path, its sandy colour whitened by the light and as nature awakened from her afternoon slumber, signs of life appeared on all sides. The silence was broken by the singing of birds that flew from the branches where they had been resting and as they sang, something of the meaning

of joy and happiness was brought back into the world. The
air carried their songs to all sleeping creatures, rousing them
from their rest until vitality was restored to the whole of creation. The earth, the sky, the trees and the birds in the air, all
seemed full of the joys of spring. There was nothing sad or
miserable under the sun except for the heart of Zainab as she
walked by herself through the fields.

Sitting in the shade of a large sycamore tree, she let her
imagination drift across the deserted landscape. The wind
rustled the leaves of the trees and water flowed by in the canal,
its surface stirred by the breeze into small waves that followed
each other with the current until they disappeared among the
reeds which grew along the banks. Sometimes a sparrow
descended from a nearby tree, chirping in the air and alighting
close to where she sat, hopping about freely before flying to
the other bank or back into the tree.

For a long time she sat there dreaming of a future so full
of gloom that she could almost touch it with her hand, her
dreams so vivid that at times she mistook them for reality.
The dire future that stretched ahead seemed to hold the fire
and torment of hell itself and the house of the man whom
they intended her to marry appeared like a tomb where myrmi-
dons* lay in wait, their eyes aglow with streaks of blazing fire.

During these long hours of pain and sorrow, Zainab would
raise her head, to the sky as if to lament the injustice of life
or to seek refuge in God from her oppressive family who
expected her to agree to something for which she had no
desire. Even her father, whom she had always believed to be
just and righteous, seemed pleased by these ill-fated rumours.

With a heavy heart and trembling body, she raised her
tearful eyes to see the evening clouds cover the sun and as it
sank to its daily resting place the sky turned crimson, informing
her that it was time to return home. She got up and languidly
brushed the dust from her black dress which hung the length
of her body from shoulder to ankle. While she was preparing
to leave she heard the rapid sound of a horse's hooves, being

* Angels who thrust the damned into hell.

urged on by its rider now that evening was drawing in and
she quickly recognised Sayyid Mahmoud, the owner of these
lands, riding home after an inspection of his crops and those
of his tenant farmers. On seeing her alone he slowed down
to bid her 'good evening' to which she feigned a natural
response in order to conceal her agitation. He asked how she
was and she replied that, of course, everything was fine. The
conversation continued and when the proprietor joked with
her about the way some of the villagers lived their lives, Zainab
was distracted from her own problems for a while. After talking
for some time, each enjoying the other's company, he asked:
    'Haven't you been working today?'
    'No I haven't.'
    The proprietor often put this question to girls who had not
been working on a particular day and they usually replied
with: 'Oh, I was milking the buffaloes' or 'I was grinding
corn' or something similar, depending on the time of year.
But today he received no such answer. All Zainab could find
to say was 'there wasn't any' as though there were no work to
be done and she had simply taken a day off to spend as she
pleased.
    They were about halfway home, the land ahead partially
obscured by trees, when the village appeared before them in
the distance, shrouded in early evening mist. The main road
was crowded with fallaheen: men, women and children with
their buffaloes, cows and donkeys. Sometimes sheep strayed
from the path and the guard dogs ran alongside them in the
fields. Their own path, however, was deserted and apart from
their conversation, the subject of which had now turned to
agricultural matters, there was no sound to be heard.
    'Do you think the cotton will do well this year?'
    'Yes!'
    He could have laughed aloud were it really such a simple
matter. But what his own sharp eyes had witnessed over the
years, from beneath those heavy eyebrows, of the changes that
come with every season made him more cautious.
    'Who knows what tomorrow will bring?'
    How many misfortunes are concealed in the future? What

happiness or distress, joys or misery lie hidden within its numbered hours? The cloak of night veils all things and the secrets of this world and the next dwell within its folds. Man awaits the future hoping for the best or fearing the worst, expecting something new or accepting a continuation of the past, but the future always comes bringing fresh trials and tribulations.

In the future lies life and death, heaven and hell; wars that humanity dreads, in which the blood of innocents flows and peace that gladdens the hearts of the free when it spreads its wings over the world. In the future lies hope and despair, satisfaction and disappointment. The great empire which confounds the mind, unimaginable even in dreams—the empire of the unknown, impossible to determine or estimate in any way. Therein lies existence and annihilation, everything and nothing.

Such was the future that Sayyid Mahmoud had to reckon with, always at the mercy of the days that follow, and he fell silent as he considered what lay ahead. He remembered past years and the dampness, worms and blights that had occurred in some, while in others the crops had flourished. Then he began to think about price fluctuations and his thoughts became more like dreams.

In those moments the rhythmic thud of the horse's hooves filled the air, its head moving up and down with each step, the rider having slackened his hold on the reins. Sometimes the horse would snort or strike the ground with its foreleg while Zainab followed a pace behind, almost oblivious to her desolation.

'Better to wait and see what the outcome will be,' the proprietor cautioned.

Their conversation moved from one topic to another until they reached the village, after crossing the road which was crowded with fallaheen. They bade one another farewell and parted, the proprietor making his way between the fields to his house leaving Zainab to follow a narrow lane with ridges on either side. On entering the village she met an acquaintance with whom she exchanged greetings then a second and a third, stopping to bid 'good evening' to each of them before coming to a group of dwellings which stood together on a low mound in the village. The only people she passed to whom she said nothing were a group of men, one of whom sported a tarboosh, Kashmiri gallabiya and overcoat. Another wore a turban over a brightly coloured skullcap, his woollen gallabiya, open at the front, revealing an undershirt with silk buttons. Between them lay a closed backgammon board on which they had been playing until it was too dark. They sat with a group of their associates on some matting spread out in front of an open doorway, beyond which was a room that looked empty apart from some rows of wooden boxes. The room was illuminated by the faint glow of a lantern so covered in dust that the light appeared red through the tarnished surface of the glass. In fact it was a new shop which had opened a month ago and in spite of its humble appearance it contained all kinds of material and spices. As a service to the better off inhabitants of the village the owner also saw fit to supply different kinds of games and various sweets and drinks, together with the socks and handkerchiefs they required. All these goods were kept on shelves out of sight or hidden away in the wooden boxes.

Zainab walked past them, continuing along the path which was crowded with passers-by. After greeting a woman standing at the door of the mill, she turned down an alley and in a few more steps arrived at her house. She exchanged a 'good evening' with her next-door neighbour before opening the slightly raised door upon which the grain of the wood and the hollows in between appeared to have been carved over the years and the latch shone as a result of the many hands that had touched it. Passing through she entered the yard which was open to the sky and was once again among her family. Opposite the main door was the hall, the only sizeable room in the house. To the left stood a small oven by the staircase which led to the roof where there was a partially enclosed room by the side of a storage area in which the family kept what they possessed in the way of wheat, barley and corn. The remainder was open to the sky and here they slept during the summer months when they were not busy working in the fields.

Zainab ate her supper and sat with her family until it was dark. When the men had prayed el-asha* and there was nothing to do but sleep, she stretched herself out by the side of her brother and sister on an old mat, with one cotton blanket covering the three of them. Her parents settled down on the other side of the hall and before long everyone, except for Zainab, was sound asleep. She lay awake, opening and closing her eyelids as she recalled the events of recent days and in the darkness many images appeared before her. Some brought joy and happiness while others caused her pain and misery so that she was moved alternately from despair to hope and from hope to disappointment with every beat of her heart. Was not her father, sleeping close by, one of those who hoped to seal her misery—in which case what was the point of staying alive? Or was it possible that the rumours were false and that the next day would be joyful after the anguish of the night? No, tomorrow would be no better than today; it was a false hope in the face of despair to comfort her in her distress. So let it be, let her father and everybody else do as they please. Did she not have the right to say 'no' and thereby resolve all her problems? As long as she had the final word she would never agree to what they asked of her and besides, is marriage a matter for force or coercion?

She imagined herself refusing, her head held high in the knowledge that the hand of God, and the government, were on her side against those self-made rulers of other people's affairs. She could almost see the disappointment on the faces of the bridegroom's party as they turned on their heels and the gloomy expressions of those who accompanied them. Everything fell still as the wind dropped outside and Zainab returned from her lofty imaginings to the darkness of the hall. Then the moon rose and a breeze stirred once more as the world was revived after its lull. The night flowers in the fields gave out a sweet fragrance which filled the air between the

* The evening prayer.

heavens and earth, bringing happiness to all creatures and painting smiles on the lips of those asleep. Zainab's thoughts returned to her parents. Would not her father have to cover his face in shame at such disobedience from a daughter he had always cherished? Would tears not be flowing down her mother's cheeks in front of all the village women, her heart broken by the insolent behaviour of a daughter rebelling against her father's wishes? How awful she felt when she imagined her mother, her eyes full of scorn and contempt, cursing the poor family's misfortune and saying: 'Shame upon you Zainab. Shame upon you my girl!' Could she really bear it when the time came, with no one to support her, having never experienced anything like it before?

And if she were to accept, would it necessarily lead to the endless misery and suffering she anticipated? Had not her mother always said that whether girls married willingly or unwillingly, after an initial period of contention they reach agreement with their husbands and the relationship becomes as sweet as honey? Then with all strife and discord between them gone they perform their respective roles in life contentedly. The husband works all day in the fields while his wife looks after the house, rearing the children if there are any and taking his lunch to him every day, or helping in the fields if the occasion demands her assistance. In this way, the months and years pass by until they reach the end of their lives. So why the terrible sadness which made Zainab wish she was dead?

In fact Hassan was most worthy of her love; a good-natured, hardworking lad, held in esteem by his family and much loved by all for his pleasant company. Indeed there were signs of gallantry in his medium build. His dark brown complexion and sharp, deep-set eyes made him resemble those brave heroes of former times, Antar and Abu Zaid. Anyone who knew how much he enjoyed listening to the poet's songs of heroic adventures, and how he longed for the return of the age of glory and nomadism under the protection of the sword, would have thought he belonged to that bygone race, more suited to expeditions and conquests than the life that destiny had prepared for him. How unfortunate that he should have been born captive to the tough physical life of a farmer, for what is that profession which so many of his countrymen live by if not a kind of hard labour?

Walking slowly all day behind the ox, beneath the heat of the midday sun which scorches the face, the peasant farmer never complains when God pours down his fire from above but trudges humbly back and forth behind the plough in silence, his back bent for hours at a stretch while he hoes the land, sometimes sinking almost up to his thighs in the furrows of the fields. And tomorrow's workload? The same as today, each bringing additional hardships. Returning in the evening, drained and exhausted, he eats his plain food and throws himself down on a mattress no softer than the ground on which the animals sleep, often without a blanket to cover himself. On either side his children sleep, together with the numerous members of a typical peasant family. If they raised their hands they would almost touch the sunken roof from where they lay. Only in the summer are they relieved of those cramped quarters to sleep in the open air beneath the sky.

Is such a life anything other than utter debasement? Yet in this respect the Egyptian farmer is no different from all his fellow workers on the face of the earth, the anomaly being that once something is accepted as normal it attracts no attention. As time goes by, even a way of life as harsh as this acquires a flavour and as successive generations become accustomed to it, the injustice seems reasonable and submission and servility appear as obedience and compliance. Having been born to such a way of life, what was Hassan's crime in Zainab's eyes? In the past she would have found no fault in him but now that he stood between herself and the arms of Ibrahim, poisoning her very existence, he was the most loathsome of men to her. She hated him with all her heart and had no desire to ever look upon his face. And was it not simply because his father had some wealth that Hassan was in a position to ruin her life? There would be no life for her except in the arms of the man she loved! In Ibrahim's arms alone would she find any happiness.

As Zainab lay on the rough mat, wonderful images appeared before her of a world filled with delights. She grasped the thread of hope which some benevolent hand held out and closing her eyes she was carried away with her hopes and fears to a world of peacefulness and sleep.

# Chapter Five

During these days in which events mocked Zainab remorselessly, Hassan's family calmly pursued their ordinary lives, accepting the affair as it stood. When the subject of his son's marriage arose, Ammi Khalil would respond with an easy heart: 'Inshallah, when we sell the cotton, God will see to it.' Then he would be silent or turn the conversation to other matters while Hassan respectfully bowed his head.

Hassan's father was a dignified man with white hair and a long chin reaching to his chest which was also adorned with white hairs. He wore his turban over a white skullcap made for him by his daughter and this fitted loosely over his forehead upon which the long years had etched innumerable furrows and wrinkles. His blond eyebrows, having all but lost any trace of their original colour, were still bushy above his deep-set blue eyes and beneath his short sharp nose a trimmed moustache covered his upper lip. Anyone looking at that old face for the first time would be inclined to think there was some western blood in it. His head was supported by a short stocky neck and his strong sturdy chest had survived all the hardships of a long life without pain or illness. Although his protruding belly seemed to merge into his two short legs, also well covered with hair, he was not what you could call fat. His self-composure, visible muscles and obvious strength showed him to be a fearless type, a thickset man rather than a fat one. Although he was comparatively wealthy, numbered among the respectable men of the village, his years tied him to the old manner of dressing so that he presented himself as a prime example of the fallaheen at the time of Ismael or before. The only concession he had made was to exchange his cotton shirt for a calico one but his woollen undershirt was so old that even his son had no idea when he had first worn it.

Standing with his head bowed, Hassan's eyes rested upon his mother sitting in her black dress and shawl, a tall woman with tough skin and a dusky complexion. From her expression it seemed that she believed in her husband and was only waiting for the remaining months of autumn to pass before her son would marry and bring a woman into the house who would carry out the household tasks, thereby relieving her of a great burden.

Besides Hassan and his parents, the house was occupied by his two brothers, two sisters, and a servant who had been with the family long enough to be considered part of it. The girls were still young and inexperienced regarding housework, so that from the time when the eldest daughter had married and moved out two years before, the responsibility for running the house fell squarely on the shoulders of the mother. Consequently, her desire to see her seventeen year old son married was strengthened by the prospect of the new wife taking over the affairs of her sizeable family. Then she would no longer have to ask her poor neighbours for help, something she found demeaning, and instead extend assistance to them when the occasion arose. In addition, she had great expectations of being a grandmother to her son's children and looked forward to lavishing the affection she had been saving for them over the years. All these factors combined to make her wish to see the marriage contract completed as soon as possible.

Many times she had waited for a suitable opportunity to discuss the matter with her husband only to hear that he considered his son too immature. Moreover, he would claim that financial circumstances were unfavourable, having recently spent all available cash to buy five feddans* of land. Nothing was more detestable to him than to have to borrow and put up with the demands and vices of the moneylenders. If anything were to happen to the cotton, God forbid, they would show no mercy and the debt would rise with substantial interest. He had seen with his own eyes how Sheikh Amir, whose house was only a few doors away, had accumulated

---

* Square measures, slightly larger than an acre.

debts over the years until he was obliged to shift his mortgage
from bank to bank or borrow from the Franks in August only
to pay them back in December at fifteen or twenty percent.
Then there was the case of Ali Abu Umar who now did nothing
but hold meetings and prepare dubious evidence to spread
false propaganda against his tenants, demanding rents that
had already been paid. Having formerly lived a comfortable
and blameless life he had been corrupted only by falling into
debt. For these reasons Ammi Khalil considered it best to wait
for a time when his son's marriage would not bring ruin on
the household and the arrival of the bride would herald wellbeing for them all.

His wife, however, was unconvinced by these arguments
and would not listen to him. One day, having lost patience
with his attempts to postpone the occasion she said:

'As you've just bought five feddans why not sell one feddan
of your land in the country if you're afraid of running into
debt?'

The thought of selling any of the land he had inherited
from his father and which he had been cultivating for years,
did not appeal to Khalil. Nevertheless, his wife's incessant
pleading day after day almost convinced him that in his latter
years he too might find consolation in his grandchildren. But
his dread of falling into the hands of the rapacious moneylenders, who neither feared God nor pitied mankind, whose
only religion was to profit from the needy, in addition to his
love for his father's lands, made it a more complex issue than
could be solved with an easy answer. It was a matter which
required him to be cautious and to seriously consider his every
move. For this reason he said as little as possible whenever
his wife raised the subject, although his conscience was never
completely at ease. Sometimes, when she persisted in her
requests it was as though a voice inside him were saying:
'Doesn't your wife have a right to expect a positive response?'

In any event he could not lightly accede to her wish. To
plunge blindly into something may result in errors which take
years to correct, if they can ever be remedied. Therefore the
best course is to be wary lest what we strive for today—

although we may hope for success—be a cause for pain and regret if we expect too much and pursue our desires accordingly. Throwing ourselves into depths we do not know is nothing more than folly leading to ruin and misery.

These thoughts passed through Khalil's mind while he sat on the roof watching the sun go down. Before it vanished from sight a full moon rose in the cloudless sky, tinted by the fire of the setting sun and as the sky gave way to the layers above, its depth appeared to increase. At that time the air was moist, carrying the evening dew which Khalil could feel on his bare chest. It was the kind of breeze that makes us forget our troubles and fears, to be carried away happily to great new worlds where our dreams run free, where everything we want we can find and where every wish we make is granted. A doorway which leads to infinite possibilities.

In these surroundings, Khalil was unable to remain with his apprehensions any longer and gradually gave in to the inevitable. He considered the brighter side of the proposition instead of the dull side and as hope took the place of fear he began to regard the prospect of his son's marriage more favourably. He thought of the children that the marriage would produce and how wonderful it would be when the house was filled with their shouting and laughter. They would be like angels in the place, a comfort from any troubles that the future might hold, and their grandmother would have plenty of time for them after being relieved of her household tasks by the new wife.

The old man took pleasure in these dreams which reminded him of his own youth and lightened his heart, heavy with the burdens of the years so that when his wife came to him, as the sun cast its evening glow over the departing day, he did not hesitate to ask if Hassan had returned from work. She replied that he had gone to pray el-maghrib* whereupon Khalil—evidently distracted him from his religious duties—went straight to the mosque where the men were lining up behind the Imam, most of them having just returned from a hard day's work.

* The sunset prayer.

By the side of the pulpit stood those who had reached the age of seventy years or more and now had nothing else to do but spend their lives in prayer and worship. In the dead of night they would come to this house of God, to recite traditional invocations by the light of one or two weak lanterns and in the sleepy hours, give voice to their prayers until the approach of dawn. At that time silence shrouds the village, broken only by the barking or howling of dogs until the voice of the muezzin splits the still air with his long call to morning prayer, adding the words 'as-salat khairun min an-naum'.* Repeating this phrase twice in a loud clear voice, he extends the vowel sounds so that they resound in his larynx, each carrying its own peculiar significance. After the morning prayer the old men return to their houses for something to eat or to continue their sleep until midmorning. During the day, you would find them stretched out in the mosque reminiscing about the past and the injustices of the ruler Ismael or discussing day to day events in the village. When the sun reaches its zenith they perform the midday prayer then retire to sleep deeply, most of them snoring quite unpleasantly. After praying el-asr* some might go to the fields to see what God is doing there while others await the pleasant evening breeze in the mosque and in this manner these venerable old men pass their time, moving gently from one day to the next, hoping for nothing more than that God will forgive them and accept their supplications.

Khalil entered the mosque and took up his customary position as the Imam raised his hands to his ears calling: 'God is great'. Behind him the voices of the faithful were raised in answer, echoing the call in a disorderly fashion. Some uttered the words in a loud shrill voice which pierced the ear while others repeated the phrase two or three times as though they were unsure whether the first would be accepted. Some broke off in the middle of a word and started again from the beginning while others rattled off the phrase in one breath. Everyone

* Prayer is better than sleep'.
* The afternoon prayer.

saw fit to join in as they pleased with no apparent cohesion, making it a motley collection of voices that resounded in the dignified surroundings at the times of communal prayer. When the Imam considered that the noise had subsided sufficiently he began to chant the Fatiha.* But before the end of his recitation a voice called from the direction of the water taps: 'God is with the patient'—and a man came running into the mosque with bare arms. Pulling down his shirtsleeves he joined the row of worshippers and raised his voice to let the Imam know that he was ready. Hardly had he made his announcement than another latecomer called: 'God is with the patient' and held them up for a few more moments. Then in the midst of the darkness which entered the mosque from every window and gradually obscured the white walls and pillars within, the worshippers bowed down. From a distance they looked like swirling phantoms in the land of the jinn* or angels drawing close together, wrapped in the veils of the sky. Night descended from the high roof of this house of God as the worshippers prostrated themselves until they were almost level with the floor, their foreheads touching the ground in submission before their Lord. When they reached the second rakat* they almost disappeared from sight and in the silent darkness they whispered their prayers which were carried upwards on the wings of night until the Imam was ready to say: 'God has listened to those who have praised Him'.

While some received these words with hearts full of the fear of the Lord, others dreamed of what they would buy at the Thursday market or secretly reckoned up the days they had worked as they waited impatiently to finish their religious duty before going to the clerk to get their wages for a day he was trying to cheat them of. Hardly had the Imam invoked the peace and blessings of Allah than they hurried away to complete their calculations. Sometimes, if the clerk was present among them, they would force him to his office to find out

* Opening chapter of the Qur'an.
* Demons or spirits.
* One complete movement in Muslim prayer.

for themselves from his records what was due to them and what was not.

Khalil prayed with them, entreating Allah for a successful outcome to the subject on his mind and when he had finished, he retraced his steps to find that Hassan had arrived home before him. They ate supper together but Khalil's head was full of contradictory thoughts that left him unable to determine a definite course of action. Nevertheless his dreams and fantasies were soon revived by the pleasant breezes blowing gently across the village which lay submerged in a great ocean of light beneath the rays of the moon.

After praying el-asha, Khalil hoped to retire and postpone further considerations until the morrow but there was no escape; his wife had come to remind him of the matter in hand. On this occasion however, he was not assailed by his previous doubts and asked who she thought would be a suitable wife for Hassan—a question which raised another difference of opinion. Should she be a young lady from a family of similar status to their own, comparatively well off, or as Khalil preferred, any respectable girl who would look after his son and his house without creating problems every month or so by becoming angry and returning to her own people? This was not a difference that had arisen recently and although Hassan's mother had decided whom she wanted as a bride for her son, she considered it better policy to refrain from mentioning her name at this time, especially as she was aware of something in her husband's attitude that upset her confidence in her personal choice. Content with Khalil's positive response she seemed to want only to arrive at a decision on which the family could all agree.

Hassan himself had never discussed the matter with his parents. Although it would have been easy for him to confide in his mother, as they were quite intimate, it was impossible for him to speak openly to his father. He was not opposed to marriage, in fact it was something he wanted, even if he did not know any more than his parents to which girl he would like to become engaged.

\* \* \*

The following week, Hassan was working in one of his father's
fields which bordered on the lands of Sayyid Mahmoud where
Ibrahim, as always, was in charge of the workers and working
girls. At midday, when they had eaten their lunch, Ibrahim
invited Hassan to play jacks in the short period that remained
of their lunchtime break. It was one of those beautiful days
at the beginning of November when the weather is mild and
the air moist, and the fallaheen rejoice at the approach of
the winter rest. The leaves which clothe the tall trees, having
fulfilled their purpose throughout the summer, were beginning
to fall to the ground although there was still sufficient shade
for those who wanted it. Hassan accepted the invitation and
they traced out their playing area, each taking two young
boys from among the workers to assist them while the others
gathered round to watch. Most were buxom girls, physically
mature yet still displaying that youthful beauty which made
even the least attractive of them desirable. Zainab sat with her
friends and companions, hardly taking her eyes off Ibrahim.
In a few moments all movement ceased and everything was
quiet as the players prepared to commence their game. After
the customary opening:

'Remember Ali'—'We remember him'

'And Iblis'—'Curse him'

'Our forefathers'—'God bless them'

'Most merciful of the merciful'

— the sound of the stones could be heard as they scattered
on the ground and from time to time the younger players
called out:

'One up!'

'Two up!'

'Well done!'

'Good shot!'

But Ibrahim's next throw was not so fortunate and reluctantly he handed over the jack to his opponent while the
spectators looked on with fixed expressions. A minute later
the two sides drew level, one with six green stones the other
with six white, and the two 'experts' began to count each
game:

'The jack, one, two!'
'One, two, three, hold it . . . and again . . . yes!'
'Right. In the middle . . . well done!'
'Now for the jack!'

Each time a contest reached its climax the smiles that appeared on the lips of the onlookers faded as excitement surged through their bodies like an electric current. Then they returned to their former state, staring straight ahead as though oblivious to anything but the game. When the contest was over, the sun passed behind the clouds and the sky turned dark and gloomy. In the distance they heard a noise to which their ears were well accustomed, one of many sounds they recognised without a thought: like the anxious warbling of birds striking the very nerve strings of the atmosphere, the gentle murmuring of water or the sound of frogs on a summer's night, filling the silence whenever the girls stopped singing. As the sound reached their ears some gazed in the direction from which it came while others stretched their arms and yawned deeply, sighing at the approach of the afternoon train that shook the ground beneath them as it passed. The clouds of smoke blown from the chimney, shot up in the air and wavered in the wind before falling over themselves and disappearing. The lunch break over, they returned to work with their usual forbearance until the sun was a red ball sinking to its resting place, warning that it would soon be departing the earth until morning. Light was fading before the oncoming night as the workers made their way to their abodes after God—or the supervisor—had finally relieved them of the day's burdens.

Ibrahim called Hassan to accompany him while the workers and working girls walked ahead or followed behind, all conversing merrily. From time to time the laughter of the girls as they parted company was carried on the breeze followed by a barely audible echo, as though rebounding off the horizon or the branches of distant trees. The two young men however, did not share the laughter of the others. To see them whispering to each other, and the serious expressions on their sunburned faces, you would realise that they were discussing a matter of some consequence. In fact, since setting out together, they both sensed that this conversation would be more meaningful than most, and after discussing everyday matters for a time Ibrahim asked his companion:

'Is it true my friend, that you want to get married?'

'Who told you that? Do you know of any suitable girls for marriage?'

'Of course! There are plenty! Don't any of these girls attract you or do you want to aim so high that you end up with someone who gets angry from morning 'til night?'

In front of them were at least three working girls who would have made excellent wives and some others too, from respectable families, who were returning from their fathers' fields. So there were a number of potential brides from whom Hassan could choose. As he surveyed the scene he remembered what he had heard about girls from wealthy families being quick to anger and return to the protection of their people. Then he considered the girls from his own social group. They would be more faithful and conscientious, he thought, and more likely to keep their obligations. As long as he did not look to those with more wealth, Hassan felt that the most promising partner would be one like himself, who had been brought up with an awareness of the value of money and knew how to handle it with respect. In his opinion they would be more reliable than the daughters of the fallaheen, who knew nothing of the value of land and never tasted the pleasure of success in their work, but lived only from day to day regardless of what they achieved or did not achieve. After a moment's silence Hassan said:

'God will see to it, my friend, in his own time.'

But something in Ibrahim's expression made him realise that he was expected to choose from the many girls in front of them, the one who pleased him most. Hassan was not inhibited in this respect but had never preferred a particular girl with whom to share his life and who would bear him the sons and daughters both he and his family hoped for. He looked at the girls who were returning from their own fields, their families as comfortable as his own. Then he turned to the sturdy peasant girls and decided that Zainab was the most beautiful of all.

For the rest of their journey the two friends discussed other matters, hastening through the descending darkness beneath which colours were fading rapidly until the eye could scarcely distinguish shape or form. When they reached the path that led to the mosque they hurried down it—Hassan, dark and impetuous; Ibrahim, nimble and sprightly—almost certain that the Imam had already started the prayer. The others dispersed, each making their own way home after bidding one another 'good night'. The black veils of the girls made them seem sad, or regretful that the tender years of their youth should be spent toiling on the land, even though their smiles made them appear content. In their black garments they looked like spirits, floating on the ocean of the newborn night as they disappeared behind walls or vanished from sight between the alleys to their houses, to spend the night in peaceful sleep.

Hassan performed his prayers quickly with Ibrahim then set off on his own and on the way he passed his father sitting with a friend by the name of Salamah on a stone bench outside the latter's house. He stopped to greet them before continuing at a more leisurely pace, now that there was no reason for him to hurry home. The two old men, worn down by the years though still robust, having been among the first to leave the mosque after the sunset prayer, now sat telling stories about mutual acquaintances or voicing their opinions on what they saw before them on the path. They considered the bull that Hajj Ali had bought at the Thursday market rather expensive at twenty-two pounds although they both agreed that it was a hardworking beast. Then a girl from the provincial capital passed by, the wife of Awad Mishal, and they discerned a certain looseness in the way she walked which led them to the view that all women from the city were undisciplined. When a group of working girls passed by, Khalil remained silent but his companion surprised him by saying:

'There, look at our fine village girls.'

And after a moment's pause, he enquired:

'Is it true, Khalil, that you want Hassan to marry?'

'Yes Salamah,' replied Khalil in a gentle voice, 'but I don't
know who to marry him to. My son doesn't like girls who
make a lot of fuss or spend their time arguing from dawn to
dusk. You know how quickly some of them become angry.
To tell the truth I'm a little confused about it.'

His companion continued in a steady tone, hoping to reassure Khalil as much as possible:

'Don't worry my friend, there's no need to worry. If those
girls don't please you there are plenty more besides. I can tell
you about one much better than them, and by God she's a
handsome girl. What have you got to say about Zainab?'

Were it not for the fact that Khalil feared his wife would
never approve a girl of lower social standing to themselves he
would have considered her an excellent proposition. But he
had given the matter much thought and knew that the atmosphere in a household where the mother-in-law does not get
on well with the new bride will always be turbulent, their
personal disputes often becoming the focus of contention
between both parents and children. If, on the other hand, his
wife were agreeable he would accept Zainab totally, even
believing himself fortunate.

Understanding his friend's apprehensions, Salamah said:

'All right my friend, then marry him to Ali Abu Umar's
daughter and see what problems that will bring you. Nothing
seems to satisfy us peasants!'

When Khalil returned home he mentioned the conversation
to his wife and although she had heard only good reports of
Zainab, her ambitions reached higher than to accept readily
a girl from a poor family who had worked all her life as a
labourer for the benefit of the rich. Her displeasure was evident
from the expression on her face but when Khalil considered
the alternative he found himself in agreement with Salamah.
He wanted to know why his wife was dissatisfied with his
choice but she would not say. And when she spoke to Hassan
later that evening about his father's attitude, he made no reply
and would not commit himself.

Although these events and conversations led to no concrete

conclusions in the minds of those concerned, the rumours in the village began to take a more definite shape as though a firm decision had been reached. Despite the fact that Khalil did not agree, the rumours seemed to suggest that everything had been finalised and that the family had agreed to accept the mother's choice of a bride for Hassan. In this way the news reached Zainab, bringing her hope once again after her spell of mortal despair.

* * *

During these days in which events mocked Zainab remorselessly, Hassan's family calmly pursued their ordinary lives, accepting the affair as it stood. Although they seldom referred to their son's marriage in conversation they were actually arriving at something more positive. Hassan's mother began to question herself whenever doubts about the 'respectable' girls arose in her mind and finally she had to acknowledge that none of them were more suitable than Zainab—or even equal to her.

In his work, Hassan seldom thought about the matter. When he did, he was inclined to think that his parents would have his best interests at heart and this gave him some hope. But he often avoided the subject completely.

In this way their lives continued . . . Until the summer.

# Chapter Six

Summer came and the rumours died down, just as everything in this world causes a commotion at first before becoming something ordinary which the eye sees or the ear hears without attracting attention. And with the summer came the irrigation shifts that disrupt the order of the peasants' lives. During periods of unemployment they stay with their families but when irrigation is in progress they work endlessly night and day with virtually no rest at all. At these times their beasts labour with them until they are also exhausted.

While the summer brought work to the fallaheen, to others its arrival meant days of rest and recreation. Hardly had spring turned to summer than Hamid and his brothers returned to the village after months spent between papers and books within the walls of the city where they rarely caught a glimpse of the horizon or enjoyed the sight of a sunrise or sunset. Their studies presented them with many problems and they would count the last few days on their fingers, looking forward eagerly to their return from the great and illustrious capital to their own small village. When the examinations were over and their bags packed, the joy of the occasion brought smiles to their faces. You would think they were migrating to the most exalted parts of the earth where they would find happiness and permanent wellbeing awaiting them. Arriving in the village they would bring out the sports balls and other items which they felt they could not be without during the first few days of the holiday and these articles would then be passed on to younger relatives who either disposed of them within a day or two or, on finding themselves in possession of something, guarded them covetously.

On the eve of their departure some were so excited that they could not tell whether the night seemed long or short. One of the younger ones spent it dreaming about his little brother from whom he had been separated the year before.

He longed to sit beside his mother and gaze into her loving face as he was accustomed to do before being sent away. One of the older ones, who had grown used to such separations found that even though the years had raised a veil of forget-fulness, he still looked forward to his return although he did not know exactly why. He was also despondent at the pros-pect of leaving the city in which he now spent the most important part of his life. The image of his mother or thoughts of his family seldom occupied his mind but he saw in his younger brother, still full of the endless concerns of a child away from home, an explanation for his own mixed feelings of happiness.

After his brothers had gone to bed, Hamid stayed up to take a last look at his room. Tapping his fingers on the desk he examined his library and the wonderful books it contained. Then he remembered his room in the village with its empty wardrobe and bare desk with no papers upon it. He imagined the evenings he would spend with the villagers, reading the papers which never came up with anything new but simply repeated what had been said before. Even so, the fallaheen would still applaud the excellent writers who knew how to rearrange the words day by day, even if their aim was merely to cram the minds of their readers with giant headlines supple-mented by inflated accounts of trivial events. No doubt, with sufficient exaggeration, they hoped to make everyone aware of what they considered it their duty to report.

In that quiet hour of the night, Hamid reminisced and almost despaired at the thought of leaving Cairo. The prospect only became brighter when he remembered the vast lands a few steps from the village over which his gaze could freely roam and where he could let his imagination wander to limits his city room could never encompass. He thought of the nights he would spend in the fields, watching the moon surrounded by stars glittering in the clear summer sky. Or sitting by a canal, listening to the croaking of frogs, the call of crickets or the perpetual humming of the water wheels that drowns the more obscure sounds of the night. Then he recalled the singing of the peasant girls, ringing in the air and carried on the breeze, filling the sleeping world with joy. In the memory of these things he found some consolation for leaving behind his room and library but an inner voice questioned him, saying: 'Have you become so neglectful that you remember the wonders of the night and the music of the fallaheen, but forget your own parents? Have you become so selfish that those whispering sounds in the darkness are more important to you than the voice of your mother calling out to greet you?'—Although Hamid loved his parents he looked to the beauty of nature for comfort. But what use is the universe and all it contains if it is devoid of a human heart which loves a man and feels for him?

In reality it was only to be expected that a young man who spent the greater part of his life with school friends in the city should return to his village in the summer to find it a place of lethargy and inertia. The people showed no signs of true community and hardly even appeared to be living together. Everyone inhabited a corner by themselves, alone in their thoughts except when driven by necessity to sit with the family at mealtimes. Even then, silence overcame them as though they were at a funeral ceremony among the relatives or loved ones of the deceased. The comradeship and frankness that Hamid enjoyed with his classmates did not exist between him and his family. Consequently his memories of nature stirred him more than the memory of his parents with whom he felt there was little to connect him other than that they had provided him with the necessities of life during the days of his childhood.

* * *

Soon they were all in their small beloved village, surrounded by wide horizons where they could enjoy their freedom beneath the clear sky. In the cotton fields the bushes had now produced buds, anticipating the bolls which were still to come, while the fields that had already been harvested were bare but for the dry roots of the previous crop which shrivelled beneath the scorching sun. During the day blazing winds blew through these bare clefts as though it came straight from the mouth of hell. The summer was fiercely hot even if its authority did not extend over the wonderful sleepless nights.

Hamid awoke having moved abruptly from the noise of the capital to the peace and quiet of the countryside; from continuous studies to the emptiness of the summer holiday. At first he did little but sleep, or recollect the days of school in his conversations with his brothers, and this other life which flowed monotonously from one day to the next depressed him. But man always has the ability to create something out of nothing and by occupying his mind in different ways he can vary the flavour of his existence.

Everything gains merit in time and the tedium of leisure to one who is unaccustomed to it soon becomes a pleasure. When a man is free to follow his imagination, he enters a world which he alone occupies, where there is no one to please but himself; a world of clear skies and perfumed air and desires that can be realised whatever they are. Such was the case with Hamid. He emerged from that period during which he created work in order to relieve his boredom and entered instead the paradise of dreams. He would spend the day aimlessly until the sun sank to its rest, then he would leave the village for the countryside where his imagination knew no bounds. Ambling through the fields with a firm but gentle step, and with no particular destination in mind, he only came to his senses when disturbed by the salutations of passers-by.

Sometimes he would come across a group of workers or working girls whom he had known before and stop to greet them or pass the time of day. On one of these occasions, when Ibrahim was supervising the pruning of the cotton bushes, Hamid walked over to see how the work was progressing. Among the workers was a young boy with a bright cheerful face, a light-hearted lad and a glib talker who left his work to join in the conversation. When Hamid asked him about his sister Fatima and why she had not come to help with the pruning, the young lad grinned from ear to ear, replying that she was married now and living in another village. Finally Ibrahim ordered the boy back to work and urged on the others before returning to answer Hamid's questions.

When Hamid noticed Zainab's sister he went over to ask
about Zainab and learned that today she had gone to the mill.
Then he spoke to some of the others, enquiring after their
sisters until the colour of the sky began to change. Carrying
on his way, thinking about the workers and what their futures
might hold for them, his memories of Zainab were reawakened
and her image appeared before him with sleepy eyes, her
shapely body concealed beneath simple working clothes. But
instead of becoming restless or agitated, his long absence and
the belief that he would never have this girl to love, caused
these recollections to have only a mild effect on Hamid's heart.
As the days followed on, however, he began to think about
Zainab more often and when he was alone in the silent midst
of nature, he remembered what had passed between them and
the times they had spent together. The most vivid memory
in his mind was of the day he had realised that he would
soon be leaving her, a few days before returning to the city.

That was at the beginning of autumn when the world
surrenders the days of joy and elation to prepare for the stillness of winter. Hamid was walking by Zainab's side casting
farewell glances at the people and the fields, his emotions
stirred by the knowledge that he would soon be leaving these
hallowed places—and the working girls. With an expression
that revealed his agitation he turned to Zainab and said: 'After
one week, I will be travelling.' Zainab responded by lowering
her eyes, sorry that they would soon be parting. She seemed
to sense that without Hamid by her side she would be no
different from the other girls while Hamid's heart overflowed
with feelings he could not comprehend. Standing close to
Zainab in the middle of the road, signs of anxiety appeared
on his brow as though he were waiting for some hidden
command. But the darkness creeping over the world at that
sunset hour only made him feel more uneasy.

Finding themselves alone on their return to the village, the
others having gone on ahead, they left the path for a small
hillock concealed from the road and sat down. A moment
later Hamid took hold of Zainab's hand, squeezing her fingers
tightly and instead of complaining or resisting, she folded her

fingers round his and squeezed them too. Then in the semi-darkness that encompassed them he leaned towards her and kissed her on the cheek. When Zainab felt it she turned away, but Hamid put his arms round her shoulders and drawing her closer he began to kiss her temples, cheeks and neck, fondling the locks of her hair which hung loose. As though possessed, Zainab gave herself up to him, embracing him in return and kissing him. Then she pressed her lips against his and closing her eyes she almost fainted while Hamid, in his intoxicated state, felt he was sucking melted honey from her tongue. Oblivious to their surroundings they remained locked in their embrace and when their lips parted Hamid kissed her again, pulling her towards him. Her burning breasts trembled with the passion contained in them and the blood rose to her temples as she lay helpless in Hamid's arms.

Hamid remembered all this and wondered if fate would be kind enough to grant him another hour like it. It occurred to him to go at once in search of Zainab, wherever she might be, unaware of how preoccupied she was now with her love for Ibrahim. Had he known he would have realised what a great divide separated them, for there is no stronger barrier than the barrier of love that excludes everything besides the memory of the beloved. But Hamid did not know what was in Zainab's heart, believing that the only obstacle between them was that she was soon to marry Hassan. Indeed, were it not that he respected the lawful relationships between the sexes, his only concern would have been to find some way to make her heart his own. What man could resist a woman so beautifully fashioned by the Creator's skilful hand?

# Chapter Seven

During those hot summer days in which folk tend to leave the cities, Aziza came to stay in the village. Even if it was only to exchange one set of walls for another, at least she would benefit from the change of environment. When Hamid learned of her arrival his only thought was to go to greet her, to sit by her side and talk to her. How pretty she had been when she was young. Lithe and quick, always ready to laugh in the days when they used to play together, never questioning their actions.

One of Hamid's characteristics was that he often felt as though a hundred pairs of eyes were studying the secrets of his soul and prying into his personal affairs. This made him hesitant but he soon felt an irresistible urge to go and meet the girl whose image in his mind was one of youthfulness and love even though he had not seen her face for four years. Not since the time her family had decided it was no longer safe for her to be alone with the opposite sex, considering that her rise to maturity made her easy prey for the devil and his temptations. Yet despite this long absence he was certain that she would be like any girl under the sun. Seated on the throne of youth and clothed with the beauty of womanhood, she would be perfect in every detail, a jewel to those who beheld her.

He did not hesitate for long. In the afternoon, two days after her arrival, he plucked up courage and made his way to the house where she was staying. With a throbbing heart and agitated mind he entered, only to find her sitting with her relatives. They all stood up to greet him, the older ladies kissing him on the forehead and after he had returned their greetings and taken a seat among them, they resumed their conversation. When he was asked why he had not been to visit them sooner he answered politely then sat in silence and although the ladies often laughed aloud at the stories they related, Hamid's lips never expressed more than a passing smile. Staring at the ground or occasionally glancing round the room, he was preoccupied with the girl whose image had accompanied his dreams for so long and who now held a position of such great hopes in his life. He was eager to see the face he had known before and which would now have reached perfection, her beautiful mouth revealing the sweetest of smiles. Then he began to wonder how she regarded him, not doubting for a moment that she shared his feelings and loved him as much as he thought he loved her!

Afraid that someone might discover his purpose he got up to leave, excusing himself despite their requests that he should stay, claiming an appointment which he had to keep. Even then he did not feel at ease, as though the ceiling had eyes that scrutinised the depths of his heart. He feared that his innermost self would be revealed and that it would become clear to everyone why he was hurrying to leave. Barely able to maintain his composure he left the house and made for a nearby garden where he threw himself down beneath a tree, beside a stream in which the water flowed peacefully. From time to time a leaf passed by in the current or a frog swam close to the bank. Unaware of himself, Hamid began to toss pebbles into the water until gradually he settled down. Having regained his composure, his thoughts returned to the girl he had tried to glimpse and he was soon transported to the realm of blissful dreams which fill the hearts of lovers or others touched by love, even if it mocks them. He began to contemplate the happiness that would be his with Aziza at his side, their conversations and the words he would whisper as they sat together in a quiet corner of the world with only the moist breezes to stir them. Then the birds would sing their touching melodies while nature showered them with blessings, immersing them in never ending joy. What sweet hours they were, imagining her so close that he had only to reach out his hand to touch her.

The following day he thought of going to see Aziza again. At first he tried to overcome his feelings, afraid that a repeated visit would betray his purpose but the struggle was in vain

and he gave in to his desire. At the same hour as before, he
visited the house only to find the same people with her, relating
their stories in the same repetitive manner. This time Hamid
felt as though his soul would flare up. He shuddered and the
signs of unrest were almost visible upon him as he got up to
leave with an excuse even weaker than the previous day.
Perplexed, he wandered aimlessly, hesitating so much at times
that he virtually stood still, at other times hurrying then
dawdling again, unsure which direction to take. His nerves
were strained and from time to time he knit his brows and
frowned dejectedly. What thing had taken hold of this young
man's heart to cause him to become distracted almost to the
point of madness? What sentence had the heavens imposed
on him for the crime of submitting himself to love? Should
allowing the soul to enjoy the most noble emotion of life
bring distress such as that which afflicted Hamid until he was
half demented?

The unfortunate young man made his way between the
fields to a canal bank where he sat in the shade of a large
mulberry tree. In his frustration he began to wonder if it
would ever be possible to wrest Aziza from her relatives so
that he could sit beside her, entreating and embracing her
until she belonged to him alone. For the rest of the day he
thought about nothing else then he spent the night dozing
fitfully until he was unable to stay in bed and got up to go
to the mosque, although he was a stranger to the place at that
time of sleep and lifelessness. As he made his way the light
of morning crept up stealthily, like hope that finds its way
into the hearts of the wretched. The sky was barely visible,
still covered by a veil of darkness as the stars faded one after
another. A deep silence covered the world so that there was
no sound to be heard apart from the cocks crowing to one
another across the village. Then the muezzin's call to prayer
split the atmosphere to the heavens.

Hamid prayed two rakats in congregation and left for the
fields which were still deserted at that hour. The air was fresh,
mingling with the morning dew, and as shapes became discernible the crops appeared beneath the brightening horizons,

having taken their share of moisture. The sky reddened in the East and the sun rose, its rays touching the earth and awakening all creatures to the newborn day. Changing colour in its ascent, the radiant orb sent forth its light beneath which the dewdrops glistened on the leaves of the trees and the grass in the pastures sparkled. The glorious fields were adorned as though with a necklace and Hamid walked through the beauty of nature, his head bowed in thought or raised occasionally to look at his surroundings.

One by one the peasant farmers set out for work, each making his way to the plot that he owned, either inherited from his father and grandfather before him or acquired by a turn of unexpected fortune. Some had a cow or buffalo with them and when they passed Hamid they bade him 'good morning' before carrying on their way in astonishment. What on earth was he doing there at that time of day? . . . He was deliberating how to be alone with Aziza with nobody watching over them so that he could disclose his feelings and hear from her that she loved him too. That was all he wanted, but how could he ever accomplish it?

His desire overwhelmed him until he began to regard the ladies who surrounded her with contempt. Neither could he tell anyone about his love for he knew the ridicule and derision which the Egyptian mind harbours towards such sentiments. That harsh mind which derides the beauty of love and the feelings associated with it because the people understand nothing about it. They believe that real life should be spent in hard work and worship as if it were a mill in which to pass the years panting with fatigue and exhaustion. Closing their eyes to anything of beauty, they consider it their duty to be content with their lot, happy with what each day brings. To be different arouses their sarcasm and bitterness, no less hurtful than the stinging whip of the cattle drover. As if the human soul were so inclined to evil and depravity that we must resist our desires and tie them down with the chains of worn-out custom as though the senses could never aspire to anything but depravity. As if the eye sees only to be defiled and the ear hears only to pave the way for wicked thoughts.

But real life exists in the knowledge that the world was created in order for people to be happy. In the stillness of the soul and the depths of the heart lies a noble emotion; to destroy it is to destroy life itself. Then indeed we would be in a vile world, filled only with materialism, the pursuit of wealth and submission to those who own it. Only when we surrender to that emotion will we inhabit a world in which we may know honour, bravery, freedom and sincerity. That emotion is love.

Hamid shuddered and was nearly stunned. Almost oblivious to the world around him, he hardly noticed that the sun was rising step by step on the edge of the sky, becoming hotter from one moment to the next. The fallaheen made their way to the fields, some in groups, some walking alone and as their numbers grew they began to disturb Hamid with their constant greetings until he was obliged to return home to be by himself in his room. But when he arrived at the house his family were all seated at the breakfast table and they called him to take his place among them. Not that this disturbed his thoughts, for the only sound to be heard was the ringing of spoons in the cups. Everyone was silent, even the children under nine years of age, as though their minds were occupied with matters of great importance. If one of them winked or said anything funny, the child opposite might smile but another would glower as though to draw his attention to an unseemly slip. If any of them asked a question they would be answered with one or two words and had to be content with that. Hamid sat with them, thinking quietly to himself and eating his food slowly until he forgot about his problems and began to feel more at ease. Not that anyone around him noticed; even the least preoccupied had no idea of the state he was in.

Hamid was restless for most of the day, wondering whether or not to go to his sweetheart's house. The antagonism which he felt towards her relatives made the thought of going there decidedly unpleasant but he continued to search for ways to be alone with the girl who possessed his heart so that he could whisper gently to her, kiss her hand and beseech her. How happy he would be then, like a prince of the world, or even happier if he could but sit beside her and caress her neck or rest his head against her breast. Kissing her forehead and mouth while she gazed at him with dreamy eyes, smiling contentedly and replying that she loved him too whenever he confessed his love for her. Such fleeting moments make life worthwhile. They bring happiness even to the most wretched among us and they were all that Hamid desired. What a moment that would be when his loved one revealed herself to him with nobody to disturb them. In his dreams he was carried beyond the confines of our world, to blooming gardens beneath golden skies in which he rejoiced by the side of his beloved or accompanied her along paths strewn with roses, shaded by the branches of trees from which birds sing their moving melodies, imbuing the air with rapture and joy.

When the hour approached in which he had already been twice to see Aziza, his dreams were disturbed and the flow of his imagination was interrupted. He could no longer restrain his yearning and set off in the direction of her house. But no sooner had he taken a few steps than he hesitated. Turning to go back he was gripped by a tremor which stopped him in his tracks, leaving him even more confused and doubtful than before.

Time never stands still and the sun had almost set while Hamid remained in his troubled state, not knowing what he should do. Finally he resolved to go to her and with a scowl on his forehead he walked to the house. When he entered, however, there were many more people than before, most of them fellow students or younger relatives, for Aziza's brother had come to spend his vacation in the peace and quiet of the countryside, away from the noise and hubbub of the town. He too would enjoy the sight of the open spaces, adorned with streams and canals, and trees in which birds take their rest.

Hamid embraced his friend and they sat with the others, discussing the days of study and telling stories about their teachers—this being the custom of all colleagues from the educated classes meeting together after a long absence. As darkness descended, those who were present began to leave but when Hamid got up his friend insisted that he stay for

supper. Hamid accepted and after their meal they spent the
rest of the evening in conversation so that it was quite late
when he finally departed, having neither seen Aziza nor heard
her speak—although this did not occur to him until he reached
his room and lay down on the bed. Only then did his thoughts
return, but the lateness of the hour soon dispelled them and
he drifted into a deep and peaceful sleep.

Time passed by and Hamid went to see his friend every
day. Sometimes he saw Aziza but he never had the courage
to speak to her other than with a passing greeting. He was
content however, in the belief that she was not indifferent to
him—for how could she not be occupied with similar
thoughts, being at that splendid age of youth and vitality
when we lose ourselves in romantic dreams and loving sentiments? An age in which feelings soften, when the heart opens
out to encompass the beauty in the world and the soul feels
the need for a partner so strongly that the prospect of a life
alone is almost unbearable, so tedious and oppressive that we
would wish to put an end to it!

Yet Aziza's heart was always imprisoned. She never saw the
sky except from the windows of the house and the only bird-
song she heard was the cooing of doves on the roof. Her
whole being was aware of the beauty of nature but she only
experienced it from within, unable to explore it for herself or
to enjoy the experience of solitude in its midst. Her soul was
split between the reality of her life and what she felt inside,
her heart straying in a wilderness where there was neither
pleasure nor pain. Enclosed within four walls she was often
perplexed by the sadness that welled up, bringing tears to her
eyes when the fire of passion burned in her ribs. Consoling
herself with hopes for the future and her desire for the happy
state of marriage, she would conjure up images of the husband
to whom she would give herself and in her ardour she would
search her mind for the man who would one day be her
beloved. Sometimes she came upon a suitable personality
whom she knew or had heard about but at other times, when
her search proved fruitless, her dreams were tinged with sorrow.

Hamid was one of those she knew and sometimes, when

his image appeared before her, she placed him at the forefront of her expectations. But he was not the only one whose image materialised before her ever wandering mind. Every day she dreamed of potential partners among people she had known in the past or who were renowned for being handsome, respectable men. So Hamid's glances did not reach the depths of her heart or enter her innermost soul and she only lowered her eyes in front of him out of natural diffidence. If, on occasion, she did feel attracted to him it was nothing compared to the feelings which Hamid held for her.

The days passed by and they all became involved in various activities in which they spent their time. Hamid often frequented the fields or went to his friend's house, both to see him and to ponder the love which mingled in his heart and seemed at times to fill his being. Sometimes his thoughts reached a state of despair then hope would return and he would contemplate how to wrest the girl from her relatives so that he could tell her of his deep emotions and inner longings. And in his dreams he inhabited a beautiful world in which he could enjoy all the things he was deprived of in reality. But when he had to face the harsh facts of life he was so distressed that he began to regard the whole world with distrust and apprehension.

One day he saw Zainab in the fields with her young companions who were all singing merrily while she remained silent and withdrawn. Hamid felt some concern for her but there were other matters revolving in his heart and mind which occupied his attention. Nevertheless, the sight of her beauty as she stood calmly amid the commotion and activity stirred him in a way which he could not resist and the memories of past times soon flooded back. Whenever he saw Zainab after that he could not help wondering why she was sad.

In this way Hamid spent the whole period that Aziza was in the village, pondering her image or occasionally visiting the house to catch a glimpse of her smile. Although he was far from content with this he found no way to be alone with her so that towards the end of her stay he became resigned to his predicament and the hopes and fears which had beset him at first gradually subsided. He began to feel more friendly towards his relatives and when he thought about Aziza in his moments of solitude it was only to enjoy the pleasant side of the memory. Sometimes he would also think about Zainab and the future or simply let the pleasant breezes play on his mind while his senses revelled in the lushness of the world around him. Ignoring his own situation, he carried on in much the same way as everyone else. When his heart did rebel during those long days of summer, it was only because he wanted a partner with whom he could share his life.

The sleepless nights which the fallaheen spend turning the tanbour* or dipping the scoop to irrigate the cotton fields helped to alleviate Hamid's concerns. He would go out, the moon straying in the ocean of the sky, bewildered by its depth while the undulating terrain extended on all sides until it became lost in the abyss of the night. Nothing much was visible except for the stars spread out around the moon, by which the peasant farmer calculates the time as he waits for them to rise to their ascent one after another; when the morning star appears he is filled with joy at the approach of el-fajr and prays in thanksgiving for the blessings of his Lord. Then he returns to work all day apart from a few stolen moments in which to rest for a while.

The corn plants unfurled fresh and green and the only uncultivated land to be seen was that which the farmers had left aside for clover. Nature was clothed in her finest attire and the fallaheen began to sense that the bulk of the season's labour was almost done. The nights of endless work and effort during the period of irrigation were over and they had only to spend a short part of the night awake in order to water the cotton. Eagerly awaiting the completion of the back-breaking succession of tasks they would watch the gushing, muddy water with satisfaction and contentment as it flowed freely in the canals and count the days that remained before the period of rest.

Then came the thinning of the corn crop, a job in which

* Irrigation device employing the principle of the Archimedean screw.

the fallaheen rejoiced and that no longer required the assistance of their working beasts which were put to graze. The workers and working girls emerged from the days of tillage and toil beneath the heat of the sun like children, shy of being seen. Some watered the plants while others helped with the thinning and in this way they moved from one hard job to another even if these latter tasks, presaging the forthcoming rest period, were more congenial and easier to bear.

Marked by her calm silence, Zainab moved from task to task with the others while the days grew steadily shorter now that summer had passed its peak. Everything on earth grows quickly and after Aziza had left the village Hamid became immersed in different thoughts although His hopes for the future were boundless. Sometimes his dreams gladdened him, at other times they made him sad but in the company of his brothers and in the wonderful universe and all it contained, he found some consolation for his many cares.

# Chapter Eight

Since Hassan first heard of his father's intentions regarding his marriage he became even more preoccupied than his mother with the search for a girl from a similar respectable family. Although his continuous work in the fields kept him from thinking too much about the matter, the hot summer days and the wonderful nights awakened in his soul those elements which determine the needs of human nature. His mind entertained the perpetual notion of joining together with a beautiful girl to find consolation in her from the pain and hardship of life while at the same time perpetuating himself and his species.

Whenever the affair was brought to Zainab's attention she accepted what she heard patiently. The only thing of which she was sure was that one way or another the outcome would be decided in the near future. Maybe events would prove her suffering and misery to be unfounded and return her to the gaiety and enjoyment of life which were presently denied.

Hamid often remembered his beloved Aziza when he was by himself but found contentment in the company of his brothers. Sometimes, in those silent hours when the morning draws its first breath and the sun rises gently from its couch, he would become enraptured by his impassioned emotions, then he would forget all about such things.

Everything grows quickly and the cotton and maize were soon so high that passers-by almost disappeared behind the tall bushes and long stalks.

As the days of summer advanced, the ripening crops brought joy to the hearts of the fallaheen although some experienced only additional burdens. Those who had to repay the debts they had incurred in the winter and on finding their circumstances unfavourable, dreaded the approach of the deadline with every day that passed. If a debt was left unpaid the tedious visits of the court ushers would ensue and they would be forced to consider any means of procuring the money, either by deceiving their wives and mortgaging their lands to borrow yet another sum or by selling enough from the few feddans they owned to pay back what they owed. Those less fortunate were forced to sell their personal possessions or look beyond their immediate families to borrow whatever they could, however small the amount, from neighbouring farmers with whom they had some degree of relationship.

One group not troubled by debt were those content to live on next to nothing by the edge of the Nile. These happy folk rejoiced when the waters rose to fill the canals that flowed between the grass and crops which they cultivated along its banks. They had only to raise the sluice gates in order to irrigate their lands, leaving the water to do the rest and enrich the parched earth with alluvium soil brought from faraway places. Then the contented farmer would spend many hours by the side of the river, leaning on a spade in the heat of the sun without a care, only moving to ensure that the water flowed evenly across every inch of his land. When the sun reaches its zenith he eats his lunch beneath the shade of the trees then stretching out for an hour, returns to spend the afternoon in a similar manner.

Autumn came and the cotton harvest was the topic of conversation among the landowners, the workers and everybody else in the village. In a few days the fields were surging with cotton pickers, mostly young children less than ten years old, hardly visible between the rows as they worked away in silence, each trying to gather as much as they possibly could and only occasionally breaking into song as they worked for daily wages. In their midst stood Zainab, drawn an hour closer to marriage with every pile she picked, her only desire being to throw herself into the arms of Ibrahim and tell him the secrets of her love. Her patience exhausted, she barely had the strength to keep her feelings to herself. Her heart was almost broken and when she saw Ibrahim at the end of a row or glanced towards him from where she stood, her body trembled and she had difficulty keeping her mind on her job. The thought of her forthcoming marriage, which it was now widely rumoured would take place between herself and Hassan, left her so dispirited that she sometimes had to call on the worker next to her for assistance.

Ibrahim was no less distracted. He forced himself to work harder in order to conceal his emotion and lowered his eyes whenever Zainab walked by. Finally he resolved to disclose his love as soon as they could be alone together. At the same time he knew that Hassan, his friend and 'brother', was soon to marry Zainab so what should he do? Were it within his power to marry her there was nothing he would not have done. But if he were to ask for her hand was it conceivable that her father would agree, now that he knew what good fortune was in store for his daughter? Maybe to preserve appearances, he would simply raise the bride price which would be equivalent to a negative reply. But why should that be? Could he not raise whatever sum was required? In all the world was there anything more precious than Zainab? He would sell their buffalo or take a loan which he could repay in a year or two from his wages. He would do anything that was necessary, even steal if he had to! Yes, he must go to her father and ask for her hand. What a life they would enjoy, sitting in their house discussing the land which they would rent from Sayyid Mahmoud to cultivate together. Theirs would be the greatest happiness between two persons, both finding bliss in each other's company.

The fields were now divided. Those which had been harvested looked dark, almost black, while the rest remained crowned with their pure white crop.

The sun began to sink in the West and they all worked hard to load up what they had gathered. When this was done Zainab slipped between the fields for her own purpose and Ibrahim went to pray el-asr before it was too late. Meanwhile the others commenced their return journey, the pack animals driven along surrounded by crowds of fallaheen who all walked beside the loads they had harvested.

On finding Ibrahim sitting alone, Zainab was too embarrassed to do what she had been wanting to do all day. Ibrahim got up to walk by her side but they both felt equally uneasy. The full moon in the sky followed their path as though it were listening to the secrets of their hearts but now it looked pale and wan; had she like them, an unrequited love? Then the sky darkened and the moon shone brighter, its enchanting rays illuminating the earth and stirring passion in all the creatures of the world.

Reaching a small mosque by the side of the road, Ibrahim asked Zainab to wait while he performed the sunset prayer. When he had finished he invited her to sit down to rest with him and after some hesitation she agreed, but they were even more silent than before. Finally overcoming his nervousness, Ibrahim clasped her hands and on this pure and holy spot, beneath the gaze of Allah and the moon, he said to her for the first time:

'I love you Zainab.'

All the happiness in heaven and on earth could not equal a tiny part of the emotion that flooded her now. The moon, the planets and the whole of creation seemed arrayed for some great wedding feast as the sweet evening breeze carried its felicitations to them through the air. Could Zainab find words to say? Would her tongue help her in any way? No! She was overcome with joy, rooted to the spot and gazing in bewilderment at Ibrahim and everything around her. Then with a single movement she threw herself into his arms, resting her head against his chest and giving herself up to him completely while he returned her embrace. Ibrahim was spellbound by the intoxicating effect which her body produced in him but after only a moment she began to tremble violently. She felt a strong urge to get away from him, to flee from the sight of his face and the burning passion it aroused in her, to wander alone she knew not where. Ibrahim was at a loss as to what to do. His strength betrayed him and he could only look at her despairingly, imploring her with his eyes to stay with him, his lips unable to speak a word. But when she got up to go her feet would not obey her. She stared at him, not knowing whether she was overwhelmed by ecstasy or whether it was sorrow that made her oblivious to her surroundings. Her

companion knelt at her feet gazing up at her in silence, unable
to repeat his declaration of love.

They remained there until evening set in and the horizon
was a belt of blackness surrounding the fields which rested
peacefully. Then the fresh breeze inspired Zainab with the
most delightful dreams. Walking side by side until they were
near the village, Ibrahim held her hand and kissed it then
they parted, neither of them uttering a single word.

Zainab went straight home where she ate her supper before
going up to the roof and while she was sitting by herself,
hardly able to contain her happiness, her brother and sister
came to be with her. The young lad sat by her side with his
head in her lap and was soon fast asleep while Zainab stared
absently at the moon until her father returned from praying
el-asha. Carrying the boy downstairs they all went to bed, but
sleep was far from Zainab's eyes. She lay awake for most of
the night and the thought often came to her to go to Ibrahim,
to lie beside him and let him embrace her as he had done on
the way back from the fields.

Those wonderful moments of bliss had brought her so much
pleasure that she earnestly wished to repeat them. But her
parents lay between her and the door and would certainly
awaken at the slightest movement.

Eventually she fell asleep, rising early next morning as usual.
She hurried to the harvest, wishing only to gaze at Ibrahim
but in the company of her fellow workers her bashfulness
returned and she could only glance furtively in his direction.
Whenever their eyes met she could feel herself shiver and
wanted to sink into the ground or lose herself among the
bushes. At sundown Ibrahim put the cotton that Zainab had
gathered to one side, intending to load it last, but there were
not enough animals and he had to wait with her for one to
return. On finding himself alone with her again he sat her
down by the side of the canal and when she was settled he
said:

'Do you remember the day we were working in the fields
next to Khalil's land and you nearly fainted—if I hadn't sprinkled water on your face . . . ?'

She blushed at the memory of the first days of their friendship and picking up a twig she began to scrape the ground beside her. But he took her hands in his as he had done the previous day and continued:

'. . . from that day I have loved you.'

So from the day that she had first loved him he had been in love with her without her knowing it. How much happiness each new revelation brought! But why had Ibrahim not disclosed his love before instead of leaving her to suffer for so long? When he saw her silent, he repeated his words and this time she replied:

'And from that day I've loved you.'

A sigh escaped the young man's lips. He drew her towards him and they gave themselves up to each other, immersed in an ocean of boundless joy. Then they sat together until a young boy came with a mule and they returned side by side, promising to meet again later.

After supper, Zainab escaped from her family on the pretence of having something to attend to outside, and leaving the village she reached the canal road where she found Ibrahim waiting for her. As she approached he came forward to greet her and taking her hand he kissed it once and looked at her fondly, expressing his joy at seeing her again.

In the vast fields beneath the light of the moon, shining brilliantly in the heavens above, the two lovers walked with their arms round each other, looking out with shining eyes into the depths of space. Smiles of contentment played on their lips and inestimable happiness flowed from their hearts so that they had no desire to disturb their feelings with conversation. In that wonderful world they let their spirits fly, intoxicated by its delights while nature looked on in silence, except for the sounds of the crickets and frogs. The night sent white wispy clouds over those glorious open spaces and the moon travelled with them or perhaps, envious of Zainab, followed her footsteps.

'Dear moon in the sky, what are you compared to the beauty of Zainab? Why should I spare you a single glance when she is by my side? Her face is full of the youthful

enchantment that you lost so many centuries ago and the
happy smile on her lips makes a mockery of the wrinkles of
age upon your face . . .' Ibrahim's dreams were interrupted
by Zainab saying:

'How pretty the moon is!'

'You're prettier Zainab.'

He put his arms round her waist and kissed her forehead
and temples, then gazed with her at the moon. But his kisses
made her anxious and she buried her head against his shoulder.
When he felt the strength of her heartbeat he turned towards
her and asked:

'What's the matter Zainab?'

But Zainab was crying and did not speak. Holding her
hand he entreated her again, to which she replied between
her tears:

'Soon we won't see each other any more . . . I'm to marry
and live in my husband's house. Times like these will not return.'

Sighing from the depths of her injured heart she leaned
against the wall of the mosque and wiped her tears. Then they
stood together in silence until it was time to return.

A few days later they met again and this time Zainab was
completely happy as she walked by Ibrahim's side, finding the
greatest pleasure in his every glance. After that they continued
to steal moments together when they would talk or embrace.
Zainab knew that she would soon be leaving him and wanted
to enjoy his company as much as possible before the tyrants
came to take her away from him.

* * *

Time passes swiftly. The season of cotton picking came to an
end and when the prices rose sufficiently, Khalil sold some
of his crop in order to raise the necessary money. Taking his
friends along with him, they went to ask Zainab's father for
her hand in marriage as a bride for Hassan. Altogether they
were eight persons, making their way through the shadows
of the setting sun as the sky darkened and daylight departed
the world for places far away. Their voices were hushed and

they all fell silent when they reached the poor dwelling where Zainab's father seemed to be expecting them. No sooner had they entered than Zainab's mother laid down a mat and began to make coffee. The custom inbred in country folk to honour new arrivals and welcome visitors made them do their utmost to treat their guests as generously as circumstances allowed.

Zainab's father received them hospitably and sitting with them, he expressed how honoured he was by their presence, saying, that they filled his house with light. They continued to exchange the customary greetings until, when the coffee was handed round, it was as though bonds of love and sincerity existed between them. Then Khalil said to his host:

'We're here to unite our families Abu Mohammed.'

'A thousand welcomes Abu Hassan. But do we deserve that honour?'

'God keep you!'

'Does this mean that we have someone suitable for marriage?'

'Yes indeed, we want Zainab for Hassan!'

Zainab's father continued:

'Nothing we have is too precious for you Khalil, but the girl is still young and she runs all our errands. In two or three years she will be the right age and her sister can take her place . . .'

On hearing this, a distinguished man with a broad chest and superior airs, the deputy mayor of the village, butted in saying:

'How can you say she's too young, Abu Mohammed, when in my day we married off girls much younger than her? A year or two ago I presided over the marriage of Abu Sami's daughter and the daughter of . . . what's his name . . . Abu Amer when they were both much younger than Zainab. How could you say a thing like that?'

He was followed by another, a landlord apparently, who addressed himself to the deputy mayor:

'Don't you remember, Mustafa, when we married the girl Masoodah? She was such a tiny thing then, but she grew to be a splendid woman. As for Zainab, she's already tall and pretty, able to look after a whole family by herself.'

And turning to Zainab's father he added:

'What do you mean she's too young man? How can you say such a thing?'

Then came the turn of the marriage official to speak:

'These things are in God's hands. As long as it is God's wish, and God wishes only what is right, then by God there's no better match for Zainab than Hassan. Have you forgotten what happened in the village of Saed Ad-din when we married Khadrah Ummu Ibrahim to Hassanin Maqlad. Her family argued for so long that somebody might have been killed before the night was out. So we drew up the contract papers regardless and of course they went on to have children. In fact God blessed them with many children and what could be better than that?'

As another of them had his say, then a fifth and a sixth, Zainab's father became immersed in a cloud of anxiety, his mind flooded by diverse thoughts. He did not know what they signified, neither did he understand them or know of any reason for the sadness he felt but a deep silence came over him while those respectable men argued their case and he listened to what they were saying without taking in their meaning. Night was almost upon them and the lamp which lit up their faces flickered gently in the still night air.

Listening from on top of the roof, Zainab was almost frantic while her mother sat uneasily by her side awaiting the outcome of this affair which she had so often discussed with her husband. She knew that he wanted to settle the matter, but when, a man finds himself on the threshold of a decision that may pave the way for the realisation of his desires, it is often both alarming and distressing. Once the step has been taken however, and the wheels set in motion, his only concern is to see the matter through to its conclusion. Zainab's parents in their poverty, pondering their good fortune, could find nothing more to say. Darkness descended, emphasising the silence as the world strayed through the night with its own hopes and fears.

Zainab was nearly out of her mind, thinking about Ibrahim whom she had been with so recently. What would become of her now? Would the events of this night really put an end to her happiness and bring instead the never ending misery that she had been dreading? Did all those present, without one of them realising their crime, really wish to seal her fate and fill the rest of her days with pain and suffering?

In his own house, aware of what was happening in the home of his beloved, Ibrahim was angry but there was nothing he could do. Overcome with anxiety and despair, he sat alone lamenting himself to himself.

Having all but convinced Zainab's father the men began to calculate the amount of the bride price. Some of them were divided on this issue but at last, when they were all agreed, there was nothing more to do but draw up the contract and for someone to ask Zainab for her consent so that her father could proceed with the arrangements.

Is this the role of a father to do as he pleases regarding his daughter's marriage and sell her to the highest bidder? A girl can hardly turn against the man whom nature has endowed with authority over her even if the irreversible outcome is a lifetime of misery and regret. Would she agree willingly or refuse outright?

Knowing that her consent would be requested, Zainab felt that all the burdens of the world were on her shoulders. The depression descending over her was the embodiment of all her fears and even the breeze seemed to pierce her heart with agony and despair. Instead of bringing her hope, her parents had brought her to this! However, they did not finalise the contract that night but were content to recite the Fatiha and postpone the signing for about one month.

* * *

During this period Zainab spent her time at home listening to her mother's repetitive conversation, or shedding tears whenever she was with her beloved. Ibrahim was also heartbroken and he would embrace her and kiss her temples only to find that his kisses increased his desire and added to his sorrow. With every day that passed their feelings grew stronger until Zainab began to think of giving up everything in order to escape with Ibrahim to a place where no one would ever find them. Somewhere they could work as they worked now and put an end to this miserable torment. All she wanted was to be with Ibrahim, to go with him wherever he pleased.

When Zainab was alone she was totally distraught; despair entered her soul and her tears flowed. Seeing her like this, her mother scolded her at first then she tried to console her. But how could she be consoled? If she could not be with Ibrahim, Zainab wanted nothing more than to wander aimlessly, tossed by events until the hand of destiny decided what to do with her. Whatever hardship she might encounter it would be easier to bear than the oppression of her parents even if she only succeeded in exchanging one state of wretchedness for another.

Ibrahim hugged her to his breast whenever she sat beside him. He tried to comfort her but it only made the pain more acute. Her despair drove her to distraction, compelling her to forsake the company of people and to go where there was no one to disturb her. More than once she spent the whole day by herself in the fields, shifting anxiously from place to place or sitting down when her anxiety weighed too heavily upon her. Sometimes her whole being rose up in rebellion, but what could she do? When evening came and the blood-red sun descended to unknown places far away, burning up the West with its fiery evening glow, there was nothing left but to return to the house which had sheltered her all her life and now wanted to throw her out.

Her parents on the other hand seemed pleased and content. When Zainab's mother was alone with her daughter she never tired of finding fault with her desolation and sadness. She would tell her stories of girls who married husbands they knew nothing about and how happy they became after marriage, saying that a father only wants the best for his child in accordance with his knowledge and desire!

When the month had passed, Khalil, Hassan and the marriage official came with their friends to the house, where they sat down amid the greetings and hospitable gestures of Abu Mohammed. Also present were friends of Zainab and her mother who had come to join the family in their happi-

ness. And in the midst of such commotion was there anything
for Zainab to say? So when a messenger came to get her
consent to depute her father in signing the marriage contract,
Zainab remained silent and did not utter a single word. Then
drawing her breath, she could no longer restrain the tears
which streamed down her cheeks. Her father was obliged to
wait, but on hearing the reason for delay the marriage official
spoke out. Shaking his head, which was crowned with a huge
turban, he exclaimed:

'Well since they're such impassioned tears, they must be
tears of joy!'

And with the formula he knew off by heart, together with
the prayers which are recited on such occasions, he placed the
hand of the bridegroom on the hand of the deputy of the bride
and asked them to repeat after him the words of the marriage
ceremony.

On the evening of the following day Zainab moved from
her father's house to join her husband's family, having shed
her farewell tears for the dwelling in which she had spent all
the days and hopes of her youth.

# PART TWO

*The harvested land, like a great cleft, seemed astonished in its nakedness, having so recently been the habitat of such luscious plants.*

# Chapter One

In the great capital at the beginning of winter . . .

The day was awaiting the sun to dispel the dusky darkness and bring warmth to the people who shivered as they
jostled one another in the streets on their way to work. The
city was awakening from a long cold night which many inhabitants had passed in silence with neither lamp nor star to
comfort them. The only sounds they heard were the voices of
the watchmen in the alleys, calling out to one another from
time to time and bringing some degree of security into the
black of night.

In that hour, as the world was coming back to life, Hamid
awoke completely relaxed from a peaceful, dreamless sleep.
He dressed slowly then went to his studies to which he
applied himself diligently and in return he derived a certain
amount of pleasure from his work so that by day he did not
need to concern himself with anything else. In the evenings
he would sit up with his brothers and friends discussing a
variety of unrelated topics one after another. They conversed
without constraint, laughing contentedly as they talked or
listened, happy with themselves and the lives they led. When
Hamid was alone in bed, images filled his head and the faces
of people he had known in the past appeared before him in
the darkness. In some he saw kindness and beauty; others
were serious and dignified. Then he would pass from this
great assembly into a wholesome sleep in which he spent his
nights. Occasionally, among the many thoughts that came
to him, the idea of marriage cropped up. Although he was
still young enough to regard it as a distant prospect, there
was no other context in which to express his longing or
conjure up the fantasies of love and happiness which are so
much a part of being young. So when the image of his
beloved came to him in the darkness he would imagine he
was embracing her and proceed in a way he could never

have allowed himself, had he not considered that one day
she would be his future bride.

But the days were filled with serious work and Hamid's
notion that marriage was something for the future gradually
quietened his dreams. The world which he had previously
imagined to be scented with flowers and saturated with love
became a calm and peaceful place in which he found his
greatest pleasure in work and thought. The people, places and
events that occupied him now became the focus of his attention and as he absorbed himself in his academic pursuits so
they dominated his mind and heart. Among the books he
read were some concerning women and marriage which opened
his mind to concepts quite different from his original beliefs
and he began to see married life as something dull and monotonous, with no appeal, convinced it was only man's inherent
foolishness that had led him to believe there was any joy or
happiness to be found there. Searching his mind for a couple
he might know who had found in the official bond of marriage
the happiness they had hitherto hoped for, his discoveries only
strengthened his conviction and he came to regard that bond
as just another of those chains of custom to which man
becomes attached simply because others have done so before
him. When one's forefathers and contemporaries, rich and
poor alike, scholars or fools have adopted this custom and
given it the sanctity of history, man in his stupidity considers
it one of life's blessings.

Consequently Hamid's memories of Aziza declined day by
day and although she sometimes appeared in his dreams, the
idea of being beside her did not arouse his emotions or
reawaken his former desire. Instead he found a great emptiness
in which to lose himself so that even when he was beset by
confusion or anxiety, he contented himself with oblivion, or
nothingness. When he thought of Zainab however, he remembered the pleasant hours they had spent together in the midst
of the glorious countryside, surrounded by trees and streams
and the birds delighting them with their loving melodies, full
of romance and passion.

These hours, in Hamid's view, had brought them close to

each other and the memory of them still held some significance for him.

Returning home from his studies one day, Hamid took off his outdoor clothes and put on the white gallabiya and skullcap which he wore in the house. As he sat thinking, and drinking the coffee his servant brought him, a group of his school friends called to visit him. Laughing amongst themselves, they entered the room and greeted him in one breath:

'As-salam alaikum.'

'And peace be with you,' replied Hamid. 'Are you all well? What are you up to?' Then calling to his servant: 'Make some more coffee, boy!'

One of his friends answered:

'The four of us met by chance and thought it would be fun to visit you. You've become quite a philosopher of late, always preferring to be by yourself. What's it all about? Listen, if you didn't already know, Asad Effendi is getting married tomorrow and we've come to ask you to go to the wedding with us.'

'Getting married? Why? The poor wretch!'

'Yes and you're not going to philosophise about that too are you? I should say he's a very lucky man!'

The servant entered with the coffee tray and five cups, one for each of them. Ali Effendi took a cigarette from his pocket and lit it, then offered one to Sheikh Khalil. But no sooner did Ali Effendi stretch out his hand towards him with the cigarette box than Hassanin snatched it from him saying:

'God forbid! You "sheikhs" are greedy enough. How could you think of smoking? Go and take your snuff instead!'

These words stirred Sheikh Khalil who began to defend his habit with all his might, breaking into a flow of eloquence and leaving no simile unturned to which he might liken his black powder. Indeed he made use of every possible allusion, metaphor and figure of speech he could think of. Then to demonstrate the truth of what he was saying he put his hand in his pocket and brought out a small tin, tapping three times with his forefinger on the lid. He opened it slowly and taking a pinch between his fingers, he inclined his head slightly as he closed one nostril with the tip of his finger and sniffed with the other. The snuff flew violently up his nose! Then after giving the other nostril its fill he returned the tin to its hiding place and took out a blue handkerchief which he held between his hands ready to use when the need arose.

Hamid, who had been staring silently at the floor, turned his gaze back to the group when the commotion had died down, only to repeat the thought that occupied his mind:

'So Asad Effendi is getting married tomorrow . . . Poor wretch! . . .'

But Sheikh Ali interrupted him saying:

'The prophet, peace and blessings be upon him, said: "Marry and multiply and I shall take pride in you, among other nations on the day of resurrection".' And Ali Effendi, after clearing his throat, countered:

'Why do think him so unfortunate?'

As though something had been unleashed inside him, Hamid replied:

'A man looks for happiness in marriage because he finds his own lonely life so unbearable that he wishes to exchange it for another. He thinks the new life will be better for him but when the first few days of delusion have passed and the reality of what he has done becomes clear, he belatedly regrets. I have searched in vain to find someone I know who has achieved the happiness he dreamed of in marriage but all the partnership seems to do is bring people down from their imagined happiness to inevitable misery. When you see the offspring suffering all manner of affliction from the day of their birth, don't you feel sorry for them and regret the fact that they were born? And later on in life we are no less wretched. Our fathers and our old people tell us that our years are the best and that youth is the springtime of life. Well, if I'm in the spring of life, with all the bitterness that I've experienced, then by God, how wretched shall I become in the future? If even the young sometimes wish to do away with themselves, won't the days and nights of old age be filled with this desire? Or do they tell us this simply to appear brave in our eyes, and worthy of our admiration?'

The tone of Hamid's voice was full of woe, whereupon Hassanin took up the conversation:

'It seems to me my friend that we spoil the enjoyment of life for ourselves and ruin our chances of happiness on earth. Personally, I think we could live happily from the first days of our life to the last if we lived among people with real feelings, following different customs to those of our own society. Our people renounce the world and ignore it, looking at the things around them with cold hearts which stubbornly refuse to love anything beautiful. They regard life from a distance, fearing everything and shrinking from situations which might disclose their feelings, while all the time their souls become eaten away with despair, and misery is engrained upon their faces. Yet they consider any alternative a digression into the realm of sin and temptation.

'Maybe I would agree that our system of marriage does not produce the bliss we dream of but it is up to each of us to strive for something else if we are sure that we are right. After all, if people only follow the customs of the past how will the world advance? Nevertheless, I don't entirely agree with your opinion. I believe that marriage supplies a framework for happiness and that it is the best system we could devise to maintain our species in the greatest security and wellbeing we could hope for.

'Imagine the situation which you envisage. Helpless children who do not know their fathers, and women with no one to support them in their times of weakness, in the midst of this urban life with all its pressures and demands. Consider the exhausted man returning from his job, looking for comfort in the words of a loved one but finding only others like himself while our women work to earn their livelihoods in order to look after themselves and their children. Surely you would agree that there is no happiness for a man without a woman who loves him at his side, and no happiness for a woman without a devoted man to care for her.

'Humanity is not sufficiently developed to allow the changes which you demand. Our situation today is the result of centuries, of millions of years. You can never deny the past with

all its rights and wrongs, even if you don't acknowledge it.
All we can do is work to change some of our customs and
introduce into the relationships between men and women
those healthy elements which are lacking. That's the right
thing to do and change is possible. How much happiness
there could be within the family if only people understood
what "family" really means. How contented they would be,
in ways they cannot now conceive. Although the true meaning
is lost to us at present you should not regard the concept of
"family" as just another manifestation of conflict and hopeless-
ness. Our lives may be plagued by bitterness and
disappointment but that is due to our incorrect upbringing.
Do you think that a boy who takes on such a load when he
is only sixteen years of age will be anything but an old man
in his twenties? Then, after childbirth, women experience
nothing of the world except from within the walls of their
houses, so that marriage becomes literally what is quoted from
the traditions of the prophet: "Marry and multiply . . ."

'Let young people love without being chained by customs
to which too much importance is attached. The long future
awaits with burdens which they can never imagine in the days
of their youth.'

Ali Effendi joined in the discussion:

'Asad Effendi will marry tomorrow as thousands have
married before him, just as you yourself will one day marry.
Picture in any way you wish the wife that you want. Make
her an ideal of perfection and beauty and create for yourself
a wonderful kingdom which you think will be yours. Yet after
marriage she will be just another woman and you will be
neither happy nor sad but the same as everybody else. If you
could clip the wings of your youthful ideals and live more in
the world of reality, you would see the truth of what I say.

'Some time ago, when I was studying in France, I knew a
girl who was a waitress in a restaurant. On my return after a
few months away she was no longer there and when I enquired
I was told that she had married a boy who was a waiter in a
cafe. And what was the reason for this marriage? They put
their savings together and opened a shop which they worked

independently for more profit. Similarly, in our country, working people get married every day not to live happily together but to make the most of their possessions. Of course a man likes a woman to care for him and share his problems just as a woman wants to be looked after in her times of weakness, and in this way each helps to make the other's share of problems lighter. But it would be a mistake to believe that people from other classes achieve more from marriage than this. If chance decrees that a husband and wife should find themselves in love they may enjoy some happiness, but this is the exception and rarely does it last!'

Night had begun to take the place of day and darkness gradually filled the room where they sat. Outside, the minarets were shrouded in mist as the muezzins climbed up inside them and a few moments later they raised their voices to break the still silence of the air with their calls to prayer. Hamid raised his eyebrows and in a sad but placid tone he murmured:

'Are dreams of love, I wonder, any easier to realise than dreams of happiness in marriage?'

Their conversation over, Hamid bade farewell to his friends at the door and returned, his heart heavy with cares. He sat down and stared at the pictures in his room of pyramids and other ancient monuments which, although succeeded by so many generations, still appear novel in the eye of the beholder. Then his thoughts drifted far away and resting his head in his hands he became oblivious to everything until he was called to eat.

When it was time for bed he stretched himself out and closed his eyes, his mind racing to the limits of his imagination. But on finding it impossible to get to sleep he opened them again and gazed into the darkness all around. Eventually he got up to pull back the curtains and looked out into the blackness of a starless sky. It was completely dark and the cold panes of glass revealed nothing of what lay beyond. Pressing his burning forehead against the window he stood there lost in thought, recalling the days of the past.

Out of the stillness a wind blew up and rain began to fall,

swept against the windowpanes so that he could hear its rhythmic thud on the glass. Sometimes it fell gently, its sound no more than a whisper then driven by the storm, the continuous pattering increased in volume—and all the while the darkness remained complete.

Listening to the commotion outside, his dreams were interrupted for a moment, but memories of the happy hours he had spent by the side of Zainab and the times he had revelled in his fantasies about Aziza soon flooded back. The rainfall played on the young man's ears as Hamid stayed up, alone with his thoughts, while in the neighbouring rooms everybody else was comfortably asleep. When the sky had discharged its load he discerned a glimpse of light, breaking through the clouds which gradually dispersed to reveal a waning moon and beneath its pallid rays the nearby walls became visible and roofs gleamed with rainwater. Calm was restored and there was no sound to be heard, so feeling somewhat disconsolate Hamid went back to bed where he spent the rest of the night amid boundless dreams.

The next morning his mind had cleared. He attended his studies, returning home at the usual time and in this manner the days passed by. As winter drew to a close, the hours of daylight began to claim back what they had lost to the night and the pleasant weather encouraged the inhabitants of the city so that smiling faces could be seen in the streets and activity was resumed in every place. The world advanced towards the spring, leaving behind the frowning aspect of winter and as the sap rose in the great trees, planted along some of the streets of the capital, they prepared to don their fresh green robes.

Sometimes Hamid was assailed by memories, at other times he forgot the past completely. When he heard news of Zainab's marriage he prayed that she might find prosperity and contentment. He hoped too that she would find some happiness to comfort her through the years of her life—that monotonous life which ends as it begins, while death creeps up stealthily all the time. As the last vestiges of youth disappear, we leave behind those days of beauty and love and an eager desire to

experience the world. Moving on from that phase of infatuation we enter a state of sombre serenity or what may be
called serious understanding. Then something akin to sadness
mingles in the depths of our being as we resign ourselves to
our fate. Looking on in bewilderment, time flies before us
and we arrange our affairs so that its passing might be easier
until life is nothing more than a waiting room which we
finally depart on the wings of a bird that carries us to our
ultimate destination.

Hamid remembered Zainab and her glances and wished
her health and happiness. Then came the spring. The world
laughed, the days lengthened, the trees were adorned and the
sun grew stronger after its winter languor. An atmosphere of
expectation prevailed, bringing joy to all creatures after the
period of inertia. The flowers diffused their scents, wafting
sweetness into the air and imbuing the hearts of men with
pure fragrances which intoxicate the soul. Caressed by such
a breeze we can only feel love for everything growing on the
face of the earth or moving in the air. Hamid began to frequent
the outskirts of the city where nature, rearranged by the hand
of man, had a pleasant, comely appearance as opposed to the
wild beauty of virgin lands. Green fields and gardens with
blossoming trees stretched out by the side of the great river
where waves rolled gently past, following each other along
with the currents from places far away until they become part
of the sea.

On one occasion Hamid met a friend and they strolled
along together discussing the landscape that had been planned
out by the tyrants during the days of despotism, to be enjoyed
today by the descendants of the oppressed. Finding pleasure
in their conversation they forgot about the time until the
sun began to sink in the West. The windows in the houses
on the opposite bank lit up and a beautiful roseate hue covered
the river as the glow of evening appeared on the horizon. The
golden disc of the sun descended quickly to its rest and reflec-
tions of street lamps danced gaily on the surface of the water.
It was the hour when nature brings forth the night. After the
first forewarnings of darkness the great abyss descends, shapes

become obscure and the evening breezes flow to the hearts of men, invigorating their minds and souls. Happiness and joy were in the air and smiles of tranquillity and contentment were painted on the lips of the two companions.

Turning on their heels they returned the way they had come, as happy as they could wish themselves to be. And while they walked, Hamid reflected that the beauty of nature outshone all other beauty even though the spring stirred his desire to be united with a loved one who would be consumed in him in the same way that he wished to be consumed in her.

# Chapter Two

Zainab now lived in her husband's house, among a family completely different from her own with regard to class, status and way of life. She was often beset by confusion when her feelings clashed with the duties of her position and looking to her innocent mind for guidance she found no knowledge or experience to draw upon so that however hard she tried to adapt, her problems would not go away. The burdens that Hassan's mother had previously borne were flung upon her shoulders so that almost overnight she became housewife to a considerable household whose domestic affairs she was expected to manage. Although her husband's two sisters helped her at first, as they had previously helped their mother, they soon realized that they could take advantage of Zainab and enjoy a laxity in her company which had never been previously allowed to them.

From the first day she felt lonely, a stranger among familiars who shared the same traditions and customs. Their conversations referred to events unique to themselves, which served to further their closeness to one another, binding them together within the family bond. Even the servant was closer to them than the new bride and when they sat talking Zainab stayed silent, speaking only when necessary. When she was by herself she felt even more desolate and the sorrow and anxiety within her grew.

When Hassan was alone with her, he would raise those matters that a husband expects to discuss with his wife but to Zainab his conversation was tedious and dull. She found it artificial, neither inspired by the heart nor stirred by feelings that required expression but simply arising out of the situation they were in. However, knowing that it was expected of her to reply in a similar vein, she answered all his questions with the customary phrases she had learned from other people. At the same time, she was aware that a situation like this could only lead to a life of regret. It was her duty to forget the past and look for consolation in the things that surrounded her. If there were to be any chance of happiness she was obliged to love her husband and invite him to love her or remain permanently thwarted, unable to experience anything in life other than pain and disappointment. Despite her great love for Ibrahim, she knew that she must try to forget him until their relationship was nothing more than an ordinary acquaintance for which no one could reproach them.

Zainab became involved in the affairs of the house, taking the greater part of the burden upon herself. Rising at daybreak she would get dressed and make her way to the watering place to fill her earthenware jar while the breeze was still moist, a journey she repeated several times. That was one of her many jobs during the summer when the sight of the streams filled with water and the life-giving sun as it rose from its couch with the dawn to disperse the darkness brought her some solace. When summer turned to winter with its long cold nights and the water in the streams dwindled away, she was directed to other tasks, only slightly less burdensome.

As the months passed, Zainab succeeded to some extent in forgetting her former love. The days began to lengthen again and the peasant farmers returned to work in the fields where a member of their family—mother, sister or wife—would bring them their lunch if they did not bring it themselves. Then they would stop for the midday break and sit down to rest in the shade of a leafy tree.

Zainab took Hassan his lunch every day, staying with him for a short time after he had eaten it before returning to the house. But the new life that permeated the world, uplifting the souls of creatures and men alike, stirred an ardent longing for her heart's desire. As spring advanced, the month of love and rapture dawned when nature is clothed in her radiant garments and the sun shining down on the fresh green leaves sends its rays into the hearts and souls of the people, rousing them from their lethargy during the winter. The whole of nature was adorned in a way that stirs the need for someone to love.

During that season of enchantment, when the month of May had arrived, Zainab made her way to and fro between the fertile fields where the flourishing cotton bushes opened their leaves to embrace the air, the light, the sun, the night and the stars. No longer could she resign herself to her situation nor could she remain deaf to the voices which called to her, as though spring itself were pleading with her to be receptive and embrace the sentiments of the season. Nevertheless she tried with all her strength to resist the emotions that flooded her heart. Indeed, she earnestly wanted to remain constant to the husband God had given her and to whom she knew she must give herself. A bitter conflict arose whenever she was distracted from her marital duties and she longed to triumph over the forces which assailed her.

Throughout this period Hassan assumed that he was in control. He behaved as any husband might towards a new bride, feeling affection for her even if it was not entirely free of that love of authority, inherited from his forefathers and condoned by the holy law. Besides, the gentler disposition of the female sex and their natural meekness whatever their upbringing, grants man a certain degree of power which he often becomes enamoured with! Furthermore, their mundane relationship, devoid of anything appetising and lacking in all aspects of intimacy, caused Hassan at first to be quite rigid with regard to their marriage. But as the days passed and the monotony of their lives increased, he joined the fraternity of all those in similar situations. As long as they find in their wives an obedient servant and a devoted worker for the welfare of their family they are content. If she will do the housework and work in the fields as well, then so much the better!

Hassan's mother saw in Zainab the fulfilment of all the hopes and desires which she had so often expressed to her husband, Khalil. Someone to raise from her shoulders the relentless burden of tasks that had become tiresome to her in later life. When she found that Zainab was of an obedient and compliant nature, something she had always hoped for in a daughter-in-law, her satisfaction increased so that she was

soon able to contemplate her further desires and anticipate
the arrival of the grandchildren she longed for. She began to
dream about the day when she would carry Hassan's son on
her shoulders or sing him to sleep, thinking of the joy that
would be hers in returning through the infant to her own
long lost childhood. Repeating over and over those heartfelt
sighs of affection, she would accompany the innocent child
to a world of calm and repose. How she longed for these
things and in her thoughts, how often she reflected on them.

Khalil too was perfectly happy, having arranged his accounts
so that there was no debt whatsoever upon him. Moreover he
did not have to sell any part of his land in the country,
whereupon he considered that a great task had been accomplished in which God had assisted in the best possible way.

# Chapter Three

Spring came, filling Zainab's soul with so many longings that she felt terribly isolated in her new life, the monotonous life of a marriage without love. Whenever she passed beneath the blossoming trees with their glowing leaves and beautiful flowers or stood listening to the joyful melodies of the birds, a persistent voice beckoned to her reminding her of the past. Stripped of her freedom she was now a captive, no longer able to pursue the desires of her heart or to escape the clutches of her husband. Yet the heart is too great to be possessed. Free, in spite of ourselves, it gives itself to whom it pleases and remains there however much we summon or beseech it. Only when we acknowledge that we are powerless, and reconcile ourselves to what our hearts desire for us, can we enjoy real happiness in which we may rejoice without restraint.

Zainab accepted that her heart wanted to be with Ibrahim just as he had been pining for her ever since she was snatched away from him. She longed to throw herself into his arms and rediscover the joy that was theirs before her marriage. When such happiness is known to exist is it not madness to remain indifferent, out of fear for some old-fashioned belief or prevailing custom? And if such happiness is all we hope for, would not our greatest desire be to achieve it and relish every part of it whatever others might say? That is what our selfish mind commands us to do but we are often forced not to listen to that egotistical voice. However much we may try to ignore it, what people say finds its way into our hearts, poisoning our happiness and turning it to misery until we are compelled to withdraw from the object of our desire.

Zainab began to fear the forces that tore her in opposing directions. Should she go to Ibrahim secretly and beg his forgiveness for having deserted him? . . . Yes, her patience was exhausted and she could not bear the burden of separation any longer. But how could she think of betraying Hassan and violating their contract as long as she remained his wife? The marriage contract that had brought her to her husband's house imposed certain duties which would bring her honour into grave disrepute if she attempted to break away from them. Did she have the audacity to face the consequences of such a crime, the very thought of which numbed her mind and her feelings?

But how harsh her father had been! Setting her on this rough path that had driven her into a situation which was almost destroying her. What words could describe his slyness and how could she respect him when he was responsible for all that had happened? Since she had come to Hassan under duress surely she was not bound by any contract, in which case there was no harm in her seeing Ibrahim so that they might kiss and embrace once more. Then at least she would enjoy a few moments of secret happiness, away from the restrictions of her miserable married life.

In this way many conflicting emotions beset Zainab's tender heart. Sometimes she longed for the happiness she desired in the heart of another who would return the affection she felt inside, a heart that contained a fire of love to set her own passions alight. At other times she resigned herself to her fate, resting her hopes in the hand of destiny that marks out the path of our lives until the end of our days when everything returns to its original state.

Finally, the life she was leading became unbearable and she realised that it was futile to silence her heart to Ibrahim's call. As the days passed by, her conviction grew stronger until one day at the market with her sister-in-law, she saw Ibrahim buying supplies. She went to greet him and shake his hand but when he gave it to her she squeezed his fingers in such a way that he was startled by her behaviour. Zainab did not usually shake hands with him at the market nor with anybody else for that matter. And why had she squeezed his fingers? Looking to her for an explanation, Zainab responded with a glance that conveyed all the hopes and fears that had been turning in her mind since the day of her marriage.

Ibrahim returned with them, conversing in his customary manner and relating stories of everyday events, but to Zainab his words spoke only of his love and how much he wanted to be alone with her. Sometimes she gazed at him, devouring him with her eyes, and occasionally she would heave a sigh as if to disclose the anxiety tormenting her soul. When she replied to things he said her words communicated the sadness she was suffering while her sister-in-law remained unaware of all that passed between them. Then, pointing to one of the fields which belonged to Sayyid Mahmoud, Ibrahim murmured:

'Tomorrow we'll be working there.'

In the course of their conversation the two lovers secretly reminded each other of their past times together and in the same furtive manner, expressed their desire to repeat them. On the outskirts of the village Ibrahim departed, taking the road which led to his house, overjoyed that Zainab had come back to him and hoping to see her on the morrow in the field he had indicated. There they would reunite, in spite of Hassan who had cheated them of their friendship.

Zainab returned to the house feeling perplexed, unable to determine whether the world looked cheerful as in her former days of freedom or whether it bore that downcast aspect that vexed her in moments of misery. In any event she could not stay with the family, discussing what she had seen and done in the market, so she went to her room, hoping to find some comfort in being alone. But solitude only increases anxiety, adding to our fears, so that when it was time for the afternoon prayer she went downstairs in search of her earthenware jar to use it as an excuse to look for Ibrahim wherever he might be. She wanted only to give herself up to him and taste the pleasure she had tasted before—there being no greater pleasure than the passionate surrender to a loved one. How wonderful to be alone with an unmarried man, in possession of his whole being, ready to give it to whomsoever he please. Surely no paradise contains a greater bliss than this—but what treachery on the part of a wife trusted by her husband!

Zainab left the house, walking past the mosque where the men were praying el-asr, before making her way through the

centre of the village to the canal road which was crowded
with womenfolk fetching water. There were also many other
inhabitants of the village, and from neighbouring villages,
walking alone or in groups on their way back from the market.
Some were young peasant boys returning empty-handed, while
others had donkeys which carried their household goods and
agricultural supplies. Then there were the merchants with their
saddlebags slung over the backs of their mules, who rode
astride their loads holding the reins in their hands while others,
whose commodities were difficult to sell, were obliged to
remain in the market until they had sold their wares. Having
done none of the things she had intended to do Zainab filled
her jar and returned to the house where she began to prepare
the supper so that it would be ready when Khalil came home
from the mosque and Hassan returned from the fields where
he was hoeing with his assistant.

Khalil was not long in coming. As soon as the Imam had
given his blessing he made for the door where he rested for
a moment before emerging into the twilight. The wind rustled
the leaves of the trees, the tops of which were still edged with
light, and the figures of the villagers were still visible as they
crowded the roads on their way home. The sky retreated
behind the cloak of night although it had not quite darkened
during those lingering moments of daylight. As the old man
made his way, earnestly glorifying God, he met an acquaintance, aged and baked like himself during the course of a long
life, hurrying back from the fields to pray the rakats of
el-maghrib in the mosque before supper. So there was no time
to discuss the problem of worms; signs of which, it was
rumoured, had already appeared in some of the villages of the
district. Invoking the protection of Allah against the havoc
the worms could wreak, Khalil arrived home slightly earlier
than usual.

As sunset approached Hassan had only six rows in front of
him which he wanted to complete in order to avoid returning
again the following day. His assistant, despite his dissatisfaction, could not leave his master by himself and was required
to stay with him until they were finished. By the time the

work was done, night had virtually erased the last remaining traces of day and they set out between the dark fields with no moon to guide them. Although the stars had taken up their positions one after another, the moon's time had not yet come. They walked together, talking in low voices, relating what they had heard about the worms and sympathising with the unfortunate victims of this wretched blight.

'Once they begin to spread,' said Hassan, 'there's nothing you can do to stop them. Their numbers multiply from one day to the next. Let's pray that God sends us two hot days to destroy them and relieve us of this burden.'

With many expressions to describe the hardships men suffer as a result of this accursed plague, Hassan and his assistant recounted the misery and misfortune that a severe infestation could cause. Discussing this and related matters they made their way down the long road as night spread its cloak over the earth. The path was quiet now with no signs of movement upon it, taking its rest after bearing the weight of the villagers returning before sunset to their homes together with their animals and all they carried with them. The wonderful breeze blew against the chests of the two young men, refreshing them as they savoured its delights. When they arrived at the house it was nearer the time of el-asha than el-maghrib although Khalil, as he sat waiting for them lost in thought, seemed unaware of the passing of time. They greeted him and explained why they were late then called for their supper and when it was served they sat down to eat their food. Afterwards they ate some of the fruit that Zainab had bought at the market and when they were satisfied Hassan asked his wife how she had spent her day. For a moment she was alarmed and remained silent as though she considered this question to be out of the ordinary, then she replied:

'It was just another market day.'

Certainly this was something to arouse suspicion and surprise! What news could he possibly be expecting to hear? Had some great change occurred on the face of the earth or some major incident—or did Hassan know the secrets of her soul and by gazing into the unseen, discern what had taken place between herself and Ibrahim? But what had taken place? It was nothing more than an everyday conversation that might have arisen between any two persons—and if Hassan did know what was in her mind then why had he betrayed her by asking for her hand in marriage? If he understood her so well would it not have been his duty, as a friend, to strive to join her with Ibrahim so that she might enjoy some happiness in life, if there were any happiness to be enjoyed?

In reality Hassan's question was nothing more than a casual inquiry and the answer he received was of no consequence. He was happy with his wife and as she had given him a reply no more meaningful than the question he had asked he paid no attention to the consternation in her voice. All he thought was that she was agitated by his late return or by some other matter which neither bothered him nor roused his concern. After a moment's silence he began to talk about other things, arranging with his assistant what they would do the following day when they had watered the cotton and hoed the land which they were going to leave dry.

Ours is a strange existence, full of mysteries of which we know but a few. Most things are concealed from us yet we consider ourselves informed about everything that happens, even believing that we have sufficient knowledge to understand the workings of the mind or the secrets of the heart. Every day events occur which we can never understand but that does not prevent us from thinking that all is perfectly clear. And on the basis of our conclusions we assess our situation and plan our lives, shaping the future according to our impotent conjectures. When we find ourselves mistaken we willingly confess our ignorance of such matters whereas if by chance we are right, which happens occasionally, we believe it is because we can see what in reality is concealed. So it was that Hassan's silence and his subsequent change of subject demonstrated to Zainab that he perceived both the manifest and hidden aspects of her soul. There was nothing left but to outwit him, to behave like somebody walking in a dangerous desert, calculating every step lest she should fall into peril.

Having convinced herself that she was right, and that everything she saw supported her view, to act in any other way
would lead to inevitable ruin.

Evening drew on until it was time to go to bed and when
Hassan was alone with Zainab he talked to her cheerfully but
she only responded with an occasional word. The minutes
passed. A lamp in one corner illuminated the room with a
faint glow just sufficient to distinguish the objects in the room,
while numerous shadows danced on the walls behind them.
In another corner stood a wardrobe, filled with Zainab's
clothes, making that part of the room perpetually gloomy by
day and by night. Dismayed by her silence and the serious
expression on her face, Hassan asked:

'Why are you so miserable tonight?'

Drawing her towards him and resting her head in his lap
he leaned over to kiss her. He caressed and fondled her then
sat her up beside him and embraced her again while she
submitted to his advances, neither resisting nor trying to avoid
him in any way. But when he let her go she was as silent as
before. She remained impassive like one who has finally lost
trust in a person with authority over them, so that Hassan
could only wonder what had happened to her.

* * *

The days passed quickly, each bringing additional burdens
until it seemed to Zainab that nobody greeted her except with
a frown or a scowl. Her husband went to work without even
saying 'good morning' and his sisters treated her in such a
way that she feared they only wanted to pry into the secrets
of her heart. When Hassan's mother gave her anything to do
she believed it was only to oppress her further and the good
old man Khalil, when he returned from the mosque and called
for his food, or called out again if it was slow in coming,
made her feel that even he wanted to cause her pain and
deprive her of any enjoyment in life. She began to regard
them all as her enemies, determined to wreak their revenge
upon her and as time went by, the belief in her own ill-fated
destiny grew stronger.

During this anxious period Zainab was distracted from the
love that had been rekindled between herself and Ibrahim.
She could think only of the misery that encompassed her and
the torment that the heavens seemed to throw upon her head.
As the tension within her grew she became more and more
distressed and a deep sadness entered her soul which appeared
on her forehead as the mark of despair. She would lose herself
in dark dreams for hours at a stretch during which she became
oblivious to everything around her, paying no heed to anything
she was doing.

Awakening with the dawn one day, Zainab set off with her
jar towards the canal. She walked down the path before the
sky had barely paled, aware only of the ground immediately
in front of her. Making her way through the fields, still resting
beneath a blanket of dew, she advanced towards her destination as the darkness gradually retreated. When she arrived the
canal was full of water, there being no irrigation work at
present, and the fresh breeze caused small waves to ripple on
the surface. Night stole away between the leaves of the great
trees on the banks to be replaced by the light of the newborn
day. She washed the vessel she had brought with her and filled
it with water then leaned against a tree waiting for someone
to help her lift it. She did not have to wait long, but the first
passer-by only said 'Hello' and continued quickly on his way.
Another, who was also in a hurry, called out 'Good morning'
while a third, crossing the bridge with his cloak wrapped
round him said nothing at all. But what was she doing all
this time, not even calling for assistance? Had she fallen asleep
where she stood, undisturbed by their greetings or was it lazi-
ness that had taken hold of her? None of these; Zainab was
roaming in a fathomless sea, travelling far from this world to
another where she could sense the joys of the past as if they
were present, but her memories only accentuated the fears
and apprehensions that now besieged her innocent soul.

Hassan prayed el-fajr then set out for work and when he
passed Zainab standing by the tree he asked her what she was
waiting for. On hearing that she was not waiting for anything
he helped her lift the jar whereupon Zainab returned to the

house as shapes became visible and the road was beginning
to be crowded with girls fetching water. Night was forced
back and the East glowed, announcing the arrival of the god
of fire and light, come to plant the kiss of morning on the
neighbouring horizons. With every step she took, the sky grew
brighter then the sun rose in its purple hue. Ascending the
great throne it clothed the fields below with light in which
their beauty and splendour shone. The cotton fields were
radiant in their greenness and the flowers which bedecked the
magnificent, sarcenet carpet glowed. Then the fields of golden
crops reflected jets of light into the sky which dazzled the eye
as the sun rose higher in its ascent. The harvested land, like
a great cleft, seemed astonished in its nakedness, having so
recently been the habitat of such luscious plants. Spread out
along the road a long line of black figures carried their conical
loads on their heads, moving swiftly but with an air of dignity
and calm. Their sunburned bodies embraced the morning air
and stirred by the fresh moist breeze, their sleepy minds opened
to a world of endless fantasy. Arriving at the watering place,
they washed their clay pots and filled them then bent down
to wash their feet, revealing strong legs which were smooth
and soft, displaying a rosiness which mingled with their light
brown skin. In their movements and conversation as they
related the news of the previous night, they seemed more like
people with nothing to do but indulge themselves rather than
poor, hardworking girls. In that rich and bountiful land of
Egypt, is there one poor girl to be found, distressed by her
own poverty?

Zainab too recalled every morning the events that had
befallen her whereupon she suffered pains which the
surrounding gaiety served only to intensify.

Finally the signs of suffering were almost visible upon her
and the expression on her face revealed the sadness that had
entered her soul. The splendour that was previously hers had
begun to wither and the smile on her lips told only of her
contempt for life. From beneath her heavy eyelids she regarded
the people and things around her with a pained expression
while her forehead remained blank, immersed in darkest

dreams. When Hassan saw her like that he was dismayed and the pain began to grow in him too.

Two marriage partners making their way down the perilous path of life. One buffeted by tempests and mocked by the wind, sometimes feeling hope, sometimes despair. The other, wanting only to be kind, confused and perplexed by everything that afflicted his companion.

Was it in the power of that working man, who had been happy with Zainab from the day of their marriage, to bring her back from the realm of despair and enjoy the good things that life has to offer? No, it was she who was taking him, from the happiness he had imagined would be his to a state of resigned sorrow and a world of anxiety and suffering . . . Then came another market day. A merry day, the merchants calling out at the tops of their voices while the villagers strolled contentedly in the knowledge that they had a few coins in their pockets. The air rang with the noise of the crowd and the sky mirrored the light of the sun which sent its rays onto the trees and shone down on the hot, dry land over which the fallaheen walked with firm unwavering steps.

Ibrahim was there and when Zainab returned to the house she was beset by confusion as to what to do. Was any value to be attached to the contract between herself and Hassan after it had been so falsely drawn up? And if her husband thought badly of her whether she had done anything wrong or not, what difference would it make if she did throw herself into Ibrahim's arms to relieve her anxiety? She had only refrained in order to please Hassan but as that did not satisfy him what was there to prevent her reliving the days of the past?

The following evening after the sun had set, Hassan returned from work and ate his supper before going upstairs where he found Zainab sitting alone, gazing through the skylight to the stars in a moonless sky. Her eyes were wandering without perceiving what was before them and the darkness of the room was only partially dispersed by the lamp a short distance away. He sat down beside her and taking her hand in his he said:

'What's wrong Zainab?'

He asked her as a friend, upset to see his partner distressed and his stumbling words told of the feelings he held for her. But Zainab sat motionless as though unaware of his presence, gazing in confusion at the distant stars and anticipating the morrow when she would see Ibrahim.

'What's the matter Zainab? Just tell me what's the matter. Has mother said something to you or has someone else annoyed you? What can have upset you so much that you seem to be burdened by all the cares of this world and the next? Is there anything you want or is it something I've done? If it's me you're angry with I can't tell you how sorry I am . . . Oh Zainab! You're not like those women who get upset over nothing. If someone has spoken badly to you, my mother, my sister or anyone else, let me take the blame for it. I'm sorry.'

Then he took her hand and kissed it twice, seeking to please her with sympathy and kindness. His voice disclosed a tenderness that would have softened the hardest of hearts, revealing his affection and the extent of his trust in her. From the day of their marriage he had been content, believing that he had taken possession of a priceless pearl among the girls of the village combining beauty, self-composure, diligence and fidelity. Thinking that his good fortune would only increase, he could not comprehend what was happening and desperately wanted to know what was afflicting his partner.

Tears welled up in Zainab's eyes but pride and shame prevented them gushing forth. She felt she had committed a crime for which she could not atone and in addition to the sadness she already felt, a new sorrow burdened her when she realised how much her husband cared for her. He had always been well-intentioned while she alone was the infamous sinner. She sought to justify herself when her husband did not even suspect her. He was the powerful one, able to dictate her affairs and control her life, yet he held himself responsible for anything anyone else might have done to upset her. There was nothing to do but throw herself at his feet, beg forgiveness, acknowledge her sin and confess all. Would it not be the greatest disrespect to turn her heart away from him when he had shown how gentle he was, ready to forgive any misdeed?

Zainab put out the lamp and went to bed, but she could not sleep. The voice inside her would not be stilled and whenever she heard its call she could feel Hassan shifting uneasily as though he was also disturbed by her thoughts. Eventually, after telling her husband that the heat of the room made it impossible for her to sleep with him, she went up to the roof to spend the night alone beneath the fugitive stars. Closing her eyes she imagined a great world where the pages of the past were spread out before her and she strayed among them without direction.

# Chapter Four

Hamid came with his brothers to spend the summer holiday in the village, having passed another year between work and dreams where he lived within four walls, apart from those occasions in the spring when he walked out along the banks of the great river. Sometimes, if the weather was suitable, he would take a small boat across the surface of the water or go to Heliopolis* where the distant horizons descend beyond the hills on the edge of the yellow sand with its blue dome. The dry wind blew pleasantly against his chest as he gazed at the desert surrounding the fertile valley. Returning along the asphalt roads, young girls passed by in black shawls which revealed their soft plump arms while their flimsy veils exposed delicate chins and rosy cheeks or wide eyes and black eyebrows below clear foreheads. Hamid would stroll along lost in dreams except when the beauty around him attracted his attention, or the wind raised the veils from the girls' faces and they would cry out or glance round, wary of Hamid's watchful eye. Sometimes he simply sat on a bench by the side of the road or met with friends in a cafe where they would talk about one thing or another until it was time to go home.

Hamid's habit of daydreaming often kept him from appreciating his surroundings but he loved the desert scenery on the edge of the city and went there frequently towards the end of term. He wanted to enjoy the 'dry' landscape and the sight of those female shapes in their elegant clothes before returning to the countryside and the peasant girls whose beauty lay concealed beneath long, straight garments. In the evening, the tramway would carry him through the open country, where the wind blew strongly, into illuminated streets bustling with carriages speeding along in every direction.

* A Cairo suburb.

For the first few weeks Hamid stayed in the village by day, only going out towards evening with his brothers, to see what was happening in the fields. Nightfall would find them sitting together on a canal bank or by a small mosque overgrown with asperto grass while the breezes blew gently overhead. Back in the village they would join the menfolk who sat with the evening papers discussing misfortunes that had occurred or complaining about the unjust and haphazard intentions of the government. Sometimes the fallaheen would chuckle between their teeth if a ministerial statement was read out which said absolutely nothing, or complain bitterly when they heard about the antics of some of the English officials. A debate would ensue if one group supported the opinion of a particular newspaper, while another held an opposing view, and whenever Hamid picked up a newspaper he was always asked to read out an article or give his judgement on an issue about which they disagreed.

One night Hamid returned to the village as the moon was rising, to find the men discussing the adverse effects on the cotton crop of the recent water shortage:

'It's the engineer, God curse him, who controls the water supply. If you grease his palm, he'll let the water flow!'

'By God I don't know what sort of conscience these people have.'

'Neither conscience nor religion! The dog in charge of our district was paid so much only the other day; but throughout this watering period, no drop has reached the fields.'

'The whole setup is corrupt in fact, from the engineer to the chief engineer, to the inspector. None have any ethics at all! Two days ago many telegrams were sent and many petitions submitted; even the inspector himself was approached. Nothing came of it! There was no response of any kind.'

'Those in power can only respond to money! We know the people of our country! Instead of the telegrams and the meetings, we should have used the money, perhaps with a little more added, in greasing the palm of the engineer. That should have secured our turn in the watering cycle and given us what we wanted!'

Their discussion was interrupted by the arrival of Sayyid Mahmoud and they all stood up to greet him before returning to their places. The servant entered with the evening papers, which Hamid placed on the table, and coffee was ordered. Then they continued their conversation, questioning the proprietor about the water supply. When he replied that it would be restored that very night they opened the papers as usual and read what was in them happily.

Sayyid Mahmoud, who had been busy all day with the engineer, had received a promise and written statement that the water supply would be resumed on a rotational basis. But after spending the day travelling and in long discussion with the government official, he was in no mood to stay at home. His feathers had been ruffled by the official who was so dedicated to serving the government that he considered anything to do with the private sector to be no concern of his. At the same time he was one of the most brazen when it came to manipulating the rules and regulations which affected them.

Taking a friend for company, Sayyid Mahmoud set out for the parched and pitiful-looking fields together with Hamid who decided to go with them. They made their way by the light of the moon until they came upon a group of tenant farmers, resting on the canal bank, awaiting the decision of God and the government concerning their livelihoods. As though the hardships that were thrown upon them at random from above were not enough, the government decreed taxes in order to increase their misery! The older men lamented the passing of the time when there were fewer needs to satisfy and fewer problems to overcome while the thin moon clothed them with its rays as it had done when they first participated in the harvest at the age of seven. At an even younger age, their mothers had carried them to the fields in their arms, leaving them to the protection of Allah while they went about their tasks.

When they passed the first water wheel and saw the attendant crouched beside it, wrapped in his cloak, Sayyid Mahmoud called to him:

'Good evening Abu Moharram. Wake up now, the water's coming.'

The old man, looking as though he had despaired of his life, got up and shook hands with them one by one. Then he said:

'My friends, even if the water comes the cotton is almost ruined. By God, people were better off in the old days. We simply waited for the Nile to rise then we would sow and that was that; and we had a bumper harvest! Why, when the water receded we caught a lot of fish. And what fish! Sackfuls of it! These days you go to all sorts of trouble to get a drop of water. It seems the past will never return.'

Abu Moharram went on to relate other stories of a time when people seemed to do very well for themselves without ever becoming exhausted or worn out, the only things they resented being the use of the kourbash* and the severity of government taxes. This old man, with only a limited time left on earth, was genuinely scornful of the government's attempts to organise the water supply and improve the situation for the poor.

Sayyid Mahmoud continued on his way, waking up the men one by one. When they opened their eyes to find that the canal was still a gaping rift they were surprised that the proprietor should have woken them at this time of night, but he quickly announced that the water would soon reach them and that they should be ready for it when it arrived. Coming to one of the more important tenants, they sat down to drink coffee and did not leave until the first signs of water had begun to trickle over the dry alluvial bed of the canal, gradually increasing in volume as it flowed over the cracks. Then they made their way to a plot of Sayyid Mahmoud's private land which was planted with rice, although no flowerheads had appeared as yet and the leaves were withered due to lack of water. Not finding anyone there they called a worker from a nearby field to stay with them until daybreak. When it was light, Hamid walked across the field inspecting the wilted

* Whip used for punishment.

plants which had lost their greenness, the leaves dull and faded
if they had not already fallen to the ground.

The sun rose and Sayyid Mahmoud returned to the village
with his companion, having seen for himself that the water
supply had been restored as promised. Hamid preferred to
stay in the countryside to spend his day by one of the water
wheels which hummed continuously in its monotonous tone
as activity resumed in the surrounding fields. During the
afternoon the burning sun, beating down with its fire upon
the land, made Hamid feel drowsy and crawling into a makeshift shelter he soon fell fast asleep. When he opened his eyes
the sun was descending from a rose-coloured sky and the
water in the canal had begun to rise again, having dwindled
during the course of the afternoon. He looked round but
there was no sign of the worker who had been with them and
as far as the eye could see the landscape was devoid of human
life. The ox turning the water wheel moved slowly as the sun
sank swiftly to its resting place and beneath the darkening
sky, the imps and spirits which inhabited that great expanse
of land seemed to creep out from all directions. A few stars
shone in the blackness but as the night advanced and no
moon appeared, their light was of little use. Demons danced
before the eyes of the melancholy young man as if they were
about to invade his shelter. The ox stopped moving and silence
descended, broken only by the sound of crickets filling the
emptiness with whistles and shrieks, and always the night
grew deeper. Hamid yawned, bringing tears to his sleep-filled
eyes, then picking up a small stone, he threw it at the ox to
keep it moving and stretched out on the ground as before.
The sluggish humming sound resumed and the water pouring
into the pool gleamed in the light of the stars which shone
steadily brighter, and in the deepening night Hamid began
to imagine all manner of catastrophes that might befall him.
What would he do if he was disturbed by hostile wolves or
worse still if they attacked one of the beasts?

For what seemed a long time Hamid tried to overcome his
fears and give himself courage until it was time to switch the
oxen. There being nobody else to perform that simple task,

he was about to fetch the other beast when he stumbled upon somebody sleeping, their face covered by a handkerchief. So as not to disturb his master, the worker who normally occupied the shelter had climbed into the enclosure to steal a few moments rest. Shaking him gently, he awoke at once and asked if Hamid had eaten the supper that had been brought for him. But Hamid had been oblivious to everything apart from his dreams and the demons in front of his eyes. Now that he had found a companion his fears were dispelled and after inviting the worker to join him, he ate his food then went back to sleep.

When he awoke it was still night although a thin moon had risen which brightened the fields. Hamid sat quietly, pondering the world around him. What unknown wonders lie beyond the horizon? How many animals or other organisms there must be close by, enjoying the breeze, the water and the stillness as he himself enjoyed them. And what of the heavens? How strange the shining stars are, smiling down benevolently upon us. Did those tiny specks really witness the dawn of creation, to remain through all eternity while our time on earth is so short? Yet in spite of their great age they appear humble as though the long succession of days has taught them the folly of selfish pride. How strange that they should be held in space, some stable and motionless while others revolve slowly in their orbits. In this world of ours can anything function without drawing on the power of everything that surrounds it?

Who knows what lies beneath the ground? The corpses of the dead and the remains of civilisations gone by, twisted roots of trees and plants, deathly silence and the rumbling of volcanoes! Within the earth are things we do not know. And how thin the moon is. Surely it must be inhabited by some form of life; creatures so infatuated that they have all but pined themselves away for love to give their planet the emaciated appearance that it displays today.

Hamid gazed steadily at the illuminated planet as it climbed the sky in its own slow and gentle fashion. Then the sky paled. The stars almost vanished from sight and Hamid knew that it would soon be morning. He walked among the plants to see how much water had reached the crops during the night, stopping at the waterline in the field of rice and glancing round as the sky darkened once more. It was the darkness which comes between the first appearance of light and the dawning of the day. Hamid returned to the shelter and called to the worker to light a fire so that they could warm the bread they had with them for breakfast.

On the far horizon the sun sent out its heralders. They made their way to the mosque where Hamid sat quietly outside staring in wonder at the fabulous East where a sky of flowing gold bathed the plants in its glow. Then the orb appeared, huge, making its way between the heavens and earth as though shaken out of bed by the angels, still covered with its rosy blanket. It ascended the lower strata quickly at first, then more slowly, giving out fire and light in which everything below seemed to dissolve and sending up brilliant shafts which whitened the blueness of the sky.

The days and nights passed by and as Hamid grew accustomed to being away from people he began to spend most of his time out of doors. One night he was gazing at the quarter moon, moving towards its evanescence, when a sweet melody broke through the air bringing joy to his ears. It was a plaintive sound carried on the wings of the breeze; the gentle sound of a salamiyya* which Ibrahim was strumming by a distant well. How much meaning there was in that sad melody! What passion and fervour it inspired. For in the mind of the player was another world, more beautiful than ours, which his sweetheart called him to. A world we reach when we transcend ourselves, where spirits fly in pairs. Hamid listened and fell beneath its spell, forgetting his own thoughts and dreams as the music played on his soul. He trembled under its influence, moved from grief to surrender to despair, then to the heights of hope and he remained where he stood until the first sign of day.

* * *

* A rural stringed instrument.

Some days later the water flowed freely, flooding the rice crop which began to flourish, becoming lush and plentiful until it was necessary to trim it back. Boys and girls came from outside the village to do the thinning, arriving on the morning train, their sickles in their hands. Baring their legs they squatted among the plants and worked away in silence followed closely by Hamid who walked behind, enjoying the sight of the beautiful crop which had become dear to him after watching over it for many successive nights. As the day advanced, the workers began to chatter amongst themselves and the supervisor had to urge one of the girls to work harder, whereupon she looked him straight in the face as though she could not believe her ears and said:

'But I haven't stopped!'

The supervisor urged on some of the others but soon began to laugh with them and in this way they experienced the bonds of comradeship which always accompany such groups in their labour. Although Hamid did not actually partake of their merriment or get involved in their verbal duels, he was not exactly neutral and often sided with one party against another. The party who won his support felt proud, not on account of their victory—for that meant very little—but because 'Master Hamid' stood by them.

The first day of thinning passed during which nothing of any great significance occurred except that in the afternoon break they asked one of the girls to dance for them.

On the second day the workers conversed more freely, opening their hearts and laughing unreservedly. One girl in particular, who thought herself more beautiful than the rest, never let Hamid joke with her without finding something to say in return.

On the third day, during the afternoon rest period, Hamid was sitting against the wall of the shelter talking to some of the workers when a group of girls came to sit beside them in the shade. The one who always had an answer for Hamid sat next to him, chatting and laughing while the others looked on askance or whispered among themselves. Hearing their whispers and guessing what they were thinking, Hamid leaned

over and kissed the young girl who looked at him in dismay
as if to say: 'Well what was that for?' The girls stared in
astonishment but Hamid hardly gave her time to turn away
before kissing her on the other cheek as well! The young boys
chuckled when she pushed him away as though she could not
believe what was happening. But no sooner had Hamid settled
down again than she threw herself upon him claiming that
she would repay him for what he had done, whereupon he
embraced her again and kissed her a third time. Whenever
he let her go she pulled him towards her and leaned over him,
ready to give him his punishment. The blood had risen to her
cheeks giving her wheat-coloured skin the flushed appearance
of a girl whose passion has been stirred. Hamid's complexion
also changed colour as he continued to kiss her or hold her
to his chest whenever she leaned towards him. Then she fell
under his sway and gave herself up to him, still claiming that
some day she would repay him for this! Finally, when it was
time to return to work they organised themselves in their
rows, sickles in hands, while Hamid followed a few paces
behind. But when he came to his senses he stood motionless,
wondering what madness had taken hold of him.

As the afternoon progressed the workers fell silent beneath
the oppression of the dumb world around them. The girl felt
weak and dizzy, lost to her surroundings as she trimmed the
plants heedlessly, quite oblivious to the glances which the girls
nearby were casting in her direction. Some smiled maliciously,
some derisively while those whose jealousy had been kindled
lowered their eyes, and on every side the silence remained
complete.

What had caused an intelligent young man like Hamid to
take advantage of that innocent working girl? However attractive she was to him, how could somebody in his position
descend to such a level?

Woman is nothing but an accursed devil, an open snare
into which unfortunate men blindly fall! She has a wickedness
concealed within her like an electric current; when touched
by a man, the electricity is released and he is thrown to the
ground, stripped of his pride and grandeur . . .

Such were Hamid's thoughts as he returned to the village after weeks spent beneath the open sky or resting in his makeshift shelter. He had left the fields about an hour after the midday break, angry with himself and crying openly, wanting to atone for his mistake. His dreams had always been pure and clean, how could he violate and destroy them in a single moment without any consideration of what he was doing? Would everybody who had known him to be upright and religious until an hour ago now reproach him—and all for the sake of a simple working girl? Woe to women who bring us down from our positions of honour and respectability when all we achieve in return is the loss of our strength, our pride and our property. Woe to existence itself that the world should be arranged in this unfortunate way. Arriving at a canal he threw off his clothes and jumped in the water to cleanse himself, asking God's forgiveness for his lapse. And whenever he saw a woman pass by he sought refuge in God from the evil within her!

Hamid spent the rest of the day with his family who were pleased to see him. They looked at his face, tanned by the sun and at his sturdy brown arms, asking him how he liked the vast expanse outside. He answered their questions but his mind was preoccupied and he felt uneasy, unable to find a way to make amends for what he had done.

When night fell he lay on his bed in the dark, oppressed by the stifling air. Tonight there were no open spaces with breezes flowing to bring refreshment to his mind and soul. No sky, with stars twinkling before his eyes, in which to gaze at length as if he might have found some inspiration there—or salvation. All he could see of the moon were the rays which reached him through the window, the planet of love concealed beyond the walls of his room. The atmosphere was nauseating and weighed heavily upon him. Where was the canal with its flowing water and the distant horizons illuminated by the light of the moon? All that had been taken away from him together with the beauty and mystery it contained. Unable to sleep he lay on his bed regretting what had happened.

Some days later he began to frequent the fields in the afternoon and his peace of mind returned when he found himself alone again, away from the world of men, so that his thoughts could continue unhindered: 'Returning to the house after eating my lunch, I found some delicious fruit which I sat down to eat even though I was full—and how tasty it was! Although I wasn't thirsty I drank some refreshing juice and that too was good. I went to say "hello" to my uncles and aunts after my long absence and they pressed me to eat some sweetmeats which I accepted and found delicious. Then we stayed up in the evening while Sheikh Saed sang to us in a beautiful voice. I listened and found it delightful. Everybody was spellbound until the Sheikh had finished his piece, leaving us trembling with joy and hardly able to catch our breaths. All these things were enjoyable but never more pleasurable than the short time I spent with that girl, caressing her and kissing her blushing cheeks as we embraced one another. What memories those moments hold, marred only by the grief that followed. Even when I pushed her away she came back and our bodies melted together. The scent of her almost over-whelmed me as we indulged our passion, both intoxicated by that wonderful pleasure we all love so much! Her warm breasts swelled as though a fire had been kindled within them, trembling with excitement whenever our bodies touched. When she bent over me open-mouthed, claiming she would repay me then kissing me without a care, her body seemed to dissolve like a wave breaking over hidden shores and sensations passed between us in which I almost lost myself. How much more enjoyable this was than all those other sensual pleasures, yet they would deprive us of it! I caused her no harm, neither did I transgress against anyone else but simply enjoyed myself in the same way I enjoy permissible things, desiring nothing more than momentary gratification. Indeed, it was a moment in life never to be equalled—except by another like it. Yet they say such things are forbidden.

'O Satan who leads us astray! What evil are you trying to induce in me? Into what great abyss do you wish to throw me? There is no relish to such passing pleasures. We sons of

Adam are born between the angels and the beasts. Either we sink to the level of the latter, contenting ourselves with the pleasures of this world, or we aspire to the former and renounce our base desires. Have I come this far only to fall, on account of one working girl, to the lowest level of all?'

After an hour spent between pain and regret, Hamid finally drifted into dreamless oblivion. He continued to sleep in the house, putting up with the oppression of his dark room, from which he could see neither moon nor stars, and whenever he withdrew into himself to reflect, he stubbornly resisted the shame that accompanied him.

Nobody else noticed any of this. They considered him to be everything an educated young man ought to be: diligent, upright and religious. To be honest he did not pray but that did not enter into the general assessment of boys still at school.

* * *

As days seemed to cancel out one another, each casting a thick veil over the one that passed, Hamid began to recover that former quietude which hung over his life like a robe in which he moved from one day to the next among his dreams and hopes and endless imaginings. Finally, when nothing remained to oppress him other than the gloomy darkness of his room and the silence of the night he decided to return to the outdoor life. The summer nights were a delight and he slept beside the raised cotton fields listening to the humming of the ox-driven tanbour. Fragrant breezes blew through the fields while the hanging stars surrounded the moon in all her splendour. By the side of his chosen spot, water tumbled boisterously in a small canal where the lights of the sky were permanently reflected. Thus Hamid returned to the natural life and after being away from the fields, away from the night and deaf to its sounds, he felt that he was returning to an old friend.

In the early morning he would return to his family for an hour or so before going to the rice fields to watch the girls thinning the crop—an added advantage for him, apart from the profit of the crop itself! When half the field had been thinned, Hamid noticed Zainab's sister whom he had not seen for some time and he asked her what she had been doing, to which she replied that she had been busy with some building work in the village. At noon Hamid took her to one side to ask about Zainab and whether she was happy in her new way of life. But his questions reminded the girl of the days she had spent side by side with her sister in the fields when they would take their lunch together at this same hour of the day. She was made aware of her present solitude, always leaving or returning to the house on her own and she began to regret the loss of times gone by.

Hamid too remembered the sweet hours he had spent with Zainab and also felt sorry. From the shadows of the past the memory came to him of that distant day when they had sat together embracing each other by the side of the road. How could he ever forget the effect that meeting had upon him? Then he remembered the night he had found her sitting alone at the top of the stairs when everyone below was making merry and he wondered how she was now and whether she ever thought about him.

The lone figures of the country girls working beneath the clear blue sky amid the flourishing green fields which stretched to the horizons, filled Hamid with joy. What beauty their sturdy bodies displayed, their protruding breasts rising and falling gently with each step while the wind plays upon their pure black garments. What great significance lay beneath that essential simplicity which blends with their strength to enhance the beauty of their natural charms.

Hamid rejected the ascetic lifestyle, the life of virtue. To him it was more like an inescapable death which assails us the moment we taste the pleasure of life, making us believe that existence is something dreadful that we should back away from in order to avoid temptation. But his upbringing created conflict in his mind and he was often burdened with guilt as a result of his desires.

'What am I,' mused Hamid, 'for all that I have done on this earth? Is the life I lead any different from that of a hermit, forsaking the world and forsaken in return? Yet in spite of that, I claim to enjoy life's pleasantries and what they call clean minded pleasures.

'What has become of you Zainab? Do you greet each new day joyfully, glad that it has come, and does you husband kiss your smiling lips when the sun appears in the sky? Or do you both live that dull, monotonous life that so many married people lead? I fear for you now lest you be sad and miserable. What times we spent together in rapturous dreams even though we denied ourselves the better part of them. Do your eyes still contain the magic that I used to see in them and does your smile, which outshone that of all other creatures, now increase your partner's joy?

'How happy Zainab's husband must be, enjoying that wonderful world in which everything is bliss, adding pleasure to pleasure and happiness to happiness. Could there be another chance for me I wonder, to see Zainab again, to kiss and embrace her and revive the dreams of the past which have all but entered the realm of extinction?'

But if Hamid were to see Zainab again and embrace or kiss her, would he not grieve and become penitent or go off in a frenzy, plunging into the water to purify himself of his deed? Would he not be overwhelmed with remorse at the depravity of his actions? No, never! From the depths of his soul he desired that kiss which alone would revive the memory of the distant past to which they and God alone had been witness.

Hamid continued to muse: 'Will Zainab have forgotten me now that she has become involved in other things? Maybe she regards me no differently from anyone else in the village, considering what passed between us to be nothing more than an innocent friendship that could have occurred with any other boy. As she merits everyone's admiration why should she consider me a special friend or lover even if I admired her more than the rest? I may have been the dominant one then; now I am a stranger. Anything I might say would only arouse suspicion and be regarded as an infringement of her marital status.

'Why am I sad that those days have gone? Do the pains

which consume us or the isolation we feel when we close our eyes to the world provide a motive for staying alive? What harsh virtue they urge upon us! Harsher than the stubborness of death itself from which there is no escape.

'Until now I have tasted little in life other than the everyday taste, neither bitter nor sweet. How can the future bring anything but despair, a stream of monotonous days rolling by beneath the vicissitudes of fate? Then a hole in which to sleep the long peaceful sleep. I bade farewell to the world on the day I was born and now I am nothing more than an insensitive object, roused occasionally by the storm only to return to inertia, moving from one state of nothingness to another without experiencing anything . . .'

Hamid gazed into the great void that surged with the light of the sun, shining on the whitewashed heavens and beyond he knew not where. There was no movement in the air and the distant trees stood completely still. In front of him the canal flowed evenly through the fields, carrying along in its current the stalks of rice which had been discarded after the thinning, and the water gleamed beneath the rays of the sun which burned down fiercely at that hour of the day. Then all was lost and Hamid could see nothing but empty space before his eyes.

The workers and working girls worked earnestly, sometimes talking or laughing, but the sound of their voices died on their lips. Hamid went to lean against the shelter where he stood looking round perplexedly, his thoughts in disarray. Finally he resolved to return to the village but looking back he noticed some of the workers sitting on the bridge and decided to return to see what they were doing. When he found that they had finished the section they were on and were simply waiting to move to the other side of the canal he left them, after saying to Zainab's sister with a wry smile on his lips:

'When you see your sister, say "hello" to her from me.'

Between the divided fields there was not a soul to be seen nor any sound to be heard as Hamid made his way along a path shaded by trees that protected him from the afternoon heat. Then he took the most direct route to the village where a few white houses stood out from the dust-coloured dwellings which looked like the remains of some ancient city, immersed in the light of the sun. When he arrived, most of the villagers were still enjoying their rest so he went to his house and standing at the door, called one of the servants by name. Another servant answered his call, informing him that the other had gone to the station but Hamid was not concerned who replied—all he wanted was some coffee, to pass the time while he waited for his brothers.

As he was drinking his coffee some of his brothers returned from the canal where they had been supervising the installation of a new water wheel, and calling for the servant to fill the large coffee pot, they sat outside debating the local news and what steps the debtors were taking these days to repay their creditors. They discussed the feddans of land which were currently for sale and various other topics then they went indoors. Hamid thought about his own affairs for a while before considering the plight of those unfortunate people who seldom realise the debasement of being constantly in debt and rarely comprehend the crises that befall them on account of the exorbitant interest charged on their loans.

The sun was still burning hot even though the air was beginning to stir and the shadows lengthening. Those who had no work to do took to the shade where they sat telling stories or playing backgammon. The branches of the trees inclined slightly in the breeze and the pond glistened beneath the dazzling light that shone on the waves rippling across the surface of the water.

As the day wore on, activity took the place of torpor, and vitality was restored bringing smiles to the faces of the villagers after the apathy which beset them during the heat of the long summer afternoons. When Hamid perceived the movement of the trees and the palm branches trembling in the air he rejoiced at the approach of the wonderful hour of sunset. Then in the distance, he noticed a rider advancing slowly. He strained his eyes but could only see a woman wrapped in a shawl with her attendant walking ahead holding the bridle of the horse. Not a sight seen everyday—maybe it was one of their relatives or an acquaintance come to visit the family and stay for a day or two in the village.

The woman's shawl hung neatly over her arms so that only her hands were visible, shimmering in the hazy air as she held onto the reins and as the horse's hooves struck the ground her body swayed from side to side in the saddle. Slowly they approached the house, becoming more discernible with every step, but even when they were just a few metres distant Hamid still did not recognise who it was. Only when she had dismounted and one of the servants had been asked about the new arrival did Hamid realise that it was Aziza!

# Chapter Five

Dear Aziza,

I rest what remains of my hopes in your hands, the verdict is yours. Either you fulfil them and bring some happiness into my life or ignore them and leave me wretched. A soul stands before you which, with only a word from you, would be on the road to contentment or thrown into a hell of misery. A soul that for so long has been torn between the hopes and disappointments of dreams now wants to emerge from its long sleep to wakefulness, either to delight in fulfilment or to remain burdened by suffering.

Yes my love, so many nights have I spent with your precious image gazing towards me, smiling and embracing me. In my dreams we would spend the night happily together until, when the image left me, I could only wonder whether I would ever experience the pleasure of my imaginings in reality. And who knows if I will achieve that?

Long months have passed while I have been waiting hopefully for that day when we might sit side by side with nobody present to disturb us. I love you Aziza but I am deprived and miserable.

Shall I tell you what I have suffered on account of loving you? Should I mention my throbbing heart and agitated mind or remind you of the days when we were young and used to play together?

Dear Aziza, I am waiting for your word and you know the bitterness of waiting. I offer you my love and devotion.

Hamid

After seeing his sweetheart again Hamid could only blame himself for forgetting her and he began to think once more about being alone with the girl to whom he wanted to open up his heart. The only way he could think of to attain that was to write her a letter and slip it into her hand, so he wrote

the above and put it in his pocket waiting for a suitable
opportunity to give it to her.

The next morning, after breakfasting with his brothers, he
made his way to where she was staying and after summoning
up all his courage he entered the house. He was determined
to do everything in his power to achieve the goal he had desired
for so long, at least a year, to be alone with Aziza and tell her
the stories that filled his head. He forgot the early spring when
he had opened his heart to the world and its beauty and the
splendour of nature adorned in her new clothing. Indeed, all
else was forgotten as his commitment to Aziza returned. No
longer could he be patient when his heart was torn apart every
hour of every day that he spent thinking about her. What great
consolation he would find in her from the harsh realities of
life.

On greeting the ladies who were present with Aziza he was
surprised when one of them exclaimed:

'Well, if it isn't our peasant boy!'

And when he sat down she asked him to tell them about
life in the country and his love for the fields—for had he not
always been a home-dweller, unconcerned with agriculture
until he had recently begun to frequent the farmlands like his
brothers?

Hamid was at a loss how to reply. He could hardly tell
them about the inspiration of the stars, his conversations with
the moon or the secrets of the natural world. How could he
relate to them the hopes and dreams that the soul entertains
when the eye looks serenely into the darkness of a summer
night and the breeze refreshes the heart, carrying the gentle
sounds of the hushed world? How could he explain the boundless joy a man experiences when he finds himself free with no
chains? They knew nothing of this and even if they had
encountered it when they were young, time had made them
forget. But should he remain silent in front of his sweetheart
whom he believed loved him and would want to hear him
speak? So he told them about that night in the fields when
he had woken to find himself all alone and how he had
searched but found no company other than the animals until

he stumbled upon the worker, asleep in the enclosure. This brought smiles of amusement to their faces and he saw Aziza laughing.

'Poor old Hamid!' said the lady who had asked him to speak, and they all began to search their memories for similar events that may have befallen them or their acquaintances. Then they began to relate other stories about things which frightened them and soon they were telling tales about the afarit.*

'You know how the saying goes—"afarit appear to those who fear them"—well, last year, so they say, Hajja Musada went downstairs one night and found a sheep in the yard with great big horns that kept on getting bigger until the path was blocked by them. But when we got up in the morning we found that it was an ordinary sheep belonging to one of Hassanin's boys!'

'They also say that afarit jump out at you if you walk in front of the enclosure belonging to Ummu Saad's boys and so now people are almost too afraid to pass by there.'

Then one of them related a story about an ifrit in the shape of a donkey, saddled and bridled, that had appeared to Ammi Jaad who guarded the palm tree enclosure. The old man mounted it and plunging a long spike between its shoulder blades, rode off to visit the shrines in Cairo, Tanta and Mansura.

They discussed the different kinds of afarit such as the 'calling spirit' who calls a man by his name. If he answers her call she takes him and throws him down an abandoned well or something similar unless he recites the Qur'anic verse: "Say He is God, the One". Other spirits would take over a person's mind and only a beautiful girl offering gifts at a Zar* ritual could cause them to depart. At this point Aziza joined in the conversation with the others while Hamid sat silently, occasionally showing signs of amazement at what he heard.

* Mischievous spirits. (Arabic singular—ifrit.)
* A ritual believed necessary for exorcising evil spirits with music, dance, incense-burning and special 'gifts'.

Hamid listened to their stories for a while then he bade them 'good day' and left, his mind at ease, content to have seen Aziza laughing and in good spirits. Sometimes she had looked at him and when their eyes met he lowered his gaze, believing that she might become aroused. But he had not given her the letter, feeling that it would have been futile to do so in front of the ladies who surrounded her constantly. Even though most of them could not read they were bound to become suspicious. Similarly he was reluctant to entrust it to someone else to pass on to her lest it fell into the wrong hands and his amorous intentions became public knowledge. Then the world would know that he was in love: disgraceful, evil, dishonourable love. The shame of it!

How can a young person in Egypt find enjoyment and happiness? He is an unfortunate victim caught between two extremes: either he remains in that deathlike state which traditional values impose on him, or he exposes himself to the corrupt practices which this unfortunate country has inherited from the happy criminal West!

But Hamid loved Aziza and wanted to be alone with her . . .

Why not send the letter among some other items which could be delivered by hand? Surely when she found it she would be mindful to let no one else see it, and as long as she loved him she would write back, to make an arrangement to meet him. After that it would be easy and only a shadow of the deprivation which tainted their enjoyment of life at present would remain. As time went by their confidence would increase until that wonderful day when each would reveal to the other the secrets that their hearts contained.

* * *

The next day he carried out his resolution, hiding the letter among some other articles which one of the younger servants took to Aziza. On finding the note she kept it carefully until she could read it when she was alone.

What great pleasure she found in the letter, and the sentiments contained within it, so that she looked back over it many times. Unable to put it away she read it again and again, trembling when she came to the end. The last line filled her with excitement and made her heart beat faster: 'Dear Aziza I am waiting for your word and you know the bitterness of waiting. I offer you my love and devotion. . . '

Never in her life had she received a letter like this, her only correspondence having been with her sister or in the form of greetings cards exchanged with friends. Now there was nothing in the world that could further her delight. She became oblivious to everything except the joy which swelled her being. Her only desire was to see Hamid and kiss him on the forehead!

These feelings remained with her, disturbed only when she was asked about affairs in the house or when she had to sit with the ladies while they told their never ending stories. Happiness pervaded her mind and body and she gave herself up to it, hardly listening to what the ladies were saying, except that whenever she heard them laughing she would laugh too, without a care for the morrow.

When her emotions had subsided she began to think what to write in reply but was beset by confusion and could find nothing to say. From the window of her room, high above the road so that passers-by could not see in, Aziza looked out at the afternoon sun, descending slowly and casting its light over the stretch of land that divided the village. Huge shadows spread out beneath the great trees as the wind rustled through the branches, and in the distance she could just glimpse the fields of cotton and corn. The narrow lanes were crowded with girls fetching water and their black robes flowed through this ocean of light as they followed one another between the green fields in an orderly procession. On their heads they carried their earthenware pitchers, sideways when empty, upright when' full, the damp surfaces reflecting the light. From the other window a cloud of dust billowed above the heads of a group of building workers so that nothing could be seen beyond. Aziza gazed perplexedly at the scene, still not knowing what to write, then picking up her pen she tried to put down some of her thoughts:

Brother Hamid,

You cannot know how much joy and happiness your letter brought me. I want to see you where we can be alone . . .

But she considered this insufficient to express her feelings. How could such a simple phrase convey her present state or give the impression of a soul overflowing with joy? Finally she wrote:

Brother Hamid,

I cannot describe to you how much happiness your letter brought me but imagine ultimate happiness—I was even happier! I do want to see you where we can be alone together but you know how difficult it is when I'm always surrounded by the ladies. Only your beloved words have drawn my thoughts away from them and from the perpetual burden that weighs upon me.

Brother Hamid, do you believe that girls like me are happy in this outmoded prison of ours? You might think we are content but God alone knows the vexation of our bitter existence which we are forced to put up with and become accustomed to as a patient gets used to her illness or sick bed.

What girl does not remember her last days of freedom without sorrow, save the most hard hearted? For me it was a day I can never recall without great sadness. That last hour of my free and noble life when I bade farewell to my uncle here in the village before returning to the town to find the cloth for my shawl and veil waiting for me in the house! That black robe, the robe of misery and sorrow.

Still I thank destiny that there is one heart in the world that beats for me and loves me. Girls are weak, as they say, in need of something to strengthen us, and I have always placed my trust in God and love.

Forgive me for revealing my innermost thoughts. Only our friendship dared me to it, my love for you and your devotion to me.

Aziza

Dear Aziza,
I too want to see you where we can be alone together.

This has been my dream for the past year but whenever I hoped to attain it circumstances have prevented me. Now at least you know that my heart is full of love for you and I long for the hour in which we can be together with nobody watching over us.

Your letter sent me into total confusion. Like everybody else I believed that veiled women were quite content to stay at home. The ladies who sit with you do not seem to mind, or they consider it unimportant, spending their time telling stories like the ones I have listened to. Now you tell me that you only become accustomed to it like a patient gets used to being sick! I do not doubt that women are tormented by their prison and I am deeply sorry for the injustices they suffer.

Let it be God's wish that we should work together to achieve the meeting we both desire. My heart is at your disposal, do with it as you please.

Hamid

Brother Hamid,
I received your letter. Some of the ladies are thinking of going out to the fields tomorrow evening with our uncle. If you come to us today they will certainly invite you. Do you think your friend the night will be kind to me too? Maybe its cover will help us to find some happiness. I too am searching for a way for us to reach our goal and maybe we are not so far away from it. All I hope is that the heavens, which I believe approve our feelings, will assist us.

Let me enjoy for the time being my present happiness and the sweet things you say. Don't remind me of the veil for the very mention of it ruins me. I cannot even think about it without suffering intolerable anguish so I have grown accustomed to ignoring my situation, accepting my fate as it is. Yet I still remember how my heart was broken when I realised what it means to wear the veil. My attendant returned, radiant with joy, from the great outside among the fields and with a grin she said: 'How wonderful the sunset was tonight!'—But what has the rising or the setting of the sun got to do with me? My family consider the pictures on the walls sufficient for my needs! Does the sky bring forth the sunset for simple folk and not for us?

But let me leave all this aside, for the memory pains me and my happiness in you keeps me from dwelling on pain. Let's be thankful that I did become accustomed to my torment and that I was able to withstand it.

O Hamid! If only you knew the loneliness we girls feel among our families and within the walls of our houses. However much our hearts are kindled by the fire in our breast we are forced to conceal and repress it until finally it dies, having eaten away the dearest and most beloved part of our lives.

Come quickly or write to me. Your words are a cure for your cousin who would be overcome by despair if you deserted her.

                                                        Aziza

Dear Aziza,

Try not to get upset for that only saddens me. Be as happy as you can. I will always be true to you and for you I would do the impossible to bring about what you desire. Today, if I may dare, I will send you a kiss upon your beautiful lips.

                                                        Hamid

Aziza felt that kiss and almost lost herself. She imagined that Hamid was standing in front of her, holding her hands in his and kissing her. What a wonderful feeling, one that she had experienced many times in dreams with various persons whose names she did not know nor where they came from. It is the dream that occupies the mind of every lonely girl when she is isolated and distressed and wants her heart to be joined with another, even in her imagination, for comfort and consolation.

That afternoon Hamid went to the house where Aziza was staying and made his greetings. And when he was seated one of the ladies informed him of their proposed outing and invited him to accompany them, which he accepted jubilantly.

The next day they all set out. Hamid walked on one side of the ladies, his uncle on the other. The ladies remained mostly silent, occasionally whispering a few words under their breaths to tell Aziza about some of the houses they passed and the people who lived in them. Only when they were beyond the walls of the village did they begin to speak freely. A young girl who was with them ran alongside as the moon rose in the sky like an unveiled bride, sending a great ocean of light into the midst of the calm and gentle night. Nearby, the trees immersed in its glow cast enormous shadows over the land, extending over the cotton bushes which seemed intoxicated, or subdued by the power of the surrounding beauty. On both sides of the road the drainage canals stretched as far as the eye could see before becoming lost in the distance.

Dividing into groups, Hamid's uncle walked with his sisters, two ladies walked by themselves while Hamid, his aunt, the young girl and Aziza formed a third party. Hamid's uncle pointed out the boundaries of the fields, telling his sisters the names of the proprietors and tenants who owned or rented them and they would show their appreciation whenever they passed the lands that belonged to their brother or for which he was responsible. The other ladies meanwhile were engaged in a conversation of their own:

'Ummu Saad came by today, saying her husband had been fighting with Hassanin Abu Mukhaimar. Apparently Hassanin made him bleed and he needed rose water to recover. Will they never learn? I mean you can't heal rifts with rose water!'

'By the prophet and the well of Zamzam, they're completely hopeless. You'd think God only gave them food to eat and water to drink in order to shed one another's blood. If people like that never got beaten, Ummu Ahmed, they wouldn't even know what rose water was for!'

On finding no conversation in her own group, Hamid's aunt joined Ummu Ahmed and her companion.

'Well did you hear Hassanin Abu Mukhaimar's wife scream last night?'

'No why? What happened?'

'Well, he got hold of his wife and beat her and wouldn't stop. What happened was that after quarrelling with Ummu Saad's husband he returned to his house saying "By God I shall kill that dog! Just let him open his mouth again!" When she replied "Oh, come on! Why don't you both make it up?" he flew into a rage and said "Even you, daughter of ____, are taking their side?" And he raised his hand in the air and slapped her so violently she fell down unconscious on the floor. Then he was noble enough to kick her in the stomach, crying "Get up! you daughter of ___, I know your tricks!" After that someone came by and sprinkled water on her face until she stood up, stunned and dazed, and stared at her husband saying "All right, all right, that's enough, let's forget it." Dear me, then she felt so sorry for herself she began to weep. But her husband suddenly raised his hand again shouting "Now you dare to cry, you pretentious women!" and he began to beat her on the other side of her face. Nobody could stop him until she screamed out and fell on the floor again as if she was going to die. When it was all over she took her daughter and went to stay in her father's house. Then they had to inform the police, so two charges were brought against Hassanin on the same night. God have mercy on us, those men are wild creatures.'

Hamid exploited the situation and managed to get rid of the young girl so that he could be alone with Aziza. But he did not know what to say to her. All he could do was hold her hand as he walked by her side feeling totally perplexed. As for Aziza, she found no pleasure in their isolation and hoped that one of the others would rescue her from her predicament. And yet was it not what they had both desired? Had they made their agreement only to let the opportunity pass them by?

Maybe they were both to be excused, for they had never loved except in their dreams and Aziza knew nothing of the ways of lovers other than what she had read in some translated novels. She knew only the unemotional life of the group. The moments she spent by herself, reading poetry or letting her

imagination take her wherever it pleased, were the closest she
had come to experiencing love.

In spite of her misgivings she let Hamid lead her further
away. Although hesitant, he was determined not to let the
moment lapse in apathy and indifference. The beautiful night
and its perfumed air inspired him with more than that and
as he walked by the side of his beloved, gently holding her
hand, he raised it to his mouth and kissed it saying:

'We don't yet know how to talk to each other, Aziza.'

She stared at the ground making no attempt to respond as
though she were searching for the reason behind them being
alone together even though it was what they had both wanted
for so long. When Hamid's uncle called they returned to the
group and Aziza was relieved when they were sitting with the
others on the bridge overlooking the canal. The small waves
that danced on the surface of the water shone beneath the
light of the planet of love and in the quiet of the night the
green grass seemed to be resting, bathed with water from
below and light from above. As they talked among themselves
one of the ladies brought out some fruit and sweets which
she placed in front of them. The world was calm, with not a
sound nor echo to be heard, all things enjoying the tranquillity of the night under the watchful eye of the moon.

They passed the time conversing in their customary manner
and when they finally got up to leave, the ladies expressed
their disappointment at how quickly the evening had gone
by. The pleasant night air was something they seldom experienced and they rarely caught a glimpse of the flourishing
fields so when they arrived home, to be enclosed for months
within the walls of the house, it was much later than usual.

The following morning, after a night of dreamless sleep,
Aziza got out of bed and recalled the moments she had spent
alone with Hamid. She remembered the kiss he had planted
on her hand—not on her lips as he had promised in his
letter—and the anxiety which beset her and made her feel,
when they rejoined the group, that she had been saved from
an awkward situation. Having contemplated the evening's
events at some length she sat down to write to Hamid.

Brother Hamid,

Do you still love me after last night? My heart tells me
how much my silence must have hurt you when we were
alone together. I feel now that I do not deserve your love, for
what has love to do with the house-buried? We live in darkness where the only pleasure we enjoy is in our fantasies. For
my part I wish no memory of me to remain with you for I
could not bear to burden you with that. It is a sin to love
someone who has been put into a convent by her family, for
we are no less secluded than the nuns even if we are less
devout.

Forget me Hamid. It was madness that made me write you
that first letter, without realising what I was saying. Yours is
the beauty of the world: the sky, the fields, the water, the
night and the moon. Enjoy those things and leave me in my
cell. I am content with my life or at least I am forced to be,
so leave me, please leave me. I am not cut out for love nor
has love anything to do with me and I implore God to forgive
me. He is the supporter of the weak and today I am in need
of His sustenance. May my heart be filled with His love alone.

The voices I heard were none other than the whispers of
Satan as he tries to take possession of girls' souls. They can
only find protection from him in men. That is the temptation
of the devil! In God alone will I seek my refuge.

Leave me Hamid to weep for my youth, maybe that will
purify me. We make such great mistakes when we are young!
God alone is able to forgive them.

Forget me Hamid . . . Forget me.

Your sister,
Aziza

Dear Aziza,

What is this that I read? Why all this grief? I never imagined that you would take it so seriously as to consider our
meeting the work of the devil! Our silence was due to the
magic of the night that kindled the love in our hearts and
left us with no words to say.

You are asking the impossible of me Aziza and I cannot

perform the impossible. The day I see my dreams fulfilled you want to destroy them forever? On the contrary, let us put aside the obstacles that stand in our way for love is stronger than you imagine, not a pleasure to taste and discard as we please. It is an emotion that controls our very being, leaving us powerless to dictate events. Even if you wish to forget me, I can never forget you. You are everything to me.

With all the impassioned kisses that I would plant upon your cheeks and temples, I hope that you will forgive my mistakes. Then I would be truly grateful.

Hamid

A few weeks after she had left the village, the following letter arrived for Hamid from the town where Aziza was staying.

Brother Hamid,

This is my final farewell. I have been informed that a marriage has been arranged for me. Although I do not want it and in spite of my constant memories of you, I know that what my family wish will be accomplished whether I am agreeable or not. Only yesterday it seems, I was shedding tears for my youth, hoping to dedicate it to God. Today I still weep for my youth, about to be extinguished by the hand of the devil.

Aziza

# Chapter Six

'When you see your sister say "hello" to her from me.' These were Hamid's words to Zainab's sister in the fields and she faithfully delivered the message the next time she saw her sister. How distant Hamid seemed to Zainab now—but how sweet were the times she had spent with him. Ever since her husband had spoken to her so affectionately she had been feeling constant regrets and sorrow. Now she remembered the days she had spent in happiness and contentment by the side of Hamid. He had been most loving towards her, someone she would have willingly given herself to if her innocent heart had been worthy of a man of Hamid's position.

Zainab went out as usual to take supper to Hassan who was working late in the cotton fields. She was in a carefree mood as though all her worries and anxieties, combined with past memories, had piled up to leave her insensitive to her own feelings. The sun was setting and a calm breeze blew gently through the air as the birds whistled beneath a red sky. When evening fell and night took the place of day she gathered her things and returned to the village.

On the day Hamid received Aziza's letter, informing him of her arranged marriage, he was overcome with remorse but the winds of forgetfulness soon began to erase all trace of emotion from his heart. Only a few days ago he had been ardently in love, writing letters full of devotion. Now he pushed her from his mind completely and released himself from his commitment painlessly and without hesitation. Hamid was surprised by his own behaviour but the surprise was no more lasting than his sadness. Maybe great sorrows are caused by events which distort our sense of reality at the time, but when the event has passed, the fire is extinguished and the sadness forgotten. Hamid's love for Aziza, which had almost faded at the beginning of spring only to be revived by her presence in the village, returned to oblivion after she had left.

One evening Hamid was returning from the fields when he met Zainab, whom he had not seen for almost a year, on her way back to the village having delivered her husband's supper. On that occasion she had been wearing girl's clothes and a headscarf which left her beautiful features open to contemplation. Today she was dressed in the manner Hamid loved and which enhances the simple attractiveness of all country girls. Her flowing garments, the veil thrown back over her head at this time, and a long cotton shawl, gave her a dignified but rather sad appearance. As she approached he put out his hand to greet her:

'Good evening Zainab, how are you?'

'How are you Hamid? Everything fine I trust?'

'You don't seem very happy, is everything all right?'

'Yes, thank you very much.'

What strange, uninformative answers! Hamid had never known Zainab to avoid his conversation before. Maybe there was something behind it!

The remaining traces of daylight vanished as they made their way along the path and a full moon appeared overhead, but although the sky was filled with many lights the thick cloak of night which encompassed the world prevented the rays from touching the earth. The green leaves of the trees were shrouded in darkness as they walked together in silence surrounded by the sweet smelling air.

Then from a heart overflowing with grief, Zainab sighed openly and Hamid could not refrain from asking:

'What's the matter Zainab?'

'Nothing!'

How could a sigh like that, betokening such a sad and injured heart mean nothing? Or was it simply that fleeting anxiety which besets us from time to time for no apparent reason, evoking a pain deep within us so that our enjoyment of life is tainted and spoiled? Maybe there was something in Hamid's proximity to Zainab which made her feel momentarily sad, in which case would it not have been more prudent to leave her alone?

As the night advanced, the light of the moon shone down gradually brighter on the path and the world became ever more quiet and still. On reaching a stone bridge spanning the canal by the side of a mosque surrounded by a low wall, Hamid asked Zainab to wait for him while he washed his hands. She obeyed mechanically and sat gazing at the moon as if trying to understand the vastness of space which separated her from that watchful planet. What was its pale face trying to communicate? In her mind she passed beyond the limits of this world to a place where everything was veiled by thin clouds beyond which she could see no further. Although she could not comprehend the meaning of what was moving in her soul, her imagination knew no bounds. She was roaming in a vast sea where indiscernible shapes circulated in total silence.

When Hamid returned he found Zainab in a daze as though in her dreams she was wandering through some unchartered desert. Very slowly and without any movement which might disturb her, he sat by her side and put his arm round her waist. Then he kissed her on the cheek and drew her towards him, asking again:

'What's the matter Zainab?'

But Zainab was not the girl he had known before. No longer an innocent child, sensing the joy of life in everything around her, who would have responded willingly and affectionately to a sincere question. No longer the sleepy-eyed virgin who would have given herself to a lover to be alone with him in some other world of happiness. She was a married woman with responsibility, regarding life with a look of sufferance and anguish. A woman aware of her duty towards a husband who trusted her.

Zainab freed herself from Hamid and with a cold expression asked if they might not carry on their way. Time was getting on, she said, and she did not want anybody to see them in a place like that. Hamid drew his breath and said:

'You have forgotten me Zainab, along with the days that we spent together.'

'No, I haven't forgotten. But I'm married. Past times are past times!'

She sighed deeply from the depths of her heart and they walked in silence to the edge of the village where they parted. But as soon as she was alone again she was saddened by memories from the past, when she was only a girl and knew nothing of the responsibilities that burdened her now. Days when Hamid's smile had brought her unrivalled pleasure that filled her with joy whenever he came from the village to meet her.

In the same way the duties of marriage demanded that she refrain from any degree of intimacy with Ibrahim and she was obliged to drive him from her heart until he no longer held any influence over her. But how could she do that? She could not even think about him without being driven senseless with longing. In all her life she had never dreamed that marriage could be as distressing as this for a woman who wished to fulfil her duty.

Alone in her room, the moon sent down a silvery ocean of light through the open window onto the mat and as Zainab looked towards it, it returned her gaze. Though pale, its tender rays seemed to be directed from above straight to the heart of the grief stricken girl. Wrapped in a cloak of moonlight Zainab journeyed to a world far from ours with all its commotion, where she strayed among her dreams until a smile appeared on her lips as though she had found Ibrahim in that other world waiting for her.

When Hamid arrived back at the house the first thing that caught his eye was the letter from Aziza which began with her final farewell. He stared at the words, reading them over and over as if some deeper meaning lay hidden between the lines. After turning the sheet of paper several times he put the letter down and sat in his chair. Picking up a book he began to leaf through the pages restlessly one after another, unable to concentrate for more than a moment before moving on to the next. Finally he put the book away and went outside where he stood in the street gazing into the darkness of the night as if to confide his secrets to the inanimate objects which surrounded him. Unable to endure this for long he re-entered the house to find his father and brothers waiting for their supper, so he took his place among them and sat down to eat.

At about eleven o'clock after they had read the papers and discussed the news, the evening came to an end and they retired to their rooms to sleep, except for Hamid who picked up Aziza's letter again. Signs of sorrow crossed his face as he looked at the lines without reading the words. Then he held the letter to his breast and raising his head with an imploring look in his eye, he entreated the moon as though there were some power there to realise his dreams. Placing the letter in front of him he squatted on his heels in the stillness of the night and burying his head in his hands, a solitary tear fell from the corner of his eye and rolled onto his shirt. The letter signified the end of his association with Aziza, and now Zainab had shown that she could have nothing more to do with him. It was all over, any hope of finding happiness had vanished as his dreams fled before him.

Hamid turned out the light and tried to go to sleep—but rarely does sleep bless the oppressed. The god of night and rest treats all who come before him equally except those whose hearts are filled with grief. The kingdom of tranquillity is denied to them, no benevolent power consoles them for their cares.

In the pitch-black room everything was still apart from Hamid's beating heart and agitated mind. All things were at peace beneath the cover of darkness besides Hamid's tormented soul. As time advanced and the night grew deeper he became more restless and his anxiety increased until he could no longer keep his eyes closed. Having despaired of going to sleep he got up to open the window and leaned on the ledge, gazing at the stars which glittered above the cloak of night. When the moon disappeared behind some distant houses, Hamid glanced at his watch to find that only two hours remained before el-fajr. But two hours in a state of desolation is a long

time and Hamid was stifled by the boredom which accompanied his depression. He turned on the lamp and began to
pace back and forth in the narrow room. Again he tried to
go to sleep but fortune was no more favourable than before
and although it occurred to him to read, he could not bring
himself to open any of the books in front of him. Eventually
he got dressed and went outside. After walking a short distance
he saw the guards stretched out in their cloaks on a stone
bench, their rifles under their heads where they lay. Only one
was sitting up, leaning on a staff that he had fixed in the
ground. Hamid approached them expecting someone to call:
'Who's there?' but they were all sound asleep, immersed in
the deep sea of night. Even the one sitting upright was as
happy in his dreams as the rest of them and just as drowsy.

Hamid found a place to sit between them whereupon the
chief guard, sensing his presence, raised himself up thinking
that he might be a member of the patrol. But on seeing no
sign of military clothing he soon relaxed again and after
acknowledging Hamid, he called to the others:

'Mohammed, Faraj! Go and patrol the village.'

Faraj sat up and leaned on his staff, followed by his sleepy-
headed companion and Hamid got up to patrol the village
with them. They made their way along the streets where the
buildings cast long shadows on the ground and the roofs shone
beneath the light of the moon. They were all silent until they
reached the palm tree enclosure where Faraj turned to his
companion and said:

'Come on, let's shake the palms. The fruit must be ripe
now.'

Hamid followed them, looking for the dates which fell to
the ground but he could hardly see at all. When the two
guards had gathered sufficient, they gave some to Hamid and
the three of them walked on, eating the dates and talking
together in low voices. The guards merrily recalled their duty
in the winter months when one of them would light a fire
while another went to the fields or the nearby storage boxes
to fetch some corncobs which they would roast on the embers.

They continued on their way until they arrived at a teahouse which Mohammed and Faraj decided to investigate to see if anyone was awake to serve them. If not, at least they could drink some water from the clay pitchers there. As it happened they did find someone willing to give them what they wanted—'On account of Mr Hamid'—whom it was an honour to serve even at this time of night. They sat for about half an hour before completing their patrol and daylight began to disperse the darkness on the horizons, announcing the approach of dawn. Hamid left them and returned to his room where he fell into a dreamless sleep which lasted until midday.

But when he awoke he saw Aziza's letter yet again. How many times he had forgotten her in the past, only to find that fate made him remember her time after time. Although he knew it was futile even to think about her, the letter still caused him pain and stirred his anxiety. How had he become so attached to Aziza when every girl he met vied for a place in his heart? Maybe it was because of what had been said when he was young: 'One day they will marry . . .' that even now he felt half demented on account of losing her. He had enjoyed the company of so many girls in his childhood, beautiful ones too, but they had all been daughters of the fallaheen. 'My final farewell, Hamid' . . . 'My final farewell, Aziza!' And Zainab too was lost to him forever.

Hamid ate lunch with his father and brothers after which they sat talking until late afternoon when some of them got up to go to the fields while others went to play backgammon. As for Hamid, the only thing he could think of which might relieve his cares was to go out riding by himself in the country. So he called for a horse to be saddled and when it was ready he mounted and set off. After about an hour's ride he arrived at some of the more remote fields. The sun was descending and the sweet evening breezes which stir the heart blew across the open spaces, bringing refreshment to all living creatures. The narrow paths which traversed the cotton fields disappeared from sight in the nearby distance so that the vast stretch of green appeared like an unbounded ocean in which the cotton bushes huddled together with no visible gaps between them.

Overhead an atmosphere of tranquillity descended from the clear sky above, embracing the whole of creation.

Hamid dismounted and walked slowly through the fields, examining the crop which was almost ripe, his horse following in a docile and compliant manner. It was not long, however, before Hamid forgot all about the cotton bolls and the beautiful yellow buds of the new crop as he drifted away into various dreams.

The sun descended quickly towards the horizon, becoming redder as it set, and crowning the earth with golden light it bestowed a farewell kiss on the wanderer in the fields. Hamid stood alone amid the great expanse, bounded only by the distant horizons which grew darker by the minute, his thoughts scattered so that he hardly knew whether he was thinking about real people or phantoms of his imagination. His mind was shifting between different worlds which he understood little or nothing about; some still, some in motion, inhabited by creatures he could scarcely imagine. The horse pulled gently on the bridle, sometimes striking the ground with its hooves and when Hamid realised that night was almost upon him he remounted, urged his horse on once, then relaxed his hold on the reins.

* * *

A week later Hamid entered the drawing room to find the clerk taking dictation from one of the village officials. When he enquired what they were doing the clerk replied that they were drawing up a register of recruits for the army. Scanning the list, Hamid noticed one name written separately from the rest and when he asked the reason he was told that Ibrahim was to be conscripted.

That evening Hamid sat up with his brothers waiting for the papers and with them sat the deputy mayor discussing the eligible recruits. He was sorry that Ibrahim was to be called up this year, especially as no one from the village had been conscripted for the past nine years, but on account of his long experience as foreman it had been decided that he should join the infantry.

In a few days Ibrahim would be leaving the village for an unknown destination, travelling first to the capital then into the unexplored regions of the Sudan and the barren deserts of the Equator where the fire burns down from above to roast the skins of those below.

Soon he would be leaving the people he loved and the people who loved him, bidding farewell to the vast lands covered with crops where he worked during the summer nights, only stopping occasionally to lean on his hoe or gaze at the moon in the depths of the sky. He would leave behind the paths which stretched to the far horizons and the canals, rippling with waves in the days of irrigation or all dried out in the winter months. And he would leave behind him a bleeding heart, a forlorn spirit whose last remaining hope in the world rested in him. He would be leaving Zainab to weep for him when he had gone.

This severe torment he would suffer not as a warlord or conqueror, but as a humble and obedient servant, condemned to spend the best years of his life in hell itself with no glory to look forward to upon his return.

# Chapter Seven

'This time next week I shall be travelling.'

These were the only words Ibrahim could find to say to Zainab when he met her returning from the watering place carrying her pitcher full of water and they struck her like a thunderbolt, numbing her senses.

She returned to the house hesitating along the way, almost out of her mind whenever Ibrahim's words echoed inside her. In spite of the pain she was suffering she carried on with her normal tasks until just before sunset, then she returned to the watering place with her empty pitcher which she propped up by the canal before making her way through the fields until she found Ibrahim. Walking a short distance together they sat down to rest against a tree trunk beside a water wheel which concealed them from the glances of passers-by. They both sat in silence, unable to start a conversation or even look at each other. Heaving a sigh Ibrahim took hold of Zainab's hand and repeated his words:

'This time next week I shall be travelling.'

So they had only one more week after which they were to be separated, maybe forever. Would they make it a week of pleasure and gratification or spend it shedding tears of mortal anguish?

How slowly the veil of night descended. As though the sun had left behind some light that refused to fade, the blue1 sky still gleamed before their eyes. In the midst of the dumb world which surrounded them, hot tears rolled down Zainab's cheeks onto Ibrahim's hand whereupon he put his arm round her shoulders to comfort her and asked her what was wrong.

What was wrong with Zainab? Ibrahim was saying farewell! Her only hope in life had just been wiped away.

Throughout this long period Zainab had always loved Ibrahim even though she had tried with all her strength to keep her honour and virtue, and fulfil her marriage duties to the best of her ability. Now she could not bear to leave him. She wanted to see as much of him as possible during this last remaining week, to hold him to her heart and never let him go.

But they could not remain there for long. Zainab had to be back at the house to prepare the supper, so she filled her pitcher and returned with Ibrahim down the deserted path, keeping close to his side until they parted, having agreed to meet again the following day. Even though there was only one week left before his departure, Ibrahim still worked in the fields by day although he no longer worked at night. So he made his appointment with Zainab for the morning, beneath the tree where they had just been sitting.

What harsh destiny dared to persecute this susceptible girl, dashing her dreams and tearing her world apart? Then to leave her in misery and despair, granting nothing in return, not even a glimmer of hope to give her some incentive to stay alive. But only the darkness was witness to her tears.

Zainab spent the night amid troubled dreams and the following morning when she met Ibrahim she related some of them to him. In one she had seen him wearing a black military uniform, walking alone in the desert at nightfall with his head bowed down. Looking up, he saw a servant approaching with a letter. Returning to the camp, another soldier read it to him and he sat crying for a long time. In the second dream Zainab was lying in bed surrounded by her mother and mother-in-law, her sister and Hassan. She was weeping and imploring them to bring Ibrahim to her while they looked on apprehensively. Then finding herself alone and not hearing the slightest sound she had sunk into a state of total peace about which she could remember nothing at all.

As Ibrahim listened he imagined himself in those hellish regions where he did not know what would be expected of him and where there was no reason for him to go other than that he was a commissioned recruit. He felt angry that no financial alternative was open to him to pay his way out of such unnecessary and meaningless servitude, but he was in no position to buy his freedom as those with the money to

do so would have done. Is this the meaning of justice?
Because one man is rich he is excused from military service
while another who is poor is driven to suffer hardship and
roast in the fire, to return bearing nothing but the scars of
his experience?

They stayed together until the sun was high in the sky and
Zainab had to go back to the house to prepare Hassan's lunch
and take it to him in the fields.

In the late afternoon as the women were fetching water,
Hamid was walking alone deep in thought when he saw
Ibrahim and called out to him to ask his opinion about his
forthcoming journey.

'I regard it as just another job,' Ibrahim replied. 'But what
annoys me is that I've no idea what I'm supposed to do. I
mean it's not as though we're going to conquer the West or
storm Tunis at high noon! And whether we go or stay the
English rulers will be on our backs just the same.'

To which Hamid could only say:

'Never mind. It's for a short time, then you'll return.'

Hamid left him and carried on his way, pleased by the reply
he had received. If Ibrahim were going out on a conquest he
would have gone willingly, looking forward to his return as
a conqueror to tell of his exploits and the deeds of his compa-
triots, proud of his leaders and military officers. But the fact
that he was being sent to carry out meaningless duties under
the command of the arbitrary rulers of his country grieved
him and weighed heavily upon his heart. At the same time
the thought occurred to Hamid that Ibrahim's view was rather
shortsighted. True, he was only going to perform insignificant
tasks at present but at least he would be representing his
country and her army. Even if there were no honour today
in being a soldier, history would remember him as the link
between former greatness and future glories. But Ibrahim, a
simple labourer, understood nothing of this nor was it in his
capacity to understand.

Walking at a leisurely pace, Hamid passed out of sight of
Ibrahim who stood watching the faces of the women coming
and going while he waited for the water to rise, casting fare-

well glances at the surroundings he would soon be leaving for such a long period of time.

Ibrahim and Zainab met every day and they would swear to each other that their friendship would last forever. For him alone would she save the love which filled her heart, whatever the future might hold, and he would remember her even among the thunder of the cannons or in the face of bloody death. Then they would sit in silence, their eyes filled with tears until it was time to part.

* * *

Tomorrow Ibrahim would be travelling and his friends had planned an evening of conversation and entertainment on his account. Hardly had the hour of sunset passed than the court-yard of the house which they had chosen for the occasion began to surge with boys and girls who came to bid farewell to their friend. Among the first to arrive were Hassan, and Amir and Hussein together with their brothers. While they were talking Atiya arrived with his drum and they all moved round to make room for him. Continuing their conversation, beneath the night sky, pleasant breezes wafted through the air so that on the faces of all the companions there were signs of happiness and contentment.

As time moved inexorably on they began to beat the drum and clap and dance as if they were celebrating some grand occasion. The evening was well advanced when they began to make their way home one by one after bidding farewell to their beloved friend. Silence replaced the noise of the crowd and an atmosphere of despondency descended over the court-yard as those who remained anticipated the parting that tomorrow would bring. Ibrahim's most devoted friends stayed with him until the last, recounting the days of the past and looking forward to his return in the near future. When the party came to an end they left with the promise that they would all be there in the morning to see him off at the station. Only Hassan remained with his friend and whenever either of them thought about the impending separation, tears clouded their eyes. Ibrahim looked up at the blackness of the sky, lamenting his poverty, but the sky at that hour was unmoved by his complaints.

Ibrahim was poor and for that reason alone he was to sacrifice his freedom. His position did not command sufficient status to receive even a small measure of justice. Deprived of his liberty and no longer able to pursue his own goals he would be forced, whether he liked it or not, into a position which in some countries might be one of pride and honour but in others means only servility and debasement. In some it would mean the defence of the realm or the strengthening of the nation against possible aggression but to Ibrahim it meant only submission to foreign rule in order to subjugate his own people further and wield unwanted authority over them. Can there ever be any justice on earth as long as there are rich and poor, strong and weak? Is it not futile for man to demand justice or complain of the wrongs which befall him when in reality he can only overcome such iniquity when he has sufficient power to rise above those who oppress him?

There was nothing that Ibrahim could do to prevent the rich and powerful tyrants disposing of his life until sufficient cooperation existed among his fellow workers for them to defend themselves and rise up against the unjust oppressors. Then they would be forced to listen to what he had to say. His words would beat upon the ears of the despots and fearing his voice, they would turn to him meekly to ask what he wanted so that they might fulfil his request.

But Ibrahim was poor, destined to be sent away from his old mother whose husband had died and whose eldest son had left the family to live with his wife. Far away from his friends who loved him for his pleasant and amiable company, far away from the green fields of cotton and clover, bordered by trees and streams, and far away from Zainab whose tears were flowing even before they parted. Snatched from the fertile beauty of the countryside to be flung into a never ending hell of barren yellow sand where nothing grew and the people were barbarous! Yet if he had possessed but twenty pounds he could have saved himself from this. What injustice could be greater, or rather what hostility could equal it?

There is no escaping fate. All we can do is be content with our lot and accept life's adversities, just as there is little to be gained through anger. For these reasons Ibrahim began to prepare himself for army life by thinking about its possible advantages. There were new countries to be seen and the differing aspects of their respective landscapes; the traditions and customs of unknown inhabitants about whom superstitious tales were told. He would also learn to shoot and parade with his fellow countrymen in uniform. These things made the prospect a little easier to bear and he was able to get some sleep before dawn.

The next morning Ibrahim accompanied Hassan to his house where Hassan's parents and sisters bade him farewell while Hassan went upstairs to change his clothes. Zainab was in her room but hurried down, hardly able to control the tremors which shook her body. Almost choked by her tears she felt now the full bitterness of this terrible hour, the hour of parting from her beloved. This was her last chance to see Ibrahim before his journey and beckoning him into the hall as though she had something important to say, she held him to her breast as soon as she was alone with him. Her tears flowed and she trembled with sadness, drawing him into her world of suffering until his world was also filled with pain. Was this their final parting, their very last embrace, after which one would be going into deserts full of dangers and the other to an unknown destination, where eternity mingles with extinction?

They stood in silence as Zainab's tears flowed and in those final moments the sacredness of their farewell and the awesomeness of their last meeting assumed great proportions. When Hassan called, she hugged Ibrahim and kissed him, almost smothered by her bitter weeping as she spoke her last words to him:

'Peace be with you, Ibrahim.'

After he had gone, Zainab remained in the hall with the door closed and there in the darkness she gave herself up to her sorrow. Losing herself completely beneath the heavy burden of her grief, so many anxieties assailed her that they

seemed to attack from every side. Her despair was complete
and shaking her head, she stared at the floor as though Ibrahim
might have left behind some token to remind her. And in
that pure and holy spot where they had spent their last few
moments together, upon the very ground where they had just
been standing, her eyes came to rest upon a large embroidered
handkerchief that had fallen from his pocket. Bending down
to pick it up, she wiped her face and kissed it several times
before placing it next to her grieving heart.

From beneath those delicate eyebrows, tears streamed from
her beautiful eyes. If she had looked in a mirror she would
have been mortified by the paleness of her complexion, her
soft cheeks having lost all their natural radiance. But Zainab
could not think about herself or her beauty, she was aware
only of the mortal anguish that was torturing her soul.

Hassan and Ibrahim walked together to the station where they
found a great host of people waiting for them. In those final
moments before the departure of their friend everyone wanted
to talk to him, to wish him well and a safe return. When they
heard the train approaching in the distance they all said
'Goodbye' and some of them embraced him especially Hassan
who gave him a big hug. The mayor of the village, taking the
new recruit by the hand, led him up into the railway carriage
while his friends and companions crowded round the window.
Then the train whistled in readiness and as they bade him
farewell Ibrahim cast one last glance, full of pain and longing,
at those sacred lands which he loved so much.

# PART THREE

From behind the battling clouds the sun broke through to
send its rays over the earth, casting its light over the fields
and roads which basked in an ocean of life and beauty.

# Chapter One

How pleasant the summer nights are, yet how quickly they pass! Carried along we forget the world and its problems and experience the utmost joy in our hearts. If desires could be realised surely our greatest wish would be that those splendid nights in which all creatures enjoy the most beautiful dreams and the moon strays in her fantasy of love, should last forever. Nights in which the silent whispers of nature commune with the heart, inspiring it to love, and the sleepless peasant with his salamiyya sends music into the world, full of fervour and passion.

But time pays no heed to desire, nor do the longings of a restless soul make any impression. In spite of ourselves the days march on into eternity with monotonous persistence, swallowing up the happy man's hours so that he can hardly feel them passing and strutting proudly before the hopeless, making their despair even more painful and agonising.

Ibrahim travelled into exile, his only sin being that he was poor, and autumn arrived to find Zainab suffering severe anxiety. After their parting she wished that she had given herself to him, then she might have found some consolation in the memory, but now she had to bear her burden without any such comfort.

Hamid finally buried the memory of Aziza's letter as oblivion erased all trace of her from his mind, but he was left with a feeling of emptiness which he desperately wanted to fill. Whenever he saw a beautiful girl he tried to get close to her, regarding her as his new found love. Then on meeting another he would forget the first and devote himself to the latter, his heart shifting from one sweetheart to the next like a bee moves from flower to flower, not knowing which to love or which to leave until he had tired of more than ten. In the end he saw a girl whose beauty so captivated his heart that he promised himself to remain constant. With every day that passed he became more attached to her and more confident of his feelings until there was no doubt in his mind that the greatest happiness rested with her alone and that she would become his lifelong partner.

When she was away for a few days Hamid did not forgot her. He stayed up at night communing with the planets, imploring the moon and the heavens to bring them together. But when they met again he turned cold from head to toe as if it had been a false dream, and he was deeply distressed. Had he really loved and cared for her, what could have caused such a change of heart when before she went away he had loved her more than anyone else?—Hearts are fickle and youth is a time of infatuation from beginning to end. If a young person falls in love only to find that for whatever reason his beloved is not available to him, that love may be replaced by another or lost forever.

Hamid began to feel indifferent. The world appeared dull in his eyes and he carried on as though he did not have a heart inside him. People, places and events held no meaning and he paid no heed to them, quite unconcerned by what they signified. His only wish was to be quiet and comfortable, to sleep his fill and do as he pleased without having to explain himself to anybody.

As the sun rose and set Hamid spent his time at home or in the houses of acquaintances, his mind roaming at random in the boundless desert of his imagination. When night fell there was the evening news and local gossip to occupy him. The villagers would discuss agricultural matters such as the water supply, the price of cotton, who was selling and who was not, before moving on to more general affairs. Someone might read out the latest prices from the newspaper or articles penned by celebrated authors until it was time for bed. Then Hamid would go to sleep, to spend the next day in a similar manner and as time went by he became more and more languid.

He looked into his conscience to see if there was anything he could blame himself for but found nothing. Sometimes he would deliberately do things that he had previously shunned without ever feeling any regret. If the pillars of the world had fallen down and the day of judgement was at hand; if God revealed himself on high while the blazing fire licked the path and the songs of the houris could be heard in the palaces of paradise, Hamid would have merely shaken his head, wondering why everybody was so afraid.

Although his state of mind perturbed him at times, his feelings were mixed with that agreeable melancholy which we experience when we accept that we do not understand ourselves or what is going on around us. Gazing out across the open spaces, engulfed by their vastness, an expression of total resignation played on his lips as though he considered his existence on earth to be something alien. Even in the fields oblivion accompanied him and he would walk with a slow, deliberate step always taking the most forsaken roads. If he approached a building he would seek to avoid it, preferring the paths which others did not take and whenever he spoke his voice was hushed and calm.

However, this was not a situation that could continue. Whatever tranquillity we might find in apathy, we are only helping the world to depress us further if we allow ourselves to remain in that state for long. Man cannot live without hopes and disappointments to give some substance to the vacuum of his life.

When Hamid realised that his days were filled with meaningless fantasies and that his only concern was to live life passively until it was time to leave it for the great eternal calm, he devised various activities for himself in order to relieve his boredom. Going out to the fields he would watch the workers and examine the crops and on his return put his observations to the supervisor, bringing to his attention any areas of inefficiency he discovered there. He soon began to find some satisfaction in this which he had not known before.

One afternoon Hamid set out for the fields with one of his brothers. The sun was fiercely hot, its rays scorching the land and while they were walking, Hamid noticed a woman on her way back to the village carrying a lunch basket in her hand. Enquiring if his brother knew who she was, they both

stared until they recognised Zainab, returning from the fields
after delivering her husband's lunch. Hamid felt himself shiver
as she approached and slowed down to meet her but her brief
greeting was returned by Hamid's brother and she carried on
her way without a pause. When they had reached their destination Hamid's brother commented:

'Do you remember Zainab before she was married? Most
girls grow fatter after marriage, but she is getting thinner!'

The two brothers sat in the shade of a tree by the canal to
observe a worker watering the nearby clover fields. A clear sky
extended overhead and an occasional sparrow hopped or flew
around them where they sat. Having tired of conversation,
silence encompassed them and they each drifted into their
own thoughts and dreams.

'Do you remember Zainab before she was married?'—the
words had made Hamid feel bitter again although he could not
explain the memories they evoked nor the sensations that were
aroused in him. But he had no wish to remain in the fields.
The silent, resigned atmosphere of the place was stifling so he
asked his brother to accompany him to the village. Back at the
house he went to his room and shut the door behind him.

Zainab was married and for that reason she protested whenever he reminded her of the past—but what did it matter to
him that she was married? He could still take her in his arms,
hold her to his breast and kiss every part of her body. The
only thing that stood in his way was a contract between her
and Hassan stating that they were bound together. But can a
written contract, however much society may respect or sanc-
tify it, prevent a man from following the call of his heart
wherever it may take him? Hamid remained in his room,
agitated and disturbed, determining at every moment to find
Zainab and acquaint her with his feelings.

The sun descended and as the sky prepared to don its cloak
of night all things gradually entered the world of darkness.
Hamid was disturbed by somebody knocking on his door,
calling him to supper, but what use were food or drink to
him when his innermost desires remained unfulfilled? Only
the voice of his father enquiring about him downstairs caused

him to calm himself so that his agitation would not show before going to greet his family. He sat at the table but hardly ate a thing and as soon as the meal was over he went outside in pursuit of his goal. Only then did he realise that the workers, who had tired themselves during the day, would now be resting in their houses and that Zainab would be resting in her husband's arms. What a harsh night!

Next morning the sun rose to find Hamid still asleep, a restless night having drained his strength and he did not get up until almost midday. After eating some food by himself he set off in the direction of the fields and close to the lands belonging to Khalil he sat beneath a tree to wait for Zainab, with no particular intention in mind. If she had passed by now he would have done nothing more than greet her, or return her greeting, and follow her with his eyes for a while. But the silence which surrounded him as he gazed in the direction from which she would come, led him to resolve upon a course of action. When he saw her in the distance he began to pace to and fro until she reached him and greeted him in her customary manner. Standing beside her, Hamid attempted to carry out his plan.

'Have you forgotten the days of the past?'

These were virtually the same words he had spoken to her previously and Zainab had no idea what was the matter with him or what he wanted from her.

'No I haven't forgotten. I'm married!'

But before he could say anything else he was silenced by the shame and humility which beset him whenever he wanted to confess what was in his heart. Would it not be tantamount to madness? How could he bear the reproach of the people and the lies which they would fabricate? Without warning, and for no reason that Zainab was aware of, Hamid held her hand and said:

'Keep well, Zainab. inshallah you'll be happy with Hassan.'

Then he turned down another path and on reaching the house he went straight to his room.

* * *

The following day Sheikh Masoud came to the village, an eminent man in the province and the leader of one of its few religious brotherhoods. Many of his followers were waiting for him when he arrived, joyful at the sight of their master and eager to kiss his hand. At the same time they were fearful lest this upright man, whom they believed to be so close to God, should detect any negligence in respect of their religious duties.

The visiting Sheikh was received by Sheikh Amir, one of the prominent, wealthy men of the village and an enthusiastic follower who defended his master's teachings vigorously. In his honour he had arranged a sumptuous banquet—which involved a great deal of slaughter of animals—and brought in cooks from the neighbouring towns to prepare the food for this great Sheikh who proclaimed the message of God and renounced the pleasures of the transient world! The reception was held in his newly built red-brick house, the walls and ceilings of which were covered with various paintings and engravings. No sooner had Sheikh Masoud arrived in the large hall, filled with sofas and chairs, than a great assembly gathered outside waiting respectfully for him to receive them. When he was comfortable they came forward one by one to kiss his hand before taking their places, until there was not an empty seat to be seen. In fact many more followers had to stand in the corners and at the entrance to catch a glimpse of their venerable Sheikh who sat impassively or spoke in whispers to his host, leaving his hand available to those who wished to kiss it. Sometimes he would touch them as they came to greet him, muttering prayers of blessing and benediction for the benefit of them all!

Tables were laid out and trays bearing the most appetising dishes were placed in front of Sheikh Masoud and the worthy men who sat with him. The owner of the house, who could hardly contain his gratitude and joy, sat beside his honoured guest and personally offered him a selection of delicacies, entreating him from time to time to bless those present with his pious invocations. Sheikh Masoud, who responded to this attention with a degree of humility worthy of his rank, raised his eyes to see close by another table laid out for his poorer followers on which there was nothing tasty at all. Had there been a soul inside him or a conscience capable of feeling, surely this man who called for the renunciation of worldly pleasures in preparation for the life to come, would have been grossly embarrassed to be sitting on a comfortable chair with delicious food before him when the good-natured workers were seated on rough mats eating food which he would not touch. And if he had realised just how idle he was, his shame would have been even greater. His only task was to roam the villages with no purpose other than to eat, drink and utter a few worthless words while the poor farm workers struggle day and night to feed the people by virtue of their labour. But what conscience would inhabit the mind of an ill-bred charlatan who followed this way of deception only to profit from it? Was not Sheikh Masoud that same person who had spent ten years between the walls of El-Azhar* without learning a thing until he despaired of ever succeeding? And when his father would no longer support him, he left the path of knowledge to those who understood more and took to the road, dressed like a dervish with his hair down! Then finding that this occupation brought him little reward he cleaned himself up and wearing a headband, went out claiming to be a spiritual leader to make compacts with the unfortunate people who believed that: 'He who has no Sheikh is led by the devil'.

After supper a recitation ring was formed in the square in front of the magistrate's house and gathering round their Sheikh the villagers began to sway slowly from side to side. Among them was a singer who raised his voice in a manner which was neither song nor chant but more like a rhythmic wailing which kept time with the movements of those reciting. In the midst of the tranquil night, beneath the light of the moon, they repeated the name of Allah with slow deliberation that gradually increased in speed with the rhythm of their swaying until it was impossible to distinguish what they were

* Islamic university in Cairo.

saying. Some of them became dazed as they shook their heads,
which hung down like ants' heads, hardly aware of what they
were doing, driven into this frenzied state only through
imitating the actions of others. The reciting was soon nothing
more than bursts of breath rising in the air, discharged with
such force and venom it seemed that the participants were
hurling the words into the faces of their enemies. As their
movements increased in vigour, an impartial observer would
have thought they were drunk, or insane, dancing about
wildly without a care for anything else. The voice of the
singer rang out in the night, urging them all to remain in
their paradise until one of them finally lost his senses and
began to shout out garbled words. He was followed by another
and another until the Sheikh had to calm them down with
some shouts of his own. The moon gazed upon them, smiling
in ridicule or mocking their lunacy, and the impassive sky
returned the echoes of their cries. They called on God until
their voices were hoarse but neither the heavens nor the earth
responded, and for all their exhaustion their efforts were in
vain.

Sensing that their strength was depleted, the Sheikh ordered
them to be silent before reciting another of the names of
Allah. They all joined in and soon began shouting again until
their throats were dry and their minds were lost. Then he
recited a third name and a fourth until at last the evening
drew to a close and the participants dispersed, eagerly anticipating the next gathering. Maybe one day their prayers would
be answered!

Hamid, who was sitting in the parlour while the recitation
was in progress, felt a strong urge to join in and shout with
the others, thinking that in this way he might atone for his
mistakes. Although he had always believed that what took
place at these meetings, and the way the villagers blindly
followed their charlatan Sheikh was utter madness, weakness
had taken hold and the sadness and anxiety that tormented
him left him open to anything, even the irrational. Yes,
tomorrow he would stand before the Sheikh, kiss his hand
and join his party. He would confess everything in order to

ease his suffering; he would even make a compact with him and become a brother to all those who feared the devil!

The next morning Hamid went to the abode of the holy man to whom he was introduced by Sheikh Amir. At a sign from his master, Sheikh Amir left them alone whereupon Hamid began to tell his story and why he had come to join the brotherhood.

'. . . I have a cousin of whom it was said when I was only six years old, I would one day marry. For this reason I had feelings for her which I did not hold for my other female cousins. I shared my things with her, sympathising and protecting her, so that after we were separated I longed for the day when we would return to each other to live together forever. Whenever I thought of her, the most delightful sensations stirred within me. At sixteen years my feelings changed, my desires were awakened and I spent long nights accompanied by her image. Then I met a country girl and I trust that you will forgive me if I don't mention her name or anything about her person . . .'

'Yes, yes.'

'The first time we met I was struck by her beauty; wide shining eyes, rosy cheeks tanned to perfection, a luxurious body and slender waist, sweet lips and glances to melt the very soul. But how could any girl rouse me when all my life I had known nothing but absolute virtue? Nevertheless, I became restless when I did not see her and an urge which I had never felt before, drove me to the fields where she worked. Sometimes I helped her or returned by her side, enjoying her company. Then I heard that she was to be married and I pledged myself to forget her, knowing that it would be treacherous for me to feel even the slightest desire when she belonged to somebody else. So my feelings reawakened for my cousin, whom I believed would one day be mine, and I began to imagine all manner of wonderful things. On one occasion we exchanged a few words but our relationship ended when she too was married. At first a great sadness filled my being but the burden of grief soon fell from my shoulders, leaving me perplexed at the circumstances of my situation. I fell into a state of melancholy, regretting everything that had happened and wondering what would become of me. Although it was not an unpleasant sensation it did not last for long, the mood left me and I found myself in the crisis which has brought me to you. I was suddenly overcome by an urgent need to possess that country girl despite the fact that she was married, but God saved me and I was able to control myself at the very moment when I was about to give in.'

'Yes . . .'

'So now I have told you everything and I want to make a compact with you.'

'Yes.'

Hamid fell silent and the Sheikh held out his hand, asking him to recite after him the words which would join him to the brotherhood. Then Hamid departed, full of happiness, convinced that this would bring him great benefit. He went to his room and sat by the window where he stayed for some time, neither thinking nor questioning himself about what he had done, his lips bearing a smile of release from his recent anxiety.

But no sooner had the day faded than all Hamid's former anguish returned, together with pangs of guilt at having confessed to somebody who did not understand. Someone who, apart from saying 'Yes', had been of no assistance whatsoever. Hamid became deeply ashamed that he should have turned to a foolish man like Sheikh Masoud in the hope of gaining any benefit. Had he not, in effect, buried his pride and self-esteem when he went to him for help? Hamid grew so resentful that had the Sheikh been standing in front of him it would have been an easy matter to kill him. But he restrained his anger and gradually calmed down.

Hamid was upset by many things, afflicted by anxiety and depression even though he was young. He wanted a heart that he could claim for himself and his lips burned with passion, longing to kiss the mouth, cheeks and temples of a girl he could love. In spite of the death which comes to all things in autumn, the beauty of nature with its rose-coloured sunsets kept Hamid searching for the kisses and embraces he yearned for. Although his head was full of regrets, his heart was kindled by the desire for a loved one who would bring him happiness. When feelings and thought are in conflict, natural instincts prevail.

Night slowly spread its cloak over the departing day, wrapping the world in darkness and bringing the sweet evening breeze to all God's creatures. Hamid emerged from his depression confused as to what to do, not knowing which path of life to follow.

A few days later he left his beloved village for the capital, hoping that the change would ease his mind and soothe his conscience so that he might enjoy a more peaceful, more agreeable kind of existence.

# Chapter Two

About a month after Hamid had travelled to Cairo his brothers returned to the house one day to find that he was not at home. They waited to see if he would arrive for supper but he did not come, and when that night and the following day had passed with no sign of him, they wrote to inform their father. He came quickly, anxious for an explanation but they had no idea what had become of their brother. Wringing his hands the old man went into Hamid's room, his eyes sunken and moistened with tears. He sat down, sad and dejected, lamenting the ill fortune that had snatched away his dearest son. Where could he be? Suicide? Surely he would not take his own life. But how could he leave his brothers and family without so much as a message and for no reason whatsoever?

The world darkened in the eyes of Hamid's father, his heart clouded with worry. Looking round he saw a picture of Hamid gazing at him with a calm, self-assured expression, unalarmed by his father's fears and unaffected by his grief. He walked across the room and stared at it, then taking the picture from its place he kissed it and held it to his breast, collapsing in tears into the chair by his side.

But his tears were of little use. He would have to go and search for Hamid even though he did not know whether he would find him alive or dead. Before telling the others of his plans, he decided to look through his son's papers and there on the desk he came across a large envelope addressed 'to my venerable father'. Tearing it open he sat down to read what was inside:

To my mother and father, brothers and relations,

I recently made myself known to a wicked man, a Sheikh of one of the brotherhoods, believing that I would find in his alleged holiness something to ease my conscience. But I found only additional burdens and suffering. Now I am going to

open my heart to you because you are the ones I love. Maybe
you will excuse the miscreant that I am, worn out with thinking
and wandering aimlessly, not knowing which road to take. I
cannot say if you will see me again after today or whether
this message will be the last you will hear of me.

Some two years ago I became aware of a persistent voice
that talked to me about love and its pleasures, depicting it as
a ripe garden filled with warbling birds. Whenever I saw a
beautiful woman and pondered the happiness she holds in
her hand, the voice rang out clearly and sweetly, overpowering
me until I began to feel that a life without love would be dull
and monotonous, a life without value. I became distracted as
I searched for the object of my desire, my hopes inspired by
the prospect of finding a woman in whom I might realise the
meaning of life and the secret of bliss. But all I discovered
was a vast and desolate wasteland in which to lose myself and
I would often return there with a mysterious longing. One
day, in a corner which neither the sun nor wind could reach,
I perceived a girl standing alone. She too seemed confused,
not knowing which path to take through the desert before
her and sometimes she raised her eyes in my direction, full
of modesty and diffidence. Gazing at her, I identified my
cousin, thrown onto the wastelands of life by the same destiny
that had befallen me, searching from her corner for somebody
to love. As soon as I recognised her I began to think: 'Two
lonely people, one to comfort the other . . .' But how could
that be when my thoughts were hovering in the air and she
remained imprisoned within the walls of her house?
Nevertheless, I was content with the fruits of my search so
that whenever I entered the realm of my imagination, I aligned
my hopes of happiness to hers and entrusted my future to
her alone.

In our own small village, among the workers and working
girls in the fields, I came upon a country girl whom the sky
itself might have sent down to earth in a time of purity as a
messenger of love. Never in my life had I seen such eyes, more
penetrating than arrows, couched beneath the beautiful arches
of her eyebrows. Her breasts protruded despite the dress which

covered them with all the protection beneath which a girl conceals herself from the desires of young men. Below her slender waist her fleshy buttocks adorned generous thighs while her glances disclosed a pure heart, full of love. I was smitten with her beauty and wanted to be by her side at all times, to take her for myself and make her the object of my desire. With each day that passed she pleased me more until, instead of going aimlessly to the fields, I felt I was being driven to where she would be.

One afternoon I found her working in a small group, removing blocks of turf from the bed of the land and placing them one on top of the other. Two or three workers stood in a chain so that the turfs could be tossed from person to person until they reached the pile safely. I greeted them and took a position next to her. I don't know why but it gave me such pleasure to stand beside her and catch the turfs which she tossed to me, that I stayed there for the rest of the day. Maybe the turfs which she had touched became precious, something to be treasured, or each time she picked one up and held it to her breast some of the warmth of her body was conveyed to me. However, my feelings for this country girl were not the same as those I held for my cousin, which I called love. I only wanted to be by her side, to hold her hand or kiss her and feel her close to my chest. Among my friends and brothers, these things were soon forgotten.

The arrival of my cousin diverted me from the fields and the working girls and I became preoccupied with finding a way to be alone with her. When I was not favoured with a suitable opportunity I spent my time between the paradise of hope and the fire of despair, waiting but to no avail. From the day I first believed that I loved my cousin, my greatest desire was to marry her. I placed my hopes on the life that we would spend together, creating an imaginary world in which I mapped out our future happiness, considering this marriage to be something predestined because they had told me when I was young that I would marry her. But on realising how difficult it was to speak to her alone, I began to feel depressed. I became resentful of our society which upholds the customs that were the cause of my disappointment. Turning my back on the establishment, I rejected the values which those who adhere to our traditions are so proud of, and the whole concept of marriage in my eyes became a subject of bitter criticism. (To this day I consider the institution of marriage defective, on account of the conditions that are attached to it. Indeed I believe a marriage which is not based on love and does not progress with love to be contemptible.)

The days passed while I tossed and turned on a bed of black thoughts and dire dreams until forgetfulness erased everything from my mind. Is there anything in life to which oblivion does not come?

When spring arrived to quicken the heart and revive the sleeping world, I awakened from my state of heedlessness. Reflecting on the country girl who had married during the winter I wished her well, and the memory of my cousin returned to dominate my heart and senses so that my only desire was to be by her side forever. Finally, I believed my hopes would be realised. We exchanged some letters and arranged the meeting we had both been waiting for . . . but it was an hour of intense silence in the midst of a speechless night.

Then my cousin was also married. She sent me a farewell letter and although it caused me great distress, almost at once my head became full of thoughts for the country girl. Her image ruled my heart and mingled in my soul until I was almost out of my mind. I determined to go to her, to hold her to my breast, to kiss and embrace her and do all the things that lovers do. Yet none of this was to be. I met her and reminded her of the past but was obliged to keep my distance when she reminded me that she was married!

After that meeting I was plunged into a deep sadness in which all good was turned to evil, all happiness to misery and all hope to despair. Had any heart been open to me at that time, in which to seek refuge, I would have done so but the only consolation I found was in myself. Unable to divulge my feelings to anyone, my distress increased until my patience was exhausted. The world darkened before me and when I could no longer see the light of hope I began to despair of my life. Then Sheikh Masoud came to the village. He set up his recitation ring and I sat watching his followers shouting in the night, calling on their Lord in fear and supplication. The sight of them appealed to me and I thought: 'If this man can reduce the burden of my anxiety I shall be the first to follow him.' I did not hesitate and went to him the following afternoon. After giving him a summary of my situation I recited the words which joined me to the brotherhood and I came away happy, but when daylight departed my anxiety returned, intensified by the shame of what I had done. A few days later I came to the capital.

From the day I arrived I thought constantly about the circumstances and events which had given rise to my ideas about love. Then my thoughts ceased and a new situation emerged which has led me to leave you all. For this reason I am writing, in the hope that you will find some consolation in knowing how I reached my decision.

I arrived here burdened with worry and although I immersed myself in my work by day, as soon as night fell my mind was flooded with memories. I saw before me a great tapestry of the past, embroidered with all the events of my life but with no sequence of time—no doubt a result of my despair. How can anyone imagine what a young man of my age feels when he fails in everything he wants, be it loving my cousin or my desire for the country girl? How can anyone understand how wretched I felt or what thorns were embedded in my heart? In any event, when we reach the limit of pain—if it does not kill—we recover some of our soundness of mind, which enables us to think. So I determined to examine my desires in more detail, and my failure to satisfy them.

The first question I asked was: 'Why did I love my cousin?' In the days of our childhood we spent all our time together until we were separated when she had to wear the veil. Then some years later, when we were not together and for no apparent reason, I fell in love with her. Was it those early memories that roused me or did I imagine her to be so beautiful that I wanted to keep her image with me all the time?

A few months later I forgot all about her. My love for her returned only when a particular event made me remember her or when she came to the village during the summer. I cannot believe that a heart so fickle is capable of true love and I doubt whether my feelings were ever sincere. Maybe it was nothing more than a fantasy which came to me in time of need—but is love itself not a fantasy, making us imagine that a woman is so beautiful that we want to live with her forever? Or was I driven by natural instinct towards any woman who would be a suitable mother for my children?

Moving on in my thoughts I sought to discover the nature of my feelings for the beautiful country girl who so captured my imagination. Why did I find such pleasure in seeing her and talking to her or accompanying her when she returned to the village? Was it love or the cry of the unborn child calling out for the opportunity to live? If it was love, surely I would not have forgotten her whenever my cousin happened to be in the village. But if it was the cry of the next generation and the drive to further the species, why did I never feel the need or desire to have sexual intercourse with her? My only wish was to sit beside her, to talk and embrace in the hope that she would return my affection.

At this point I was beset by confusion for I could not comprehend my feelings for either girl. Then an idea came to me that made me shudder. If my only desire was to talk to the country girl and to be alone with her or kiss her, what did I hope to achieve in the long term? Was it not in fact, to achieve more and fall into the natural trap of procreation even through self-deception and trickery? Certainly she was a fine-looking girl, with a strong healthy body full of the scent of youth. The child born to us would have inherited these qualities and others besides, thereby advancing mankind another step forward on the path of progress. But enough of such thoughts, which echo the philosophy of European thinkers! Is it not enough what our forefathers have taught us—to advance in slow stages and safeguard the stability of society? Why should I break down the barriers of convention and pay attention to fanciful theories?

Nevertheless I triumphed over my preconditioned beliefs and my mind began to think more freely, laughing at the inhibitions that blocked its path, although at the same time I was aware of a bitter regret on account of the difficulties these obstacles create.

Turning my attention to the age-old custom of marriage, I was struck by the way our society regards any relationship between a man and woman, outside of marriage or the family, as vile and despicable. Whether it be pure love, or mutual friendship or admiration, it is considered to be something evil. Any display of intimacy is seen to express our animal nature; a crime against the unborn child, conceived as a result of physical lust. I myself grew up to despise the idea of sexual relations between unmarried men and women . . . Then the thought occurred to me that people only pursue marriage in order to satisfy their carnal desires and I applied this theory to the circumstances in which we live.

The world is a wheel turning, the origin of which we do not know. Every drop in the ocean is an integral part of this cycle and the present generation is like a wave in the ocean of humanity. Behind the birth of every creature lies the act of procreation. This is what destiny decrees and our universe functions in accordance with this law. People arrange their relationships in order to maintain their integrity while they perform nature's function of reproduction. In former times, maybe, the family performed its duty to nature more success-fully than it does today. The practice of slavery enabled those who were successful in war—men of great physical prowess and therefore the best equipped to produce healthy offspring—to buy the partners best suited to them. Although this practice did nothing to promote meaningful relationships between men and women, it satisfied the needs and desires of many. Indeed, were it not that this system paid no heed to the rights of women I would say it was the best suited to the needs of nature, and also the most honest. Regarding the situation that exists today, although it may appear more humane, it is no less disturbing however much people may think that things have improved. Young men and young girls are married and expected to spend their lives together without even knowing each other!

A man looks for three qualities in a partner: she should be pleasing to him, fertile, and in conjunction with the father, a good parent to the children. And in the absence of any real freedom of choice an individual may settle for the first person he finds who satisfies at least two of these conditions. So I wanted to marry my cousin because she was the most suitable of the girls I knew who might bring me happiness and fulfil the purpose of nature. As for my acquaintance with the country girl, although I thought that I was driven only by my desire to kiss her, to hold her to my breast and enjoy the pleasure of her company, I realise now that I was also being driven to achieve nature's goal. The only reason I did not think of marriage is that I was brought up to believe that I would only marry someone from a similar social background to myself. But nature is not concerned with the traditions which we set up in order to preserve the fabric of society, on the contrary it scoffs at them, and in all honesty I consider that it would have been no fault on my part if I had married the country girl whom I admired. Yet I did not marry her! Someone else did that and I felt it would be more worthy of me to let her honour her contract in the best way that can be expected of a wife.

When it was obvious that neither my cousin nor the country girl were available to me, I knew that I would have to search for another besides them. So I began to think about leaving everybody and isolating myself in order to achieve the object of my desire. I appreciate the enormity of the task I have taken upon my shoulders but I only conceived of it after becoming so weary of life that I had begun to detest it. In fact this resolution is easier to bear than the decision to stay which would have been harder for me and for everybody who loves me.

Now I must take my leave of you. I hope that you will not suffer on my behalf, for life is too short for worrying. Thank you for everything you have done for me. Goodbye.

Hamid

When Sayyid Mahmoud had read his son's testament he was filled with dismay. The afternoon sun, weak at that time of year, shone through the window onto the floor of the room and descending further, the rays of light reached to Hamid's bookshelves as if to point out to his father the real reason behind his son's despair. Hamid had often spent his time reading love poetry and the tender words enticed him away from the realities of life. He was also influenced by romantic stories, of heroes who die for the sake of their loved ones, until he became convinced that a life without love was not worth living. Then he began to contemplate how wonderful a life of love would be, spent in dreams by the side of a sweetheart who holds a man's happiness in her hand.

But his father was distracted from the sun and the books; his only concern was the safety of his son. Wondering what he could do to ensure his return, he stayed in the room until the light of day faded and night began to occupy the vastness of the sky. When his other sons arrived, after watching a football match at school, they called for their supper and Sayyid Mahmoud sat with them, his thoughts in disarray, unable to eat or utter a single word.

The next day the following note arrived from Hamid:

My dear father,

I realise the suffering I must be causing you but I implore you not to worry on my account. There is really no need to be concerned. I am living an agreeable life, working and looking after myself from the fruits of my labour. Not for one moment have I ceased to be thankful for everything you have done for me and I sincerely hope that one day I will return, to throw myself into your arms and the arms of my mother.

I blame myself when I think of you suffering because of me but I am well and living comfortably . . . so until we meet again in the near or distant future I send you my greetings.

Hamid

How could his father be consoled by a message like this? In fact it made his grief and sorrow more intense. Had he learned that his son was dead he would have been overcome with despair and at least despair is a form of relief. But he knew that his son was alive, without a friend, aimlessly struggling to earn a living. Nothing is harder for a father to bear.

Yes, Hamid was still alive, searching for someone to love but finding no one as if a barrier existed between him and every girl he met. His father returned home distraught. Sometimes he bore his burden calmly, sometimes fearfully, but the safety and wellbeing of his eldest son were his only consideration.

The unjust society around them remained indifferent to the anxieties of father and son, whether the former died of remorse or the latter of a broken heart. And somewhere in her quarters was a girl even more distressed than Hamid who could not find her way to him. Nor could she leave her father's house, having been raised there in comfort, to search for the man she loved. Only when these two meet will they extinguish their mortal anguish with love and revive those noble feelings which alone offer hopes of happiness and consolation from the hardships of life.

# Chapter Three

Three days after Ibrahim's departure, Zainab was sitting alone in the hall where she had bade him farewell. In her hand she clutched the handkerchief she had found there and whenever she looked at it she was reminded that her beloved was on his way to an unknown destination. The suffering that filled her being overflowed in hot tears which fell from her eyes without her being aware of them and rolled gently down her cheeks.

For three nights she had hardly slept. Every time the night receded her streaming tears seemed to revive its deathlike darkness and pain racked her chest as she lay awake in bed. If Hassan asked her what was the matter she would complain of nausea or colic, saying that she expected it to pass by morning. By day, the bustle of activity distracted her from her anxiety and at times she almost forgot her sadness. But when she was alone she suffered pains that nearly killed her.

That evening Hassan ate his supper as usual, then went up to their room. Finding it empty he called his mother to ask where Zainab was but she did not know. He started to feel uneasy, wondering where she could be at this hour after the men had prayed el-asha and returned to their houses. Eventually Zainab came upstairs but she would not say where she had been, having no desire for her husband to know where she spent her hours of private recollection. When she persisted in her silence he asked her again, more determinedly this time, and signs of indignation and exasperation appeared in his voice. Finally, overcome with anger, he shouted at her:

'Tell me where you've been. I won't tolerate your deceitful silence any longer. I demand to know where you've been tonight. Otherwise we shall go our separate ways!'

What could Zainab reply when she had simply been sitting in the hall? What would she say if he asked her what she had been doing there? She could make up a story to explain why she was sad and in pain then at least she would not be deceiving him with her silence! Maybe that would quieten his suspicions and stop him accusing her—but might he not take her words as further proof of her cunning and trickery? In the end she said nothing, leaving him to think whatever he wished. As long as her own conscience remained at ease she could not be found guilty of doing anything wrong.

But her conscience did not remain at ease. No sooner did she lie down on the bed than her worst dreams materialised and she could not control the pain which gave rise to her sighs. She felt stifled and the sobs which she tried to suppress found their way to her husband's heart, keeping him awake and forcing him to listen to the pitiful sounds that issued from Zainab's chest. Then his mood began to soften as though her tears had extinguished his blaze of fury or as if God were inspiring him, in the darkness of the night, to show some compassion. Every sigh became a knife which cut into his heart until he could no longer be silent and asked her gently:

'What's the matter Zainab?'

Hardly had he spoken these words than she gave herself up to weeping like a child who has lost its mother. Tears streamed from her eyes as her sadness and anxiety spilled into the night and her sighs rose to a wailing pitch, combining with intermittent moans of pain which seared Hassan's soul. He got up to light the lamp and knelt at her side, fondling her as a mother fondles her young ones. He showed affection now, believing that his anger and accusing tone had upset her, for in truth he had only known her to be trustworthy and honest.

Frequently, when we wish to make amends, it is difficult to admit that we are in the wrong and we attempt to put things right by every possible means other than acknowledge what we have actually done. On the other hand, with people we care about and who occupy a special place in our hearts, it is easy to say too much in the way of confession.

Our love for them may even cause us to blame ourselves for things we have not done if that will make them happy. Hassan

was of the latter, accusing himself of being rude, apologising
for his insinuations and asking Zainab's forgiveness for his
outburst. But this only made her suffering more acute, adding
another tribulation to her already severe distress because she
could not open her heart to a kind and loving husband.

'What's the matter Zainab? Let's not be like small children,
crying over every little thing, or nothing. Just tell me what's
the matter, I have a right to know. If what I said upset you
I'll never say anything like it again. But you must realise that
I worry when you're nowhere to be found, afraid that you
might have gone off to the fields or to some other place, and
the weather is so cold at nights. Please don't cry.'

So Hassan was afraid for Zainab because of the coldness
of the night, and her tears upset him! Dear God, if you wished
to give Zainab to Hassan could you not have induced her to
love him? Why did you not bring them together at a time
when she regarded every young man as a potential lover?
Maybe then she would have found in him a companion with
whom she could share her life and be happy. Instead of her
tears, and Hassan's anxiety on their account, they might have
enjoyed a carefree life. But after all her efforts to be a good
wife to her lawful partner, can Zainab be blamed in any way?
Could anyone accuse her of being wanton or speak of her
with disrespect? Having tried her best to give her heart to her
husband when it already belonged to somebody else, should
we not excuse her and lay all responsibility on the harsh
circumstances that led to her plight?

Anybody seeing Zainab's sad, despairing face at that hour
of the night or hearing her sighs piercing the silence, would
be full of sympathy. Anyone who realised the extent of the
conflict between her feelings and her duty, would know what
a terrible struggle this was, in the face of such a cruel destiny.
Hassan could not remain beside her without tears falling from
his eyes, no less bitter than those of his wife.

Two partners bearing their burdens: one weeping silently,
fearing for his companion; the other shedding tears of confusion and despair, buffeted by so many opposing forces that
she could find no guidance on the path of life.

Hassan put his arms round Zainab's shoulders and cuddled
her in a way that was full of affection. Caressing her tenderly,
he tried to console her with gentle words:

'Still cross with me Zainab? I didn't mean what I said. If
I'd known that you were going to get so upset over a couple
of words I would have behaved like those who prefer to say
nothing rather than show any concern for their wives. But I
spoke as I did because I know you're intelligent and I thought
you'd understand that I was afraid for you. If you need to go
out at night I just want you to tell me.'

His words reached the depths of Zainab's soul and she felt
that she alone was in the wrong. However, it is in the nature
of human beings to justify their actions and fearing that her
silence would only make Hassan more concerned, Zainab
explained between her tears:

'I was sitting in the hall from suppertime until I came
upstairs.'

Hassan stared at her, bewildered by her reply. What on
earth was she doing in the hall, and why hadn't she said
anything until now? But his faith in her prevented him from
asking the questions that sprang to his mind so that he only
censured her for saying nothing before. Then he drew her
towards him, relieved and content.

He continued to caress her until she calmed down then he
put out the light and lay beside her on the bed. He talked to
her gently about matters of no consequence, hoping that sleep
would soothe her anxieties but it was not long before he fell
asleep himself, exhausted after his day's work. As for Zainab
she could not close her eyes but spent the night suffering
pains more intense than anything she had experienced during
the past three days. Sometimes she blamed herself for upsetting
her husband and wanted to open up her heart to him. She
even tried to sever her relationship with Ibrahim forever with
one final, steadfast resolution but a voice inside her whispered:
'Can you really do that?' Then she imagined her lover standing
beside her smiling, slipping his arm round her slender waist
and saying 'I love you'.

What power the image of a loved one can have, making

us forget our misery and distress along with the world and everything in it until only the image of the beloved remains. Just as in life, the presence of a lover embracing and kissing us brings ultimate bliss, so the memories of their words and actions provide us with the most delightful dreams.

Zainab raised herself from the bed on her wrists as if to bring the image closer, under the cover with her where they could kiss and embrace. When her wrists would no longer support her weight she lay her head on the pillow, her spirit wandering in a boundless sea. Finally exhaustion overcame her and she fell into a deep and peaceful sleep. But it did not last for long. The cockerel was calling from the balcony and she awoke full of determination, as though the dreams in which she had spent the latter part of the night had compensated for the brevity of her sleep.

Hassan got up to pray el-fajr and when he arrived at the mosque he found his father there before him, reciting the Qur'an with his aged companions. No sooner had he finished his ablutions than the voice of the muezzin rang out from the top of the minaret, inviting the faithful to the house of God, the darkness echoing his call in every corner. Ending with the words: 'Prayer is better than sleep', the muezzin climbed down the staircase which was so narrow it was only the fact that he was accustomed to it that prevented him from striking his head. He led the worshippers for the two obligatory rakats then returned to his house, hoping to find something hot to eat before teaching the boys at the Koran school. Some of the congregation made their way home while others stayed to praise and glorify their Lord. Hassan was among the former and when he arrived at the house he found that Zainab had prepared him some breakfast before going to fetch water.

* * *

Zainab left the house as day was struggling to dislodge the canopy of night. The roads were covered by a layer of dew and the early morning light brought a blueness to the sky which encompassed the fields where the corn plants grew.

Everything was calm as the sweet, moist air revived the weary, bringing happiness to their hearts and encouraging all creatures to wake up from sleep. The whole of creation appeared content with the rest it had taken during the night.

When she had covered half the distance she recalled what had passed between herself and Hassan and aware of a sense of urgency, as though an impulse which she did not understand was driving her back to her husband, she hurried to the canal where she quickly filled her pitcher before returning to the village. But when she reached the house he had already left for the fields with the waterer, so she emptied her jar and set out on the second round. She did not know why she wanted to see Hassan, nor what she would say if she found him, but we are often beset by strange desires which we cannot understand. Although we may regard them as whims, they are often the result of events that have taken place and left their mark upon us.

The road was now crowded with workers and women fetching water. Among those whom Zainab met were Ummu Saad, Ishta Ummu Ibrahim and Nafisa Ummu Ahmed, walking at a leisurely pace as they made their way to the canal on their first round. When Zainab greeted them they stopped to tell her what they had heard the night before about Sheikh Masoud going on hajj* this year, asking her if it was true that Ammi Khalil was going to accompany him, but Zainab did not know. No one in the house had asked for provisions or for anything else to be prepared, so even if the rumours were correct the journey must be planned for some time in the future. While they were talking they heard a voice down the road calling 'Good morning girls', and Hajja Zahra came to join them. When she found them discussing El-Hejaz* it awakened the memories of her own pilgrimage, which all women who have been to Mecca love to share. If an opportunity presents itself they seldom let it pass without recalling the places and events which they have seen and witnessed

* Pilgrimage to Mecca.
* Western province of Saudi Arabia where Mecca and Medina are situated.

with their own eyes. After adding to the facts with tales of
their own imagining, you would think they had been in a
magic land among people whose speech was all inspired and
who received everything they possessed directly from the
bounty of heaven. So Hajja Zahra told them all about her
pilgrimage: the shaft of light she had seen above the city of
Medina, the Arabs she had met and the worshippers circum-
ambulating the Kaaba. She described the events in a haphazard
fashion, relating the stories which she always told on these
occasions until the girls were amazed at what they heard and
from time to time they extolled the good fortune of those
who were lucky enough to visit the birthplace of the prophet.
Their attentive listening so encouraged Hajja Zahra's imagination that Zainab almost forgot what was on her mind.

From the red horizon the circle of the sun ascended in the
East, bringing life and energy back into the world. The women
reached the canal where the water flowed peacefully, covered
with a thin veil of light while the trees on the banks bore a
sorrowful countenance, anticipating the coming of autumn.
Some of the girls filled their earthenware jars, others washed
their clothes, and from time to time a farmer passed by with
a cow or buffalo.

When Zainab returned on her final round, daylight
prevailed in every corner. The sun swam in the sky sending
its rays onto the stalks of grass and the leaves of the corn
plants. The dew that the night had left behind sparkled and
the surface of the water shone with light. As she washed her
pitcher, Zainab heard the sound of a bull lowing which she
had heard many times before and looking round she saw the
animal asleep under the tree which Ibrahim had tied it to in
the days when 'Antar' had been his faithful companion. When
this bull was hitched to the water wheel it would never stop
but worked at a constant, steady pace. Even when shackled
with another to draw the plough, it never tired or gave its
master any trouble. To Zainab it seemed that the beast was
lowing for Ibrahim and she wanted to run to it and kiss it in
the hope of finding any trace of her beloved to calm her
troubled mind. She stared at the tree where she had so often

sat with Ibrahim but the leaves had turned yellow, sad at his departure. That sacred spot next to the mulberry bush, and the thicket surrounding it—did not all these things lament the loss of a friend like Ibrahim? Zainab felt they must share her suffering, otherwise they would not be communing with her so mournfully.

Every time Zainab came across a reminder of her beloved she was beset by anxiety. Soon she would be consumed by grief. Her face was beginning to show the signs of her sadness and her body was shrinking on account of her abstention from food. Preferring to be alone she would spend long hours in dark thoughts and as time went by her condition deteriorated. Her heart became resentful, her body would tremble, and her face turned pale until the grief within her overflowed in tears that ran down her cheeks, but there was nobody to see them.

With every day that passed, Zainab grew more anxious and more inclined to solitude. During these periods of isolation she would give herself up to weeping until she was no longer aware of herself or the things around her. Although she suffered terrible loneliness, which increased every day, there was no friend to whom she could turn among the world of people. The silence of the universe and the lowing of the beasts were more comfort to her than the talk and tumult of the crowd.

As autumn advanced, nature appeared more desolate. The once proud cotton bushes were left without a leaf upon them and vast areas of bare land spread out bleakly across the earth. The corn plants looked decrepit with their clothing stripped off, shrivelling before their oncoming death. The water in the canals dwindled away, leaving just a trickle in the dried up beds from which both men and animals drank. Nights turned cold and the long awaited sun, when it rose, seemed to announce that it would soon be setting, while the wind which blew from the north made the rich people shiver. Only the fallaheen welcomed it, rejoicing at the prospect of the days of rest which lay ahead. Everything was approaching that state of inertia during the winter months when there is no work and little activity.

The world appeared ever more gloomy and Zainab become more sad and grief stricken until the change in her appearance was evident to those who knew her. When she began to suffer fits of coughing she believed that she had caught a cold but she would not stay indoors and keep warm for that would deprive her of the reminders of Ibrahim which she saw in the fields, like the tree that had witnessed what had passed between them. In spite of the cold morning winds that make teeth chatter, she would go to the canal as the sun cast its first rays of light on the land. When the canal dried up completely and the women had to go to the railway station in the afternoon to fetch water from the steam train, Zainab would cast her looks of resentment and hatred at that coal-hearted machine with its black face that had taken her lover away. Whenever she saw the tree or the train or any other reminder of Ibrahim, clouds of anxiety descended upon her from which there she no escape other than in her bitter tears. Then the cough would attack her chest, shaking her body and bringing to her pale cheeks a shadow of their former rosiness which vanished as soon as the cough subsided. Returning to the house she would shut herself in her room, or in the hall, where she would sit for hours on her own and if Hassan enquired about her health, she would reply that she had caught a chill which troubled her constantly.

The year drew to a close followed by the month of January and the season of planting. The fallaheen worked hard to sow the new crops and soon the fields began to unfold with the fresh shoots of bean plants, clover and cereals. The dried out canals that traversed the countryside, waiting to be dredged during these last days of winter, appeared despondent and resigned while all around, the green earth stretched to the far horizons. From time to time the animals pasturing in the meadows bellowed, filling the still air with their noises, and groups of larks alighting on the silken carpet, hopped and chirped, bringing a hint of gladness to the wintry atmosphere. Sometimes Zainab's mother met her at the watering place and she would always ask about Hassan and his mother.

Occasionally she would visit them in their house, bringing with her some fish or cucumbers according to the season and if she ever saw anything for which Zainab should be reproached, she never hesitated to give her advice. Returning home she would tell her husband in tones of happiness and contentment how dearly Hassan's mother loved Zainab and that his sisters regarded her with great respect and affection. If she happened to meet Khalil, he would enquire politely about her affairs and assure her that Zainab was doing very well, praising her as one of his own, and if she questioned him further he would insist that all he said was true.

When Zainab's mother met her during this latter period, she was startled by the paleness of her daughter's face and her apparent absent-mindedness. She wondered whatever could have happened to her and the cough, even though it might only be a simple ailment, concerned her when it continued day after day. So she considered it her duty to advise Zainab not to go out unless she was well wrapped up against the cold. But what was the use of such advice, now that the illness had gripped the girl's chest? It would not be long before she showed all the signs of a mortal consumption.

# Chapter Four

My dear brother Hassan Abu Khalil, may you live in peace.

After wishing you well and a peaceful life we would like to inform you that these days we are in Umm Durman. We are all quite well and only hope that you are also in good health, which is our greatest wish from our Lord. The staff sergeant has informed us that he will be sending a battalion in the direction of Sawakin but I don't know if our company will be included. God willing, when it is decided I will let you know if we are part of it and send you a letter from Sawakin. I apologise for the delay in writing till now but they have been moving us about a lot and I didn't know whether I would be staying or be posted. Anyway you can always send letters under my name to Umm Durman and I will receive them. Even if I go to Sawakin they'll send them on to me. I met Ahmed Abu Khadr here from our district, the son of Abu Khadr Abu Ismael, who sends his greetings to you. I also met Saed el-Birhemtushi and he sends his greetings. I have also met Khalil Abu Awad Allah and Saed ed-Din el-Habashi and Ali Abu Mahjoob who all send their greetings too. Please say 'hello' for us to Hussein Abu Masoud, Abu Ahmed, my mother, your parents and your brothers and sisters. Also to Hajj Hindawi Abu Atiya, Ibrahim Abu Saeed, everyone else who is dear to you and all the people who ask about us. May they live long.

Written on behalf of Ibrahim Ahmed.

P.S. Best wishes to all your family—may they enjoy a long life.
Ibrahim.

Since the day Ibrahim had left, nobody had heard any news of him so when this letter arrived for Hassan informing him that his friend was in good health and that his greatest hope was that all his acquaintances in the village were enjoying good health too, he hurried to tell Ibrahim's mother. As soon as she heard the news she threw her skinny arms round Hassan's neck and began to kiss him profusely. A nervous tremor took hold of her and tears fell from her eyes but Hassan could not tell whether they were tears of joy because her son was well, or tears of sorrow at the pain of separation. In reality whenever she remembered Ibrahim or thought about his distant exile, the sadness which had come over her on the day of his departure returned. At the same time she was glad of the good tidings that Hassan brought and praised God for the safety of her beloved son. These conflicting emotions made her heart rise to her throat and her lean, worn-out body trembled as the tears rolled down her tawny face upon which time had etched innumerable wrinkles.

This was the first message to reach her from Ibrahim for six months. After leaving the village he had travelled to the district capital then to Cairo where he stayed for a few months in the barracks at Abbasiyya and from there he and his countrymen were posted to the unknown regions of the Sudan. In order to reach those desolate lands, where every poor ablebodied recruit would take his share of misery, one virtually has to pass beyond the grave to the tortures of hell itself. And when it was over he would be sent back to his country having earned nothing but the right to wear a twelve-inch tarboosh and a jacket and trousers in which to parade before his companions for a few days following his return. Then he might join the idle who spend their lives asleep or in conversation, wearing yellow leather slippers and a white gallabiya with a turban wound over a brightly coloured skullcap. Or, if necessity demanded, he would rejoin the ranks of the unfortunate workers and labour as he had done previously, earning his livelihood by the sweat of his brow.

Hassan told Ibrahim's mother the news after hearing it himself from one of the clerks in the mayor's house. Then he went to inform his family of what he could remember and that Ibrahim sent his regards to everyone. Zainab was longing to hear what was in the letter, earnestly hoping that someone would read it out to them, but she could not make her desires known lest her husband became aware of the secrets of her heart. Maybe he was only waiting for such a sign to rage at her again and disclose what he harboured against her in his soul. She wanted to know whether Ibrahim had said anything about her or mentioned her name—but did he even think of her now, being so far away and unaware of all she was going through? Maybe she had vanished from his mind completely, forgotten in the realms of the past. Was there nobody present who might read the letter to them?

The days when Ibrahim used to sit under the tree waiting for Zainab had gone, but how could he forget what had passed between them? Did nobody want to listen to Ibrahim's letter—not even Ummu Jaziyya, Hassan's mother?

After a moment's silence Ammi Khalil asked his son:

'Well, do you think our friend Ibrahim Abu Ahmed is happy?'

'Oh yes,' replied Hassan, 'completely happy. He says he might be going to Sawakin, or maybe not, because he still doesn't know whether his regiment will be travelling or staying put.'

'Never mind Sawakin,' retorted Khalil. 'A man should stay in one place. Too much moving around confuses the sanest mind!'

While they were talking, one of their neighbour's young sons came to ask if his mother was with them because she was not at home and he was afraid to stay in by himself, whereupon Ummu Jaziyya said:

'Sit here and soon she will come for you.'

He sat down and they asked him what he was doing in school. Then to see how good he was at reading, Hassan brought out Ibrahim's letter for him to read to them while they all listened attentively. Zainab edged forward as close as she possibly could, listening to every word with rapt attention. From time to time Hassan told the boy to repeat a phrase that he had mispronounced, having heard the correct pronunciation at the mayor's place.

In the middle of the letter the boy's mother came to enquire about her son but when she saw what he was doing she stood still and listened quietly, her breast swelling with the pride and satisfaction of a woman who believes herself to be the mother of a gifted child. After reading 'written on behalf of Ibrahim Ahmed' in the clear voice in which he was accustomed to recite the Qur'an at school, the boy fell silent. Zainab felt her heart heaving in her chest, having heard all those whom Ibrahim remembered without so much as a mention of her name. He had asked Hassan to pass on his regards to his sisters but had it not occurred to him to say 'and to Zainab also'. Her hopes were dashed still further when the boy turned over the sheet of paper and read the postscript which contained nothing that might have consoled her. Then the boy's mother took him back to her house, leaving the family to settle down for the night.

Retiring to their winter sleeping quarters in the hall, where Zainab lit a fire every day before sunset, Hassan climbed under the blanket and went straight to sleep, leaving his wife to put out the lamp. She lay beside him in silence, apart from the cough that shook her from time to time and made her cry out loud when it seemed that her inflamed chest was about to crack. However, the noise of her sighs no longer prevented her husband from sleeping now that he had become accustomed to it and after working hard all day, when he did lay down his head nothing could wake him until the morning.

Two months had passed since Zainab first became afflicted by her cough. At first she had hardly suffered any pain and it was only accompanied by the phlegm that accompanies an ordinary cough, which she brought up occasionally to relieve her chest. A few weeks later there was a general fatigue and loss of strength so that any task she performed exhausted her and when pains began to accompany the cough her complexion lost its ruddy hue and her face turned almost white. The signs of sadness upon her were evidence of the affliction she was suffering and aroused the sympathy of those who noticed but at the same time, her ever increasing lassitude stirred those who only looked at her beauty to believe she had grown lazy and taken to sleeping during the day. So she tried not to let anything interfere with her work and carried on with all her usual tasks whatever that cost her in the way of weariness and exhaustion.

In the darkness of the warm hall Zainab thought about Ibrahim's letter, wondering why he had not mentioned her name when he had mentioned so many others. Was it not the greatest neglect on his part, to have remembered Hassan's mother and father but to leave her forgotten? Maybe he had found other things in his new surroundings to occupy his mind, and other girls who would give their hearts to him so that she no longer held a place in his memory. On the other hand, just as Zainab could not mention his name in front of her husband how could she expect him to mention hers—and did not his silence indicate that he was thinking about her but feared in the same way, that others would discover what was in his heart? Had he not written in the postscript which the boy had read when he turned the page, 'best wishes to all your family' having previously wished the same for 'everyone else who is dear to you'? Did not all this indicate that he might still remember her and be keeping his promise?

Whether he was in Sawakin now or still in Umm Durman, all Zainab could contemplate was the time of his return so that she might enjoy those blissful moments again. Meeting every day, they would recall this period of separation along with the sorrow and grief that accompanied it. She imagined him greeting her, arms open wide, and with tears of joy falling from their eyes they would withdraw to the sacred tree to relive the days of the past.

As these pleasant images revolved in her mind, the happy memories they evoked calmed Zainab's anxiety until somewhere among the gardens of her dreams she became oblivious to her sadness. But in the days that followed her thoughts were not always so kind and her fears returned, bringing many black hours filled with sorrow and pain.

Then she would go and sit by herself where the weak rays of the winter sun dispelled some of the cold, remembering

Ibrahim and his letter and suffering alone the torment of this cruel separation. Sometimes when she stood up, she felt so tired that she almost fell down again and in these moments of weakness, the cough would wrack her body until she felt as though something was crawling in her chest.

At last Hassan became aware of his wife's loss of strength and began to take notice of her cough. He considered it best that she should go out only when there was some urgent need, otherwise she ought to stay indoors and keep warm so that the cold would not make her condition worse. He forbade her to go for water because the effort involved was too great, especially now that the canal had dried up and it was necessary to go to the railway station. The only concession he made was to allow her to walk within the village if she wished, although he preferred her to stay in the house at all times.

Such considerations, however, did nothing to comfort Zainab. Certainly she was tired and suffered pain when the cough struck, after which she would spit out blood, but although she was aware of the swift decline in her physical strength she still longed to see the sacred places she loved and to sit there alone whenever time allowed. So she resisted her husband as best she could, saying that she did not wish his sisters' share of the work to be increased because they already had enough to do. But Hassan was firm and demanded that his instructions be carried out without fail. If his sisters were not able to perform all the tasks required of them, any servant girl could take Zainab's place and do her work for her until she was well.

After these orders Zainab did not leave the house for a week, yet those hallowed places were never far from her mind. Something urged her towards them as though the lifeless objects themselves were calling to her to share with them in remembering Ibrahim or as if the destiny which hung over her, vying for her soul, had revealed that she would soon be leaving all these things behind. However much Ummu Jaziyya tried to ease her worries and make her laugh, her efforts were in vain and she was obliged to be quiet when she saw that the smiles which Zainab allowed herself only made her look more sad.

By the end of the week Zainab's patience was spent and after lunch with her mother-in-law and Hassan's sisters, she left the village without saying where she was going. The fields spread out before her, covered with the green shoots of new crops, their beauty enhanced by the larks and wagtails that hopped among the plants. In this late winter season the great trees looked mournful and the horizons appeared forlorn. Zainab took her customary route to the watering place where she found the bed of the canal dried up, filled with the alluvial mud of the Nile. The tree where she used to sit with Ibrahim stood close by and beneath it three wagtails and a sparrow hopped along the edge of the canal. Near the bank a water wheel had been dismantled and laid down for its winter rest, the hole left behind covered with straw while an all sides, the farmlands stretched into the distance. Zainab stood gazing at the tree which seemed cheerless and pitiful, more desolate than the rest, and an ominous silence hung over the place like the silence of death. But she could not stand for long; her legs gave way and she sat beneath the tree, communing with the inanimate objects about their memories of Ibrahim.

While she was daydreaming the sparrow approached cautiously, pecking at the ground beside her and picking up a worm in its beak before flying a short distance away. After digesting the worm it hopped about again but this time, when it was by her side it fluttered its wings and perched on her knee. As though realising that there was no cause for the fear which usually accompanies such small creatures lest a careless hand should brush them aside, it made no attempt to fly away. Instead it raised its head to gaze at her with its tiny eyes and a moment later it flew to her shoulder and onto her hand. When Zainab felt it she was not startled but drew the bird closer and with a tender expression, full of love and sympathy, she looked at the little creature that had come to enquire about her grief. Then she raised the bird to her lips, wanting to kiss it, but the sparrow flew to the bank now that the wagtails had departed.

Meanwhile clouds had covered the sun. All movement ceased and in the gloomy atmosphere everything looked

morbid and melancholy. The colour of the green shoots darkened and as the wind dropped they became rigid as though
awaiting a command. The scene seemed to complement
Zainab's mood, providing her with some consolation and a
suitable arena for her thoughts. When would Ibrahim return?
When would they meet again? Arriving on the evening train
he would enter the village surrounded by his companions,
struggling to get away from them so that he could come to
her and fall into her waiting arms. What bliss they would
enjoy on that wonderful day. Returning to the tree, they would
sit in the shade while he told her stories of his days in the
army, his journey to Sawakin and all he had seen in Umm
Durman. Zainab tried to picture the place where Ibrahim was
staying, the landscape and the people among whom he lived.
She imagined him in his military uniform, conversing with
his fellow countrymen and when they mentioned those they
had left behind, Zainab was the one that Ibrahim remembered,
the sweetheart he would never forget.

Only a few months ago they were together beneath this
tree, savouring its beauty, but now that Zainab was alone the
whole of creation appeared sad and forlorn. Instead of the
flourishing fields of corn and cotton the land was clothed
with small winter shoots and the trees which had lost their
leaves stood barren and forbidding.

As the clouds amassed, the sky darkened again until the
light of day had all but disappeared. A light drizzle began to
fall and a breeze stirred the plants which soaked up the precious
water. Then the breeze became a wind, causing the rain to
fall more strongly over the vast expanse of green and as the
sky poured down its load, the vegetation huddled together.
Zainab moved behind the tree to protect herself but the wind
was blowing in all directions and she could not avoid the
downpour. She remained there for a quarter of an hour until
the storm began to abate and for a moment daylight was
restored. From behind the battling clouds the sun broke
through to send its rays over the earth, casting its light over
the fields and roads which basked in an ocean of life and
beauty. But it soon became veiled again and nature reverted

to the sorry state in which it had been before. Zainab stayed where she was, the rain making her more and more miserable until it seemed that her whole body was clothed in sadness and despair.

Finally the storm clouds scattered and the sky became a great blue dome from which the sun shone brightly on the fields below. In her wet garments Zainab made her way back to the village, sadder and more distraught than ever and while she was on the road a gust of wind blew up which made her shiver, causing her to cough violently until at last she reached the house and hurried into the hall to change her clothes.

Shocked to see his wife like this, Hassan demanded to know where she had been, to which her only reply was 'outside', and in spite of his persistent questions Zainab would not say what she had been doing. Hassan shrugged his shoulders and fell silent, shaking his head in resignation. But his questions had caused Zainab further distress, her body trembled and she could not contain the cough which took hold of her. It was an acute attack during which her temples and eyes reddened and anyone witnessing it was made to suffer every tremor which gripped her body. When it was over Zainab spat blood. Hassan's eyes moistened with tears, his mouth twisted with suffering and his youthful face expressed both pity and affection. He spoke to her gently:

'Don't you see what the cold does to you Zainab? Wouldn't it be better if you listened to me and stayed in the house while you're not well. I know you wouldn't want me to shut you in or confine you to your room but please stay indoors until your cold is gone and your cough has stopped.'

Zainab too, still believed that her thinness and coughing were due to a cold, but they were both mistaken. The malady eating away at the girl's chest was stronger and more severe than anything they could have imagined. It was abominable consumption threatening her life.

* * *

In these Egyptian villages where the air is fresh, the sun shines and life is peaceful, it is rare for anyone to be aware of an illness like consumption. Most people would think that the sick person had been smitten by the evil eye or simply caught a chill or something similar. It is also a rare disease, making it hard to imagine for people who have never witnessed it. Moreover, the fact that a person afflicted by such a disease would often be left until their last hours or even until death without being seen by a doctor, only reinforces the ignorance about these matters. So Ummu Jaziyya ascribed Zainab's weakness to the work of the evil eye and attempted to cleanse her by putting alum in the fire. As it burned, they imagined they saw someone they knew in the changing shapes which they believed to be the cause of the evil. Then they would spit into the flames in order to break the hold over the afflicted person. But none of this was of any use, the illness from which Zainab was suffering was the tragic culmination of her overwhelming anxiety and sadness. Throughout those long sleepless nights spent in pain and misery, the illness had continued to sap her strength, making her weaker with every day that passed.

Ammi Khalil came home at the end of the day, sad and dejected and his wife hurried to see what was the matter. On hearing that Hajj Saeed, the deputy mayor, had been taken ill and that he might pass away this very night her first reaction was one of relief because it was not something that concerned them directly. But she still remembered the funeral ceremony and the food to be prepared, so she returned to discuss it with Zainab, paying no regard to the girl's health except insofar as it affected her ability to cook and serve. While she was talking, Hassan returned from the mosque with the news that some of the men were saying that Hajj Saeed was on his deathbed.

No sooner had they finished their supper than a mournful cry pierced the silence, coming from the direction of the deputy's house—the cry of his wife, heartbroken at losing him. During the course of her wailing, dogs began to howl sadly on the roofs as though they too mourned the passing of the deceased to the abode of his Lord. Then the cries ceased

and the village was enveloped in the silence of death as Azrael*
spread his wings. Hassan's family spoke together in hushed
tones, humbly pondering the hour when they too would leave
the surface of the earth to be buried in its belly. The hour in
which we depart this tangible world where we know our place
to the darkness of eternal extinction, full of unknown horrors
and direst dreams.

Only a few stars shone in the sky and the stillness of the
night brought the thought of death closer, chilling their souls
with fear. In the midst of the darkness the wailing voice rose
again, this time accompanied by others, then silence fell once
more.

Ummu Jaziyya made enquiries about what would be needed
the following day and finding that they would be expected
to bake some bread on their baking trays she asked her daughters and Zainab to see to that. She told Hassan to go at first
light to the house of Awad Allah, the butcher, to order sufficient for themselves of the cow that would be slaughtered,
and finally she instructed the waterer to get up early and go
with the girls to gather vegetables from the fields. Then she
settled down, reassured that everything would be ready in the
morning.

A great commotion ensued, the waterer climbing to the
top of the roof to throw down some firewood while the two
sisters started to mix the dough. Zainab tried to light the oven
but the exhaustion she suffered with every movement she
made, together with the cough which troubled her all the
time, meant that she had to ask one of Hassan's sisters for
assistance. When the work was finished, they all went to bed
but Zainab's cough would not let her sleep. She lay thinking
about the dead man who had reached a fine age on this earth
only to leave it like those before him.

The next morning the commotion began again. Zainab got
up feeling worn out, her condition having deteriorated during
the night. Her skin had turned pale in contrast with her
bloodshot eyes which bulged from her scrawny face and she

---

* The angel of death.

looked round in bewilderment as though the things she saw today were not what she usually saw. Then she sat by the fire thinking about the funeral while Hassan and his father joined the long procession which passed slowly in front of the house towards the mosque, where prayers would be said before moving on to the cemetery where the deceased would be buried.

A few trays of food were brought out at lunchtime but at sunset a host of women and girls gathered round the entrance to the tent which had been erected, some bearing dishes or trays of food on their heads while others carried dining chairs. They stood outside, waiting for the family of the deceased to arrive with their trays and from inside the tent the voice of the Qur'an reader could be heard chanting softly, every verse he recited making the villagers feel more keenly the sadness of the occasion. When he had finished the chosen sura the family arrived and the women jostled their way into the tent with their goods, among them Hassan's eldest sister carrying their tray.

Hardly were the days of mourning over than Zainab suffered a severe fever which shook her body from head to toe, forcing her to stay in bed. With this additional burden she became even weaker, gripped by alternate bursts of hot and cold. And whenever the fever subsided the cough would return to shake her shrinking body, causing those who saw it to suffer with her. When Zainab's mother learned of this development she rushed to see what was the matter, but all Zainab could say was that the incessant cough still troubled her until she thought she was going to die.

Sitting by her side her mother lit incense and alum to no avail, with every moment that passed her daughter was exposed to more severe pains. When she saw her spitting blood and pus after a bout of coughing or looked at her lean and tired face, she remembered the health and beauty that were previously hers. And in the middle of the darkened hall where Zainab lay, her mother's tears flowed along with her sighs as she covered her face with her hands to hide her anguish from the others.

Seeing her daughter's illness advancing day by day, her mother suffered too, but Zainab would give no indication of the nature of her ailment except in the sighs and groans that she uttered. Whenever she was strong enough she would go into the courtyard clutching an embroidered handkerchief that she raised to her lips when nobody was watching. In this way she reminded herself of Ibrahim although it only made her torment worse. She desperately wanted to hear his news, but she did not know how. And nobody guessed what was on her mind.

# Chapter Five

Apart from attending to her household affairs, Zainab's mother now spent most of her time by her daughter's side. She kept her husband informed and sometimes he went himself to see how she was, but Zainab could not look at him without an expression of pained reproach that struck his heart and which he almost understood. Ummu Jaziyya devoted herself to looking after Zainab, leaving her only at the obligatory times of prayer when she would go to pray in her room. At night Hassan stayed with his wife and she had no need of anyone else.

A cloud of sadness hung over the house and the faces of all who came or went showed signs of grief. Even the dust-coloured sun which sent a pool of rays round the bed where Zainab lay, seemed sad as if it were aware of the anxious hearts that its light embraced. The leaves of the acacia trees in front of the house had blackened and when the wind blew through the branches they swayed dolefully, shaking their heads in sorrow.

Sometimes Zainab was visited by her friends, full of the freshness of youth, but on seeing them she remembered her own days of freedom—and how bitter to be reminded of our former strength and beauty in the days of our decline and weakness! When they departed, they left behind a broken-hearted girl whose tears of anguish flowed from her wide eyes and trickled down her pale cheeks.

Every day the cough made her weaker until she was so thin that in bed there was virtually no trace of her except for her face.

Perceiving nothing but misery all around him, Hassan finally despaired and went to tell the magistrate about his wife's condition. The magistrate criticised him for leaving her so long without being seen by a doctor but the fault for this lay with Hassan's parents who had always replied whenever he

suggested treatment: 'God is our doctor. Our Lord cures . . .'
So Hassan's mother had continued to burn incense and alum,
convincing herself and everyone else that Zainab was merely
suffering some evil visitation which would soon pass away if
God so wished.

But God did not wish and Zainab had continued to grow
weaker until Hassan was obliged to resort to the village magistrate to complain of his parent's obstinacy. The magistrate did
not hesitate. He ordered the telephone clerk to request the
provincial doctor to come at once and Hassan promised to
provide everything that was required when he arrived.

The doctor came on the first available train, reaching the
village as the sun entered its last quarter. The magistrate greeted
him warmly and called for a servant to make coffee while they
exchanged pleasantries. The doctor was a good-humoured man
and his youthfulness endeared him to the people of the district
who always welcomed him cheerfully with open smiles on
their faces. When the formal greetings were completed and
the two men had drunk their coffee they began to talk for a
long time about politics. They upheld the opinion of the party
they belonged to and supported the newspaper to which they
both subscribed, believing their representatives to be almost
infallible. In praising their leaders, they enhanced their conversation with appropriate expressions of acclaim and admiration
as they recalled the most recent articles written by their polit-
ical heroes. At the same time they scorned the politicians of
the other parties, considering them all to be totally misguided,
if not actually insane:

'They would never have permitted the publication of that
article two days ago. They're clever at talking but actually do
nothing!'

'They argue every word, kick up a fuss over every little
thing, repeating "long live" and "down with" until they give
themselves and everybody else a headache. Meanwhile the
English and the Khedive remain in their positions of power.'

In this manner they discussed the leaders of the parties, the
ministers of government and the government officials, especially those of their district. Then the doctor told a story about

the chief of police who constantly flattered the Governor of
the province and who was invariably hypocritical. This so
pleased the magistrate that he stood up to embrace his
companion—the least reward he could bestow on him for
ridiculing the libertine who forced the magistrates at his meetings to make contributions to meaningless causes, buy books
that they did not need and subscribe to newspapers which
they despised. Although they had to be content with the
decisions of the chief of police and accept what he said, at
least in defaming him they found some relief from their
burdens! So the two friends indulged themselves freely, each
exchanging one story for another until they had had their fill.
When the doctor asked why he had been called out, because
he was in a hurry and wanted to board the eight o'clock train,
the magistrate finally ordered one of the guards to summon
Hassan Abu Khalil.

The sun descended in the sky and as if unable to control
its movement, sank quickly towards its resting place. The wind
shook the branches of the trees and palms, rustling the leaves,
and on the surface of the pond the waves grew bigger as they
approached the bank, then disappeared. As far as the eye could
see the roads were virtually deserted except for the main road
where the women passed to and fro, carrying their earthenware
jars on their heads. They walked slowly and deliberately, their
bodies swaying from side to side with every step and in the
hazy distance they appeared like angels of the vast spaces over
which they strode. The silence which reigned over the countryside encompassed the village where all was quiet and calm.

Hassan came quickly. After waiting anxiously for hours he
was at his wits' end. He hung his head gloomily and the signs
of sadness upon him touched the hearts of the magistrate
and the doctor. The magistrate asked him to sit down and
tell the doctor what was the matter—but what was there to
tell? That Zainab was sick, her condition pitiful and the very
sight of her made his eyes stream and his heart weep? That
every day she grew weaker than the day before and the girl
he had once known to be healthy, strong and beautiful was
wasting away? Was it in the power of the young doctor who

sat twiddling his fingers and looking at Hassan sympatheti-
cally, to relieve her affliction and restore their peace of mind
so that they might enjoy life once more and find some
meaning to existence?

When the doctor and Hassan reached the patient's bedside
everyone left except for Zainab's mother. The doctor's first
question was whether any member of her family had been
taken ill in the past but her mother was there before him
strong and healthy, and her father was no less active. So he
enquired whether there was anything she wanted, to which
she said 'no', then he asked about a number of routine matters,
none of which received a convincing reply. Finally he requested
to be left alone with her whereupon he proceeded to banter
like a mother coaxing a child, hoping to find out anything
she might reveal. But he was far from satisfied with the answers
he received and maybe he was asking for more than she could
give. Whatever faith we may have in a doctor and his science,
we can never easily divulge something for which we think we
will be blamed, however confident we may be that our trust
will not be betrayed.

Having despaired of Zainab's answers the doctor asked her
to cough, but no sooner did she raise herself up to respond
to his request than she was beset by the most severe fit of
coughing she had yet endured. When the doctor saw the pus
that she spat out afterwards he raised his eyebrows and
shrugged his shoulders as if to say: 'It's too late for a cure,
now that the illness has reached its most crucial stage.' But it
made him shudder to see this girl, on whom the remnants of
a former resplendent beauty were still visible, shrivelling up
and hastening to her death.

Looking upon her with compassion, he explained that there
was still great hope of recovery but that it depended on her
telling him what was raging in her breast. Zainab sighed, her
wide eyes full of entreaty and supplication which made him
pity her even more. She wanted to tell him what he needed
to know but she hesitated and withdrew as if her story were
too sacred to be shared with another human being. Noticing

her hesitation, the doctor encouraged her by all possible means until she agreed to tell him a little about herself. In fact he did not need to hear very much and after reassuring her, he allowed the others back into the room and went outside, followed by Hassan.

As they crossed the stretch of land that separated the magistrate's house from the rest of the village, the sun had begun its descent and the shadows of the buildings lengthened. The first signs of night appeared in the sky although its blueness remained, clear and untainted, reflected in the pond where the breeze stirred the waves that followed one another across the surface of the water.

In the magistrate's house, the doctor took out his pen and notepad and wrote a prescription which he gave to Hassan. He told him to purchase the necessary medication from the pharmacist first thing in the morning and to follow the instructions precisely, at the same time advising him that his wife should spend at least two hours outside every day before sunset.

Hassan left them and when they were alone the magistrate asked the doctor about his patient's condition, to which he replied:

'Well although it's true that she may get better, it's also possible that she will not.'

Then they discussed other matters until it was time for the train that would take the doctor back to his district.

* * *

Hassan made sure that his wife took her medicine in accordance with the doctor's instructions and that she went out every day between midday and the time of afternoon prayer. He decided that she should go to their own fields, so the next day at noon Zainab set out with Hassan's sister who carried his lunch. They found Hassan sitting under a tree, having spent the morning ploughing the land in readiness for the sowing of the new cotton crop. Beside him the two bulls ate their fodder and in the middle of the field the plough divided the right side which was unturned from the left which was covered with tilth. When he had eaten his lunch his sister returned to the house and Hassan resumed his work, leaving Zainab to sit by herself. Looking out across the lands belonging to Sayyid Mahmoud, she remembered the day she had almost passed out and Ibrahim had sprinkled water on her face while she rested in his arms. She imagined him in the fields, looking round as he used to do, then digging his spade in the ground and gazing towards her as though inviting her to come to him.

In the opposite direction Hassan drove the plough, cutting the dry earth into strips and teasing the bulls occasionally with his whip. The animals pulled with all their might, scattering clods of earth on either side. Reaching the end of one line he would lift the plough on its side before twisting it onto the next and in this way he would continue for the rest of the day, backwards and forwards along the length of the field beneath the heat of the burning sun that blackened his face. Meanwhile, tired of being alone in that place, Zainab got up to leave and when Hassan saw her he came to ask what she wanted. Replying that she wished to go home, she set off towards the village but after walking a short distance she felt as though something were driving her back to the field. She stopped beneath the shade of a tree and turned round but she could not stand for long. Overcome by exhaustion which beset her whenever she made the slightest effort, she sat in the shade staring at the fields, recalling the past and the days of her youth. That wonderful time when the heart is free to do as it pleases, drifting from one person to another until it finds its eternal partner. Those delightful days when Zainab could give herself to the person her heart desired.

Now her beloved was far away and there was nobody to whom she could reveal the secrets of her heart. The star of her life was setting, leaving her only with memories which sometimes consoled her but at other times brought the most excruciating torment. If her parents had not been so selfish, sacrificing her wishes in order to marry her to Hassan, she would still have been happy and healthy. Nature herself, by her own inspiration, guides us to the right path. Blind prejudice turns us from it!

When a passer-by asked her why she was sitting alone,
Zainab continued her progress until she reached the canal. As
it was nearly time for the water round, she sat down to rest
against a tree trunk and picking up some pebbles, she threw
them one after another into the water that flowed gently by,
reflecting the colour of the sky. The banks of the canal were
smooth after the dredging with no grass or greenery upon
them and the light of the afternoon sun, slanting across the
landscape, cast shadows almost as long as the objects that
stood in its path. A gentle breeze blew through the trees,
shaking the leaves almost imperceptibly.

The first of the water fetchers arrived and after rinsing and
filling her jar she called Zainab to help her lift it onto her
head. Encouraged by her presence, Zainab assisted, but no
sooner had she sat down again than the deathly cough almost
choked her, making her eyes water and her veins swell until
she had thrown up the blood and pus on her chest. The other
girls hurried to see what was the matter but with eyes streaming
and her heart bleeding in horror at what was happening to
her, Zainab could only say:

'It's nothing. I'm all right.'

Then realising that she could not avoid their questions as
long as she remained with them, she forced herself up and
returned to the village. Approaching the house she saw her
mother on the doorstep grinding pepper with a pestle and
mortar, occasionally glancing down the road as though she
were expecting her and hoping for some improvement. But
Zainab was no different. Always weary, her strength sapped
further with every move she made and the raging cough
besieging her from one moment to the next.

They entered the house and went upstairs to the roof where
Zainab rested her back against the wall. Her mother sat beside
her, gazing at her face but the eyes which had once been so
alluring now pleaded for mercy. The expression contained in
them held her mother captive, unable to refuse any request.
Seeing her daughter like this made her feel so helpless that

she wanted to beg forgiveness, although for what crime she did not know. After a period of silence she asked her how she was.

Zainab's heart was overflowing with memories of her absent lover in the wastelands of Sudan and she longed to disclose what she was keeping hidden, but the reproach that she imagined her confession would provoke made her hesitant. If her mother heard anything like that she would surely be full of rebuke, which Zainab could not bear. And if death were already close by, she would wait for it patiently until it came to take her to a place where there would be neither sadness nor torment, only the stillness of the final annihilation. Yet before that moment came was it not her duty to expose the crime that her parents had perpetrated in marrying her against her will? When her mother repeated her question, Zainab summoned up the courage to reply:

'My condition is as you see. I will probably soon be dead and all because of you. When I used to weep and tell you that I didn't want to marry, you said lots of people get married against their wishes and the relationship always becomes as sweet as honey. If only you'd given me a husband I could have loved I would have nothing to say but now I want to sever the ties between us forever. Tomorrow or the day after I shall die and I warn you mother, when the time comes for my sisters to marry, don't force them against their will for as you can see, it is a mortal mistake.'

Her eyes full of tears, Zainab could say nothing more. The effort had been almost too great and her mother, on hearing this, felt as though a stinging arrow had pierced her heart, inflaming her breast so that she too was unable to speak. They sat in silence and the sadness hanging over them only deepened the atmosphere of gloom.

Zainab trembled and the cough struck again, ripping her chest until she collapsed in pain, almost unconscious. Realising for the first time the full import of her daughter's suffering, her mother supported her in her arms but Zainab was hardly aware of her surroundings. Placing an emaciated hand on her chest she raised herself up, bringing a hint of colour to her pale face, but after another bout of coughing she threw herself down again, weak and exhausted.

In the afternoon Zainab wanted to go outside and in spite of her weakness her mother agreed to accompany her to the fields. She was surprised when she did not take the road which led to Ammi Khalil's land but she could no longer resist her in anything. The humility she felt on account of her daughter's suffering meant that even if Zainab had asked for the impossible she would have done anything in her power to grant it to her.

Spring was in the air, new life unfurling in every corner. The sun's rays shone on the leaves of the trees and water was flowing once more in the canals. Larks and sparrows hopped on the dykes or hovered in the air and from time to time a flock of doves flew by, rejoicing in the sun and the season.

Followed closely by her mother, Zainab reached the watering place where she hesitated, unsure which path to take. Perceiving her consternation, her mother waited patiently for her to continue but when Zainab moved on, bearing left towards the tree, she fainted, totally drained of energy.

Having taken its share of spring decoration the tree was adorned with new leaves that shaded the earth below and the whole of nature was clothed in the fresh garb of springtime except for the clover that had been left for the cattle, wilting now as it awaited its coming death.

Zainab's mother tried to revive her, sometimes shaking her gently as if to wake her from a deep sleep, sometimes sprinkling her face with water but Zainab, lying prostrate on the stones, was unaware of anything her mother was doing. Despair crept into her mother's heart and with tears welling up in the corners of her eyes she lay beside Zainab's motionless body. Wrapping her arms around her she began to weep like a child as her beloved daughter in the prime of life and the spring of youth bade farewell to this earthly abode.

Zainab's words when she had accused her parents, echoed in her mother's ears as she lamented the fate of her hapless girl, imploring the heavens to show some mercy lest two families be bereaved of their dearest. Straying among her thoughts, she felt Zainab stir beneath her whereupon she cuddled her like a baby, entreating her in the hope of any sound which would reassure her that she was still alive. And as though relieved for a moment of the burden she was carrying, Zainab sighed and opened her eyes. Then she tried to stand up until with her mother's help, she was propped up against the tree. Although she had regained consciousness she could not tell whether she had woken from a peaceful sleep or an awful dream and turning her eyes to the things around her, she sighed again and hung her head to the ground.

Her mother could find no words to say. Whenever she tried to speak something restrained her from moving her lips. At last she asked:

'Is there anything you want Zainab?'

Zainab did not reply but remained with her head bowed, so weak that she could not speak, and in her silence she experienced the dull sensation that a drugged person feels or someone so numbed by pain they are no longer aware of it, or anything else. When she did regain a little strength all she could say was:

'O mother, I'm going to die.'

Knowing that her worst fears were almost upon her Zainab's mother held onto Zainab and tried to lead her back towards the house, but Zainab's legs would not carry her. She could not walk and her mother had to decide whether to carry her on her shoulders as she had done when she was an infant, or whether to wait for someone with a donkey. But what was there to stop her from carrying her now? After the emaciation she had suffered under the onslaught of a fast approaching death she was barely heavier than in the days of her childhood. And in the closing stages of her daughter's life would anyone question the action of the mother who carried her? While she was wondering what to do, a farmer passed by, returning from the fields with his donkey so she called for help and they returned to the village where she entered the house with Zainab.

But no sooner did they reach the room than Zainab started

to cough up pus and blood and was stricken by fever which left her unconscious on the floor. She began to talk deliriously in broken speech and her mother shuddered when she heard her shout 'Ibrahim!' with her last remaining strength, after which she became so still that there was not even the sound of her drawing breath. She grasped her hand but it was cold. Her eyes were shut, her lips pale, all the signs of death visible upon her. In front of this terrible scene her mother's eyes were scorched with despair. She bent over her daughter, clasping her hands and crying: 'Zainab, O Zainab . . .?'

Then she fell to the ground like a collapsed mountain! Alone by the side of her eldest daughter, sinking in the sea of extinction, she whispered:

'It's over.'

At that moment her younger daughter arrived. Returning from her day's work to visit Zainab and seeing the cause of her mother's grief she crouched against the wall trembling with fear, then bursting into tears, she rushed downstairs. Ummu Jaziyya met her halfway and realising that something was seriously wrong she hastened towards the room. Zainab's sister reached the door where she met Hassan returning from the mosque with Ammi Khalil. He grabbed her by the hand but she managed to free herself and ran home to her father. Before he could ask her what was the matter, she told him between her sobs:

'Mother's weeping over Zainab!'

On hearing this he stumbled, as though struck by lightning, but quickly got up and hurried to Khalil's house. Finding the old man sitting alone, staring in front of him with the expression of one bereaved, he said:

'Has she died Khalil?'

But Khalil did not know.

In the room of death the two old women sat on either side of the dying girl. Her eyes rolled upwards and her mother knew that she should not be moved from the floor where she lay. Hassan sat by the door, his head in his hands, and tears of anguish which he had never shed before, flowing down his cheeks.

Zainab asked her mother to fetch an embroidered handkerchief from the cabinet and taking it in her hand she held it to her lips then placed it over her heart, her last words being that the handkerchief should be buried with her in the grave. In the middle of the night her eyelids closed and as she passed away into the depths of peace the wails of the two old women rose up, proclaiming in the emptiness of space, the death of this innocent girl.

* * *

# Darf Publishers

Chewing Gum by Mansour Bushnaf
Translated from the Arabic by Mona Zaki

Translating Libya: In Search of the Libyan Short Story by Ethan Chorin
Short stories translated from the Arabic by Ethan Chorin & Basem Tulti

Oh, Freedom! by Francesco D'Adamo
Translated from the Italian by Sian Williams

Ebola '76 by Amir Tag Elsir
Translated from the Arabic by Charis Bredin & Emily Danby

Maps of the Soul by Ahmed Fagih
Translated from the Arabic by Thoraya Allam & Brian Loo

African Titanics by Abu Bakr Khaal
Translated from the Arabic by Charis Bredin

Twilight in Jakarta by Mochtar Lubis
Translated from the Indonesian by Claire Holt

Libyan Twilight by Raphael Luzon
Translated from the Italian by Gaia Luzon

The Apartment in Bab El-Louk by Donia Maher, Ganzeer & Ahmed Nady
Translated from the Arabic by Elisabeth Jaquette

Hurma by Ali al-Muqri
Translated from the Arabic by T.M. Aplin

Farewell, Damascus by Ghada Samman
Translated from the Arabic by Nancy Roberts

Suslov's Daughter by Habib Abdulrab Sarori
Translated from the Arabic by Elisabeth Jaquette

The Travels of Ibn Fudayl by George R. Sole

The Confines of the Shadow: In Lands Overseas, Volume I by Alessandro Spina
Translated from the Italian by André Naffis-Sahely